MONTANA SKIES
Kay Stockham

Enjoy!
Kay Stockham

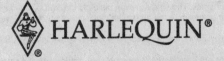

HARLEQUIN®

TORONTO • NEW YORK • LONDON
AMSTERDAM • PARIS • SYDNEY • HAMBURG
STOCKHOLM • ATHENS • TOKYO • MILAN • MADRID
PRAGUE • WARSAW • BUDAPEST • AUCKLAND

ISBN-13: 978-0-373-78140-9
ISBN-10:   0-373-78140-7

MONTANA SKIES

www.eHarlequin.com

Printed in U.S.A.

ABOUT THE AUTHOR

Kay Stockham has always wanted to be a writer, ever since she copied the pictures out of a Charlie Brown book and rewrote the story because she didn't like the plot. Formerly a secretary/office manager for a large commercial real estate development company, she's now a full-time writer and stay-at-home mom who firmly believes being a mom/wife/homemaker is the hardest job of all. Happily married for fifteen years and the somewhat frazzled mother of two, she's sold four books to the Harlequin Superromance line. Her first release, *Montana Secrets*, hit the Waldenbooks bestseller list and was chosen as a Holt Medallion finalist for Best First Book. Kay has garnered praise from reviewers for her emotional, heart-wrenching stories and looks forward to a long career writing a genre she loves. For more information on Kay's work, surf her Web site at www.kaystockham.com.

Books by Kay Stockham

HARLEQUIN SUPERROMANCE
1307–MONTANA SECRETS
1347–MAN WITH A PAST

Don't miss any of our special offers. Write to us at the following address for information on our newest releases.

Harlequin Reader Service
U.S.: 3010 Walden Ave., P.O. Box 1325, Buffalo, NY 14269
Canadian: P.O. Box 609, Fort Erie, Ont. L2A 5X3

To Johnny L. Evans, Emergency Medical Services Pilot, for answering too many questions to count. Any mistake is entirely my own. Thanks, Johnny! To parents everywhere struggling to do your best by your child and raise them right. To the FNGs—for more laughter, friendship and love than I ever imagined. I am so blessed. Thanks for making it all fun—or at least funny!

And, as always, for Chad. You are a hero in so many ways...just don't let it go to your head. ;)

CHAPTER ONE

RISSA MATHEWS glanced into the rearview mirror and groaned when she spotted red and blue flashing lights. "Oh, great. Oh, this is just *great!*"

She took her foot off the gas pedal and rolled to a stop off the road, the police cruiser following closely behind. Swearing under her breath, she reached beside her for her purse.

It wasn't there.

Mouth open in panic, she leaned over to feel beneath the empty seat beside her. Had it slid in between the passenger seat and the door? "No, no, no, you've got to be *kidding* me."

"Put your hands where I can see them," a deep baritone ordered from her left. "Slowly."

Raising her head, she found herself staring into a pair of thickly lashed green eyes set amidst a sun-browned face and sharp, angular features. A broad-rimmed Stetson covered the officer's head and a khaki uniform shirt stretched across his wide chest, but it was the sun's reflection off the man's badge that had her imagining it was laughing at her.

She'd been pulled over by North Star's very own sheriff. What were the odds on *him* letting her go?

Rissa straightened—slowly—and immediately noticed from her higher position in the truck that his hand rested on the butt of his gun.

"Ma'am, do you know how fast you were going?"

"Not exactly." Who had time to pay attention to the speed limit when summoned by an irate principal?

"You were driving seventy-nine in a fifty-five. License and registration, please."

"Oh, ah…"

"Is there a problem, ma'am?"

Rissa looked at the empty seat beside her, her hands fisted in frustration. Why today of all days? "I don't have it," she admitted, her voice low. "M-my license. I mean, I *do* have a license, but it's— I don't have it with me." Her embarrassment heightened when one of the sheriff's eyebrows rose in response to her words.

"I see…. Your name?"

"Rissa Mathews."

"And where were you going in such a hurry in the Rowlands' new truck, Ms. Mathews?"

The casually posed question didn't disguise the underlying query, and Rissa realized if she didn't talk fast, she'd not only wind up with a ticket she couldn't afford, but also a free trip to jail until he could determine whether the truck was stolen. Then where would her daughter be?

Probably right beside her.

"Do you know the Rowlands?" she asked, hopeful. "I'm Maura's cousin—I'm staying at the Second Chance and helping Seth and Grace. You can call and confirm I have permission to drive the truck."

The sheriff stared at her, his gaze assessing. Maybe loosening up a little? She and Maura resembled each other, had the same hair and build passed on from their mothers.

"I just might do that," he drawled with a bit of a western twang, "but first tell me why you were speeding. Are you on an errand for the ranch?"

She wanted to say yes, but she would be lying and she was a horrible liar. The Second Chance was a fully operating year-round ranch and vacation resort, one for physically impaired guests and their families. Guests could ride horses, fish, snowmobile and ski with full thought and consideration given to any special needs. Maura had made two trips to town this week to obtain something for a guest so trips into the small town weren't unusual.

"No, but…I'm late. I ran out of gas and had to

walk back to the ranch and borrow the truck. Now my daughter's waiting for me to pick her up at school, I'm late for appointments I *can't* miss, and—" She clamped her mouth shut. If he were going to give her a ticket there was nothing she could do about it. Rambling certainly wouldn't help, and doing so only reinforced the typical first impression most assumed when they spotted her blond hair and curvy frame.

But pride or no pride, she couldn't afford a ticket. Smothering a moan, she rubbed her aching temple. "Look, Sheriff, I know you've probably heard every excuse under the sun when it comes to people trying to get out of tickets, but I had my purse in my car when I left the house. *Really.* I must've left it behind when I switched vehicles. And I know I was speeding," she reluctantly added, "but I had the truck under control, no one else was on the road—"

"*I* was on the road."

"And most highway speed limits are seventy now so I wasn't driving *that* much over the norm." She tried to appeal to his sense of fairness. "Surely you've been late at least once and driven faster than you were supposed to?"

Her direct question earned a slight lifting of his lips at the corners, and Rissa chose to take the gesture as a sign the lawman was softening. Hope soared, and she gave him a rusty smile. Why not? Her appearance was often a hindrance to her goals, and it was definitely a hindrance when it came to her job. A female pilot in a male-dominated world, she'd often downplayed her looks. Maybe this once they would help?

Without comment the sheriff's gaze shifted from her eyes and face to where her arm rested along the window, his expression carefully neutral. "Give me your social security number and spell your name."

She did and watched while he wrote them down. "Keys?"

He lifted his hand, palm open, the calluses on his skin rough against hers when they brushed together during the exchange. A tingling sensation shot up her arm.

"Don't move."

Rissa watched him in the rearview mirror, unwillingly noting the masculine grace in his long-legged stride.

A couple cars passed, and she wanted to sink down and hide when the occupants rubbernecked to get a look. Ignoring them the best she could, Rissa leaned her head back against the seat and stared out the window up at the cloudless sky.

She pushed aside the upset she felt at herself for making such a stupid, costly mistake, and thought about the long list of things she needed to be doing instead of sitting by the side of the road with her fate in the sheriff's hands, awaiting what would probably be a huge fine.

Minutes passed, and with them her impatience grew until she spotted a bird flying high overhead in the vast sea of blue and focused on it instead. Dipping and soaring, gliding, the sight brought a smile. Some women took hot baths to relax, she liked to skim the treetops. But since 9/11, pilots had become a dime a dozen in the flailing market, her wings clipped, and that left Jake's brand-new Dodge Ram pickup taking the honor of being the fastest thing she'd piloted after selling her BMW Z4.

"Ms. Mathews?"

She started at the sheriff's return, but if he noticed her reaction, he didn't let on. Instead he studied his notepad, the broad-rimmed hat shading his face until all she could see was his mouth and chin.

"It seems speeding isn't new to you, and you received a ticket a little over a year ago for the same problem. Were you running late then, too?"

Rissa straightened the hem of her light pink T-shirt. "Actually it was a family emergency. My…my husband and daughter had been in a car accident and—" she pictured Skylar lying in the ER hospital bed, cut and bloody, hysterical, screaming for her dad on the other side of the curtain "—my husband didn't make it. My daughter couldn't be sedated because— The hospital said to hurry so I did." She wasn't about to apologize for it, either.

Silent, the sheriff shifted his weight and tapped the narrow book against his fingers twice. Finally he flipped it closed with a heavy sigh.

Rissa blinked at him, confused, until she took in his expression and realized she wasn't the only one who'd known loss and pain.

"If I let you go…"

"It won't happen again," she promised huskily.

"Make sure it doesn't. You might be running late today, but no one is hurt. Slow down and keep it that way so that your daughter isn't trying to get to the hospital—*to see you*."

"You're letting me off?" Relief swept through her, and she caught her breath at the wry twist of his lips she received in response to her question. It softened his angled features, made her heart do a little jump, skip and thump she didn't expect.

"Yeah, I'm letting you off—with a warning to slow it down or else pay the price next time."

"Understood. Thank you, um—" she glanced at his name tag "—Sheriff Taggert. Seriously… thank you."

He held out the truck keys. "Drive safely."

"I will." Rissa flashed him a grateful smile and started the engine, waiting for him to step away before she slowly eased back onto the highway. Within moments the sheriff's broad-shouldered image faded in the distance, but she had a hard time making him disappear from her thoughts. What had happened to him to put that look in his eyes? What kind of pain had he endured?

Fifteen minutes later she still contemplated the questions to keep from having to think about her own problems—namely her daughter—when she pulled into North Star Middle School's parking lot.

The office was located on the other side of a vestibule, and she continued through the second set of doors, pausing when a woman heard her and raised her head. A wary, dread-filled expression crossed her face before she quickly masked the look and pasted on a smile. "Mrs. Mathews?"

Rissa's stomach tightened. "Yes, I'm Rissa Mathews."

"Delia Kline, counselor for the middle and high school students. I was away at a meeting the day you registered your daughter."

The woman held out her hand and Rissa shook it. "Sorry, I'm late."

The counselor dropped several files on a nearby desk and waved Rissa deeper into the reception area. "No problem. It gave me some time to clear my desk while Mr. Kline and I waited."

"Didn't you say your name was Kline?"

She nodded. "Yes. My husband is the principal here. This way, please."

Suddenly awkward, Rissa smoothed her hands over her jeans and looked around, trying not to breathe too deeply. The school smelled of bleach and artificial air fresheners, the remnants of lunch and old paper.

Delia Kline's matronly form led the way down a short, tiled hall past several other offices, one of which had the woman's name written on it. Skylar was nowhere to be seen. They entered the office at the end of the hall, and a balding man in his late forties or early fifties stood, his weary expression declaring it had been a long day.

"Mrs. Mathews, welcome."

Once again she held out her hand and made sure to keep her grip firm. "Mr. Kline."

"Please, sit down." He indicated the two chairs across from his desk. "I'm sorry to request a meeting on such short notice, but we decided it might be best."

O-kay. Rissa seated herself, but wished she'd waited when Mr. Kline rested a hip against the desk in a casual pose and his wife remained standing two steps away. Both stared at her, their faces pitying.

The principal cleared his throat. "Mrs. Mathews, let me begin by saying we realize the first week at a new school is always trying, but we do our best to make sure new students are welcomed. However, I must admit your daughter has not made this experience easy."

"I gathered that by the phone call."

"Yes, well, I don't know how to put this other than bluntly, but your daughter's physical appearance has proved to be a little daunting to some of our students."

They thought the students were daunted? A belligerent teenager had taken over and changed her daughter from the inside out. Removed her girl-next-door, fresh-faced appearance and changed it to Goth Girl, Child of the Night.

"Moving so far away from a place where her appearance might have been accepted can't be easy, and a period of adjustment is called for," Delia Kline offered. "That's why we didn't immediately call you when she had trouble earlier in the week."

Rissa shifted on the uncomfortable chair, the knot in her stomach growing with every word. Skylar's appearance hadn't been the norm at home, either. "What kind of trouble?"

Mr. Kline exchanged another glance with his wife. "The first was a spat, a group of girls arguing in the hall between classes. They were warned to behave, and the incident dropped. Today, however, there was a full-fledged fight." He cleared his throat once more, his solemn gaze meeting hers. "One of our teachers witnessed Skylar throwing the first punch."

"As I'm sure you are aware, our duty as administrators is to protect the student body and teach them, guide them, and to set examples when confronted with bad behavior," Mrs. Kline murmured pointedly.

"Meaning?" The question came out soft and thready, revealing too much.

Delia Kline's mouth tightened. "I'm sorry, Mrs. Mathews, but along with today's punishment, Skylar has been issued detention after school all next week. Two hours a day, all five days. We understand this might be an inconvenience for you being so new to town, but we think detention is better than expelling her under the circumstances, with the school year ending in a matter of weeks."

It certainly *was* an inconvenience. Staying two hours after school meant Skylar couldn't ride the bus out to the ranch. Rissa would have to come pick her up, the drive nearly an hour round-trip.

"I understand," she murmured dazedly. What else could she say?

"May I suggest something?" The counselor unfolded her arms and walked over to sit in her husband's desk chair.

The move drew Rissa's attention and that's when she noticed the credenza behind the desk where a collage of framed photographs on top showcased the bright, smiling faces of their family. Older kids from the looks of it. What could it hurt to get advice from people who'd survived teenagers? "Of course."

"Perhaps you could talk to Skylar about blending in more, easing up on the makeup and concentrating on making friends?"

Did they think she hadn't tried that? "Individuality—"

"Is important. Absolutely," the principal confirmed, evidently sensing the beginning of her parental defense. "But right now and in this small community, Skylar's individuality is a little *too* different. It's frightening to some. Especially after all the news reports of school shootings resulting from teenagers thought to be outsiders."

Rissa stood, her hands clenched into fists. "You've *profiled* her."

"We've done no such thing," the principal argued. "I'm simply relaying to you the thoughts of other parents. Parents who have seen Skylar this past week and are concerned. They've voiced their apprehension to me, and after observing Skylar with the other students, well, it appears the children are projecting the same attitudes in regard to her appearance."

"Mrs. Mathews, losing a loved one is difficult on anyone," Mrs. Kline interjected softly. "We understand that, and her last counselor documented Skylar's changes in behavior and personal appearance very well, enabling us to grasp the enormity of what Skylar underwent with the accident and loss of her father. But I'm sure you are aware not everyone retreats behind a mask, and the fact that Skylar has changed so *drastically* in the course of a single year…it only adds to our concern." She glanced at her husband quickly before focusing on Rissa again. "There are professionals who might be better equipped to help your daughter."

"She's seen them." Three-hundred-dollar-an-hour shrinks who knew what they were talking about. Didn't they? "I was told to leave her alone and let her express herself how she wants. To *wait* until she's ready to talk about what happened. She simply needs more time."

"I don't doubt that's true, and a good idea in theory, Mrs. Mathews, but the reality is we must stand firm. Skylar's behavior cannot be allowed to continue. Violence is unacceptable in our school, and we won't allow Skylar to upset our student body—or harm them."

JONAS HAD WATCHED Rissa Mathews pull onto the highway before he'd walked back to the cruiser and climbed inside. Driving home, his mind remained preoccupied with the beautiful blonde and the information her social security number had revealed.

He didn't need the computer to tell him that New York City was big and bustling with too many people. Too much everything. Crime, poverty, wealth and everything in between. Everything North Star wasn't.

Topping twenty-plus miles over the limit and not carrying her license, he'd had no intention of letting her off with a warning. But the look in her eyes, her expression when she'd told him about the last ticket she'd received, had gotten to him. Who wouldn't have done the same in that situation?

You'll probably find out later she lied.

If that were the case, so be it. But until then, he'd give her the benefit of the doubt and keep an eye on her for future speed violations. Her record showed she hadn't received any drug-related citations, and the standard check for alcohol and drugs turned up nothing. She was clean. Just speeding. Which is why he'd listened to his instincts and let her go. People deserved a break every now and again, and he'd given Rissa Mathews one. Just one. Nothing wrong with that.

Jonas stepped inside his house only to come up short when confronted with Caroline's thunderous expression. His daughter stalked toward him from the kitchen.

"What's wrong?" he asked, the car already parked in the driveway when he'd pulled in giving him a good indication.

"I'm *not* going." Her mouth flattened into a mulish line.

Jonas glanced over her head to the kitchen beyond before shutting the door behind him. "What is it this time?"

"*Ballet*. It's boring! Dad, please don't make me go."

"Your grandma likes taking you to new places. You've never been to a ballet before. Maybe you'd enjoy it."

He watched her cross her arms over her flat chest, then did a double take when he suddenly realized she wasn't so flat anymore. When had that happened?

"You'll go, too?"

"We'll talk about it later."

"Uh-huh. That's what I figured."

Jonas ignored Caroline's put-out tone and listened to the sounds of his ex-mother-in-law's weekly visit. The dishwasher was running in the kitchen, the washer and dryer were on in the hall, and the sweeper sat out in the living room.

He frowned. "Did you tell her we'd—"

"Yeah. Do you think she thinks we did anything right?" Caroline rolled her eyes. "The dishes had a film on them," she informed him sourly, "the clothes are too wrinkled and she saw a speck of dust on the floor." She shook her head. "Like, how hard is it to clean? It's not calculus."

Jonas took his hat off and hung it on the peg by the door. "I'll talk to her. Anything happen at school today?"

"No."

It was the same answer he'd received every day for a while now. The same look. What happened to the little girl who used to burst into the house talking ninety miles a minute?

"There you are. Caroline, why didn't you tell me your father was home?"

His daughter made a face her grandmother couldn't see, and headed down the hall toward her room.

"Dinner's in—"

"I know!"

Marilyn shook her head at Caroline's response. "Jonas, really, you need to take her in hand. She's rude."

"Trust me, you don't know rude until you've seen and dealt with some of the kids out there."

"Still, there's no time to waste. She's getting to an age where…"

Jonas tuned out while he sorted through the mail lying on the entry table. Sweepstakes, credit card application, credit card bill, electric bill, mortgage. Marilyn droned on, and he kept flipping. Water bill, eBay flyer—

An acrid scent reached him and he paused, sniffing. "Is something burning?"

Marilyn stopped midrant. "The bread!"

Grimacing, Jonas followed her into the kitchen, and winced when he spotted the smoky haze filling the air.

Marilyn grabbed a pot holder and yanked open the oven door. Smoke billowed out. "I told her to watch the bread. One little thing she could've done to help me, but did she? Now it's ruined. *Ruined!*"

As though waiting for the climactic moment, the fire alarm went off at the height of her cry, and Jonas waved one of the flyers beneath it to clear the smoke.

Caroline reappeared in the doorway. "Grandma, I'm sorry! I forgot the bread."

"How could you forget? It was one little thing!"

The alarm sputtered, squawking twice more before ending. Jonas tossed the paper aside, opened the patio door and motioned his daughter to his side.

"It's okay, Marilyn. It's not ruined, see? A little black on the bottom. We'll peel it off, and eat the middle and top."

"Like we always do, right, Dad?"

He chuckled, wondering if they'd hold the record for the most burnt ready-made biscuits if it were ever added up. "Right."

Marilyn wasn't amused. "It took me all day to make this bread. To prepare it and for it to rise, and—*look* how unappreciative you are!"

"Grandma, I'm sorry I forgot." Caroline battled back tears until her face brightened. "I know! Maybe we can get you a breadmaker for Christmas."

"A *what?*" Marilyn's self-pitying expression turned to one of horror.

Jonas squeezed Caroline's shoulder and locked his jaw to keep from laughing—and arguing. Every week the same scene played out in one form or another. If not because of burnt bread, then for spilling something after Marilyn had finished cleaning or not eating themselves sick to prove they wouldn't starve. There was *always* something.

"We're very appreciative," Jonas murmured, feeling guilty at his thoughts. Since Lea left, Marilyn tried hard to help out. And he was grateful. He just hated feeling like Marilyn's generosity was an anvil held over his head, a reminder that he'd done wrong by not being exciting enough for her daughter to hang around.

"Grandma, we love you."

"Yeah," he added when Caroline nudged him. "What would we do without you?"

His mother-in-law's eyes filled with tears and she held open her arms. Glancing at him quickly, Caroline stepped forward into her embrace.

"I love you, too, Caroline. I'm just in a mood today since your grandpa's business trip was extended. All's forgiven. And I'm so looking forward to our evening out, aren't you? I knew the ballet would make a wonderful birthday gift. Of course, I'd rather it be us, but I understand if you'd like to bring one of your little friends along."

"Wellll—"

"That's very generous of you, Marilyn. I'm sure Caro would love to invite someone."

Marilyn smoothed her hands over Caroline's unruly red hair and smiled. "This is going to be so much fun! We'll have to hurry, though. There are only two months left to find an appropriate dress, but I know the perfect color—*pink!*"

CHAPTER TWO

"STAY HERE."

"Why can't I come in? I'm thirsty."

Rissa ground her teeth together. Her daughter acted four instead of fourteen. "Skylar, I *need* this job. Seth and Grace are being very gracious by letting us stay in the old cabin in exchange for housekeeping help, but we have no expendable income until your father's life insurance check comes through. I'm not buying a soda at double the price we can get it from home."

"It's only a buck or so."

"Fine. You want one—pay for it yourself."

Skylar's black painted lips turned down. "Geez, Mom, get a grip."

A grip? A *grip!* Staring at the creature who used to be her baby girl, Rissa inhaled deeply and fought the urge to scream until she couldn't scream anymore. Her daughter's long blond locks were gone, chopped short and dyed jet-black in a page-boy cut. Chalky powder hid her skin, and black eyeliner, black blush and black lipstick lined her eyes, cheeks and lips accordingly. A tiny black teardrop adorned her cheek below her left eye. Dressed from head to toe in yet more black, Skylar looked like an extra from a vampire movie.

"We'll discuss your behavior when we get home. I can't do this now, not when I'm going in there for an interview."

"It's a freakin' diner. Why do you want to work there, anyway?"

"Watch your language," she ordered automatically. "And for the record, I don't *want* to wait tables, but since I haven't found a pilot's job yet, what do you think I should do? We have bills to pay or have you forgotten?"

Skylar's eyes widened. "You're blaming *me* for the bills?"

"Only the one you made. Now for the last time, stay *here*."

"What*ever*." Skylar slumped in the seat and lifted her booted feet onto the dash, the decorative chains rattling. "It's not like there's anywhere else to go in this stupid town."

Meaning the mall, the music stores or other forms of entertainment. North Star *had* been a surprise. It remained quite old-fashioned despite the modern conveniences available in the nearby state capital.

Simple was good, though. No mall meant no more surprise shopping sprees. No more thousand-dollar credit card charges racked up by a daughter who had slipped out of the house one morning a young girl and come home a vamp.

Rissa slammed the truck door closed and ignored Skylar's glare. "It's a freakin' diner," she muttered, using one of Skylar's favorite adjectives. "You've flown in treacherous winds, rescued flood victims and kept your cool while SOBs tried to put the moves on you midair. Waiting tables again will be a breeze."

Ignoring the voice in her head snickering at her pep talk, Rissa made her way down the block and into the diner on the corner. It was six-thirty and already the dinner crowd had thinned. Maybe it wouldn't be so bad. The ad specified evening hours. Thin was good.

And so were tips.

"Can I help you?"

She pinned a smile to her face and tried not to fidget. "I'm Rissa Mathews. I spoke with Porter earlier today about an interview?"

The older woman nodded, her mile-high hair bobbing up and down in sync with her chins. "Porter, she's here!"

A door separated the kitchen from the counter and dining area, and Rissa jumped when a hand slammed against it. An older man emerged, his bushy eyebrows rising high when he saw her.

Without greeting or comment, he took in her appearance of jeans and a T-shirt, his mouth pursed. Maura had told her to dress casually. Bad advice?

The man glanced at the waitress standing by the cash register. "What do you think?"

"Her looks and newness to town will sure draw 'em in, but…you got any experience, honey?"

"A little. I waited tables in high school." For three whole days before she got fired for dumping a plate of spaghetti on a patron's head after he'd groped her behind.

"You're hired." Porter nodded at the waitress. "Charlotte'll get you an apron and things. Be here at five-thirty sharp. You'll stay until we close at ten and then help clean up. Weeknights are slow. We're usually out of here by ten-thirty or quarter 'til. That a problem?"

"I—" Rissa wet her dry lips. "No, not at all." Except next week she wouldn't have time to pick Skylar up after detention, drive her back to their cabin at the Second Chance and make it back here on time.

Four hours in a car unattended? Her daughter was a walking, talking disaster waiting to happen.

"You don't seem too sure," the waitress added suspiciously.

"Oh, I'm sure. I want it." She nodded firmly. After all, it was only a week. "I'll be here. Thank you, Porter…Charlotte. I'll see you tomorrow." Head held high, Rissa gave them a cheerful wave and left, ignoring her nerves, the sick twist in her stomach and her aching head. But halfway down the block she spied a bench out in front of the barbershop and her body refused to take another step. She dropped down onto the weathered surface and buried her face in her hands, not caring who saw her looking so utterly pathetic. She needed a moment of peace, a chance to regroup.

She'd gotten the job. When added to the fairly steady tips she received by working at the ranch as the temporary housekeeper, and what money she'd managed to put back from liquidating everything before their move, she should be able to make all her payments with some creative timing. But while the job ended one worry, she dreaded the night—the next week—to come.

The Klines' comments resonated in her head, and a self-indulgent moan sounded, followed by the sharp sting of tears.

Larry, what happened to her? What did you do?

Blinking away the moisture, Rissa shoved herself to her feet and retraced her steps to the truck, her gaze zeroing in on Skylar once she was close enough to make out her daughter's dark form.

Before her Goth change, Skylar had looked like the best of both her parents. Her daughter had gotten her blond hair, blue eyes and curvy figure from her and had taken after her father when it came to his height, bone structure and blinding smile. An anchorman for the local television station, Larry attracted attention with his wide grin and jaw-dropping looks the camera loved. Sadly, it hadn't taken too many trips through the sky flying Larry to and from the special assignments he covered with him murmuring outrageously flirtatious comments into her headset for her to agree to his whirlwind proposal.

They'd been the perfect couple. The one people talked about when they entered a room. But it had all been a sham—looks were deceiving—and even before finding out proof-positive about his affair, she'd suspected his infidelity for years. Nearly from the beginning.

Rissa climbed inside the truck and waited, wondering if Skylar would comment. Seconds passed. Skylar ignored her, didn't ask if she'd gotten the job. Unbelievable. Rissa stabbed the key into the ignition, more than a little tired of Skylar's indifference.

The accident had done some major damage emotionally, she *knew* that, but something had to give soon. Otherwise she feared she'd lose Skylar forever. And a big part of herself.

JONAS KNOCKED on Caroline's bedroom door and waited until she said he could enter. She'd already showered and now wore a T-shirt and gym shorts, her long red hair pulled back in a ribbon.

"Didn't we wash your pjs?"

She shrugged. "They're getting too small."

Already? When he added that comment to what he'd noticed earlier in the evening, he knew he'd been given the perfect opening to discuss…things.

"I, uh, talked with your grandma before she left about taking you shopping." He cleared his throat, the sound emerging louder than he'd intended. "For some new under—uh…things."

"Dad, you *didn't!*"

He walked over to stare out the window, easily able to imagine Caroline's face blazing with embarrassment, much like his probably was at the moment. "She'll do fine."

"She likes *old* stuff. Can't I go by myself?"

"You're too young."

"I'm almost fourteen!"

Like he didn't know that? Wasn't reminded of it every time he looked at her and remembered the moment she'd been placed in his arms mere seconds after she was born? "If your mother were here—"

"But she's not." Caroline stomped over to her dresser, her head down. "And I *am* old enough. There's a store by the grocery now, and they have stuff like that. Couldn't you wait in the car while I went in? That would work, wouldn't it?"

He'd forgotten about the little shop that opened up a year ago, The Blooming something. But what did his daughter know about shopping for bras? *What did he know about it?*

Jonas ran a hand roughly over his face. "I thought since you and Marilyn had to go look for a dress, you could get some things then."

"Grandma will order one before we ever get a chance to go shopping. She thinks if she buys things, I have to wear them." She grabbed a handful of CDs and pulled one from the middle. "Dad, you know how she is, she wants me to wear *pink!* I'll never get a dress I like." CD in hand, she stomped back across the room, and the bed squeaked when she flopped on it.

"Whatever you get will look great."

"Uh-huh. You don't have to wear it and look like a redheaded bag of cotton candy. Everybody knows red hair and pink dresses only work for movie stars."

He rubbed the muscles in his neck in a poor attempt to ease the tension. The teenage melodrama was getting to him. "Look online for a few

dresses you like and then send her some sugges-
tions. Your Grandpa Dave can print them off at
work and give them to her."

"Why can't we do that with the other stuff? Just
order something?"

"You'll need to try things on, sweetheart. To,
um…get the right size." Jonas felt his face heat again
and cursed silently. There were some things dads
weren't meant to discuss with their daughters. That's
where mothers came in. Knowing your little girl was
growing up and having to follow the process firsthand through underwear sizes was just cruel.

"But if it's wrong, we could send it back and
order something else."

"What about the shipping charges? Sweetheart,
the answer's no." He glanced over his shoulder at
her. Disappointment clouded her face, and he
sighed. Against his better judgment, he thought of
a compromise. "I guess if you really want to go
to that store by yourself, I could call and ask one
of the saleswomen to help you."

She covered her face with her hands. "That's
even *worse!*"

"Why?"

"*Because!* Everybody knows about Mom
leaving us and if you call for help and I go in to
buy *that* stuff, they'll give me those funny looks
people give us sometimes."

He knew exactly which looks she meant. Pity, curiosity. Thoughtless scorn that they'd driven their small-town princess away. Jonas turned to face her and found Caroline watching him. Her gray eyes revealed the same thoughts, the same doubts about herself. Insecurities they'd both gained from Lea's desertion.

"We'll do all right and get things taken care of, Caro. Don't worry."

Once again she left the bed, but this time she padded over to where he stood, sliding her freckled arms around his waist and laying her cheek on his ribs. Jonas hugged her tight and kissed the top of her head like he had nearly every day since her birth.

"I'm sorry, Dad."

"For what?"

"That you have to do this stuff. Maybe Mom would've stayed if—"

He squeezed her to silence her. "No, honey. She wouldn't have stayed. Your mom wanted to leave North Star long before we ever got together, *before* she got pregnant with you. Some people are meant to live in small towns, others aren't. It's as simple as that." He kissed her hair again, then her forehead. "You did absolutely nothing wrong, you hear me?"

She nodded, but the movement lacked substance and belief.

"Sweetheart, no amount of helping around the house or extra good behavior would've changed things. She didn't leave you, honey, she left me."

"But she didn't leave until after—"

"*Trust me,*" he ordered, anxious to drop the subject before she became upset. "I know what I'm talking about, and you aren't to blame. Now...homework done?"

"Almost." A heavy sigh left her chest. "I can't believe we get homework on the weekend. It *sucks.*"

He chuckled. "Finish it up tonight then and be done with it so you'll have the rest of the weekend free." He loosened his grip, but she held tight, her nose pressed into his chest, her forehead hot pink.

"Dad...think maybe we could go to The Blooming Rose tomorrow?" Her words were muffled against his shirt. "Things are kind of tight."

Which meant she hoped to get her things before school on Monday, with or without help. Jonas sighed and rubbed her back. "I'll take you on my break, how's that?"

"And I can do it by myself? *Please,* Dad?"

"I guess you can't get things too wrong."

"Really?" She hugged him again. "Thank you!"

"I love you, baby. Don't worry so much about things, okay?"

Caroline nodded, not looking at her dad when she released him and walked over and seated herself on the bed. She grabbed a pillow to hold in front of her, and waited for him to close the door behind him, smiling when he looked through the space one last time before he pulled it shut.

A second passed. Two. Tears filled her eyes, but she didn't let them fall.

Her dad was a good guy, the best. People liked and respected him. Came to him for advice. She knew he only said those things about her mom leaving because he was trying to make *her* feel better.

She dropped to her side and grabbed the photo album next to her bed, cracking the CD case when she put too much weight on the plastic frame. Ignoring that, she stared down at the proof right there in the album.

Newspaper clippings and photos, announcements. All the stuff her grandma had collected over the years. Her mom had danced, cheered or played sports every season of the year from grade school to high school. She was pretty and popular, a model for local TV and print ads. She'd worn the latest styles, always looked neat and clean and great. Always had a cute boyfriend. Wrote words like "smooches" and "kiss-kiss" in her notes.

Caroline rolled over onto her back and stared up at the poster of Harry Potter tacked to her ceiling. How many times had her mom told her she was a mess? Complained that her hair was too wild, her teeth too crooked, her freckles too dark? She didn't stand right, didn't walk right, always looked weird because she stood out. The only redhead in her class and smart, too.

Sniffling, she pulled her ponytail over her shoulder and looked at the frizzy split ends. Why couldn't she have been pretty like her mom? Like Mandy or the other girls in school?

She swung her feet off the bed and padded over to her computer desk, wishing she'd win a trip to one of those makeover shows. Now *that* would be an awesome birthday present. She bit her lip and found her mouse, clicking on the box to maximize the screen, and going back to what she'd been reading online before her dad had come in. She told herself to forget about it, but she had to know what they said about her. Every day.

Inhaling deeply to get rid of the lump in her chest, she read to the bottom of the chat-room posts, and this time she couldn't hold back the stupid tears no matter how hard she tried. Caroline slumped in the chair and hugged her knees up to her chest.

Her mom definitely hadn't left because of her dad, she'd left because of *her*. Because of how embarrassed she was to have such an ugly loser for a daughter.

Everybody thought so.

"DON'T YOU walk away from me!"

"He's a moron!"

"He's your principal," Rissa countered, "and he says you've got to get your act together or—"

"What? He'll expel me? I hope you told him to go for it," Skylar taunted gleefully.

Rissa strove for calm, for patience, knowing without a doubt Skylar would like nothing better than to be expelled from school. Permanently. "What about your future? What happened to becoming a lawyer?"

"Lawyers suck."

"Lawyers are our only chance at winning this lawsuit, Sky. They play an important role in the world—just like your principal and your teachers *and* you. Regardless of what you do when you grow up, you can't survive unless you're able to support yourself. *Why* are you throwing your education away?"

"Because it's *not* important! What's it all matter if you get nailed in a car crash or—or get a disease? What good is it then?"

"That's just an excuse to live your life in fear. Skylar, the last thing your dad would want is for you to blame yourself for what happened or throw your life away!"

Skylar rolled her eyes and whirled around. She stomped out of the small living area into the even smaller kitchen, her boots thudding every step of the way.

Rissa watched her for a moment before she tossed her purse—found in the passenger seat of her car exactly where she'd left it—and keys onto a table, wishing she could sling them across the room into a wall. But to do so wouldn't quite portray the calm, patient example she needed to set.

"Can we please talk about what happened today without it turning into a shouting match?"

"But we do it so well." Skylar's lip-curling sneer was back in place once more.

It took two deep inhalations and a count to ten, but Rissa managed to ignore the expression. "You punched a girl and now have detention. Why?"

"She deserved it."

"*Why?* What happened?" Skylar didn't respond. "Sky, I need you to hear me—to *talk* to me. Tell me what's going on so I can try to help you."

Her daughter glanced over her shoulder, her black gaze flat. "*Help* me? You just want to *control* me! That's why you moved us to the middle of nowhere."

"You need control in your life, and if you washed your face and wore your regular clothes, you'd be more readily accepted and you know it."

"Why should *I* change? I like me this way! It's not my fault you don't."

"I love you no matter what, but you can't blame me or the school officials for not understanding why you've changed so much! All it took was one look at your old school pictures and grades from New York, and it was obvious to the Klines that you need help."

"Help, huh?" Skylar shut the refrigerator door with a slam, the force causing a box of cereal on top to fall over. "Go ahead and say what you really think—I'm a freak!"

"I *think* you're hurting," she snapped, her tone not as sympathetic as it could have been due to Skylar's belligerence. "I *think* you're confused and angry and lashing out, and I'm trying to understand why, but that's hard to do when you act like this! You won't talk to me!"

"Like you talk to Grampa?"

Oh, her daughter knew how to push her buttons. And then some. Her dad's marriage to a much younger woman had rocked her, angered her to no end coming just four short months after her mother's death.

"Of the two of us, trust me, I'm the one you want to deal with. If your grandfather ever saw you looking the way you do—"

"Screw this, I'm going to bed."

"We're not finished!" Rissa hurried to get to the stairs before Skylar, wondering how she'd stop her. Her daughter might be similar in weight, but Skylar topped her in height by a couple inches.

Thankfully, Rissa made it there first, her arms outstretched to bar the way. "I know how different North Star is from New York City, but I know if you'd only try—"

"You don't *know* anything!"

"Then tell me." Rissa focused on the psychiatrists' advice to be supportive, open, willing to listen. *Nonjudgmental.* No matter what it took, she'd do it. Somehow. What choice did she have? "Tell me," she ordered, her voice hoarse with pent-up emotion. "Tell me about the clothes, about the paint. Tell me why you should be held accountable for something you *couldn't* have prevented."

Skylar's mascara-layered lashes lowered, nearly brushing the tiny black teardrop drawn on her pale cheek, before flicking up again and piercing her with a pained glare. "It's not paint," she said dully. "This is *me*, Mom. When are you going to get it?"

"It's not you." Rissa kept her tone just as soft. "Somewhere under that mask you're wearing is the *real* you. Look at me," she urged when Skylar turned away yet again. "Sky, why are you doing this to yourself? I miss your dad, too. We didn't always get along, but—"

"Dad was such a *jerk* for cheating on you! If he hadn't cheated and run around on us then—"

Skylar broke off and Rissa opened her mouth to comment, but just as quickly closed it, her focus gone. What could she say? Her very handsome husband *was* a jerk, along with quite a few other foul descriptives she could think of, but dead or alive, she wouldn't bad-mouth him to their daughter. Skylar had witnessed her father's infidelity firsthand, she didn't need to hear her mother spouting anger and pain on top of it. Not doing so was a promise she'd made to herself from the beginning, a way to maintain what dignity she'd had left after learning the truth.

Skylar needed her to be strong. And now that she had finally emerged from her year-long, drama-induced daze, she focused on the task at hand, that of treating Skylar like the child she was instead of the adult she resembled.

"Baby, we've talked about this. You aren't to blame for your dad and I not getting along. We had problems, but they weren't your doing, and telling me about the affair had nothing to do with the accident. Don't feel guilty—*it wasn't your fault.*"

"What if you're wrong?" Skylar turned to face her, every muscle in her body, her stance, her expression, challenging. "What if he *did* try to commit suicide with me in the car because he hated me for…screwing things up?"

Oh Lord, help her. She hated that Skylar carried

that doubt in her mind. Hated that she thought her father so angry over their marital situation and separation he'd want to kill her.

Rissa walked toward her. She wanted to hold her, comfort her, but Skylar distanced herself again, the couch now between them. She stopped, her hands at her sides, her arms empty and aching for the little girl who used to snuggle up with her every day.

"It's *not* true, Sky. Your dad wasn't perfect, but if he'd had any thoughts of suicide, he certainly wouldn't have endangered you. He understood why you told me. He *did*. You were hurt and angry and confused, but he understood! Let it go. *Please*. Try to remember what Jake said about the inquiry being normal, and stop blaming yourself. The policy was a large one, and the delays… It's the company's bureaucratic way of holding onto their money as long as possible, that's all."

"How can you be so sure?"

Beneath the steady weight of Skylar's stare, Rissa faltered. And prayed she'd say the right thing, find the missing piece. "Because your dad was a lot of things, but first and foremost, he was a father. For all his faults, he *loved* you like no one else. You were his princess, daddy's little girl. He loved you so much he'd have died—"

Skylar flinched.

Rissa clamped a hand over her mouth, regretting the words the instant they left her lips, unable to believe she'd said something so insensitive in her rambling explanation. She held out her hands in apology. "Oh, I didn't—Skylar, I'm sorry! That came out wrong. I didn't mean—"

Skylar made a break for the stairs leading to the tiny bedroom loft. Rissa turned, but knew she didn't have a chance of stopping her this time. "Skylar, I'm *sorry!*"

She kept going, her boots loud on the wooden treads.

"Skylar—"

"God, just leave me alone! *Leave me alone!*"

CHAPTER THREE

THE NEXT MORNING Jonas leaned against the outside of his cruiser and lifted a hand in greeting to Ben Whitefeather. The old man drove by slowly, and Jonas watched his progress, wondering if he should stop Ben to chat and discreetly check for alcohol. Depending on the man's arthritis pain, the old saying applied— Ben could be sober as a church mouse, or drunk as a skunk.

Jonas decided to let Ben continue on when the truck didn't waver. He'd never stopped Ben for DUI because the old man typically did his drinking at home, but he had been called out to Ben's house by the man's teenaged grandson when Ben had gotten drunk enough to forget the pain in his legs, and managed to get his helicopter up in the air believing he'd seen smoke in the hills. A flame chaser from years back, Ben was determined to put the fire out before it spread through the forest. Twenty minutes later, he had landed safely a hundred yards from the overgrown helipad, and promised not to drink and fly again.

Jonas sighed and leaned his head back to ease the tension in his neck. He'd parked under the shade tree planted to the right of The Blooming Rose, and it was a good thing he had because Caroline had been inside almost an hour already.

While he waited, he'd chatted with a few of the townspeople, something he'd done often before Lea had left. But once she was gone, all the questions and nosy busybodies had driven him to not be so accessible, and he hadn't realized how much he'd missed it until now.

Jonas straightened, prepared to walk by the glass door to look inside even though he told himself to give Caroline another fifteen minutes. He was smart enough to know his daughter would be mortified if anyone saw him staring into the clothing store while she was inside.

"Is something wrong?"

He jerked his head toward the now familiar feminine voice so fast he nearly gave himself whiplash. Rissa Mathews stood a few feet away. Smiling, her blue eyes friendly. Wow.

At five-seven, she was tall, yet had a woman's lush, rounded figure. Full breasts pressed against her blue-green T-shirt, making her eyes appear darker than he remembered. Khaki shorts hugged her hips, her long legs the perfect size and shape for a man to grip without fearing he'd bruise her.

Jonas froze at his thoughts, the temptation, and nearly groaned aloud. "Mrs. Mathews," he murmured, dipping his head in a nod of greeting that hopefully hid his juvenile reaction. "Uh, no, nothing's wrong."

"Good. But, please, call me Rissa."

"Okay." Was it his imagination or did she seem as nervous to be talking to him as he was talking to her?

"I, um, just wanted to say thank you for letting me off on the ticket."

She glanced over her shoulder, and Jonas followed her gaze. Maura Rowland and her new sister-in-law, Grace, were strapping Maura's twin boys into grocery carts.

"You didn't call the ranch and confirm my story about having permission to drive the truck, but I told Maura and Grace what happened." Her shoulder lifted in an embarrassed shrug. "Want to see my license now? I have it with me today," she informed him with a soft laugh that sounded a bit rusty. "My purse was in my car, right where I left it."

Jonas returned her smile, liking the way her eyes sparkled, the way her smile lit up her features even more. She was pretty, no doubt about it. A woman who'd have the gossips gabbing. "You probably won't ever forget it again, will you?"

"Not a chance. Money's, um…kind of tight right now." Her cheeks flushed. "Anyway, I just wanted to say again that I appreciate what you did. I don't know how I can repay you."

"Just don't let it—" He broke off and glanced at the store. Still no sign of Caroline. Was it too much to ask? "Would you like to repay me in full? Right now?"

Rissa looked a little taken aback by his questions. "I guess that depends on what you have in mind."

Unable to help himself, he grinned at her, at the suspicions he saw lurking behind her expressive eyes. The same thoughts in his head. But he warned himself to keep it casual. "I'd like to borrow you for a few minutes, that's all."

Maura and Grace stood talking to one another by Maura's minivan. The women glanced toward him and Rissa and then started talking again. Matchmaking. He could spot it a mile away.

"Borrow me?"

He shifted his attention back to Rissa. "If you have time. Do they need you?" He tilted his head toward the waiting women. Maybe it was just as well.

"No, they'll be fine. They're grocery shopping for the guests. Grace told us this morning there's a big hotshot coming from California. He's bringing his entire company and all their families, and rented out the whole ranch." She shook her head, her smile wide. "I've never seen Maura in such a tizzy. Guess you have to be a chef to get excited over fixing two gourmet meals a day."

His worry over Caroline was momentarily replaced with interest in Rissa's comment. Every sheriff had to know the goings-on in his town. "Any names mentioned? It's not some movie star, is it?"

She laughed at his horror, the sound not so rusty now. "No, no one like that."

"Good." That was a relief. The last thing he needed was a bunch of paparazzi following to snap pictures. "But if you need to go with Maura and Grace to help, I won't keep you. Don't worry about what I said."

"No, I have time. I wasn't supposed to come at all and only jumped in at the last minute." She made a face. "My daughter and I had a huge fight last night and it carried over to this morning. Grace and Maura decided I needed a distraction."

He winced at her words.

"What? Did I say something wrong?"

"Not at all. It's just that's why I, uh, need help— with *my* daughter," he explained when she looked confused. "But it sounds like you've had enough girlish temperament today."

Still no sign of Caroline. She'd be mad if he went in, but it shouldn't have taken this long and he had to get back to work.

"No, forget that," she said, waving a hand in the air between them as if she were erasing the words. "What's up? Where is she?"

He stared at her a long moment and saw the sincerity in her expression. "She's in The Blooming Rose picking out some…things, and she could use a woman's advice."

"You mean you want me to—"

"Just check on her," he begged, desperate to not have to go in the store himself. "If I get within twenty feet of the entrance I'll be blasted for humiliating her." Jonas hesitated, clearing his throat. "Rissa, I'm sorry to ask this of you, but you'd really be helping me out here because my ex…she hasn't been around for a while now," he informed her, unsure of exactly why he wanted to make that clear. "And moments like these aren't easy on a single dad's ego."

She laughed again. Not a little laugh, either, but a throaty, deeply appealing belly laugh that made him want to—

"Oh, believe me, I understand perfectly when it comes to girls and clothes. What does she look like?"

"Red hair, freckles. Five-three, about a hundred

pounds. She's thirteen going on thirty. You can't miss her."

"Got it. Be back soon."

She started to walk away and Jonas reached out, his hand gently surrounding the warm, soft skin of her arm, the need to touch her overwhelming. "Rissa, thank you. I really appreciate it."

"You're welcome."

"Could you…do me another favor and not let her know I sent you in?"

Her smile widened, blinded him and teased him. Made him think things best left alone because she seemed completely unaware of the power behind the simple act, the effect of it.

"Working undercover, huh, Sheriff?"

"Jonas," he immediately corrected, reluctantly dropping his hand and letting her walk away. But not until after he'd slid his fingers down the length of smooth skin to prolong the moment. Rissa Mathews was trouble with a capital *T*.

IF D'S WERE BAD GRADES and A's were good, how come bra sizes were backward?

Caroline fought the urge to run out of the store. How stupid was she that she couldn't figure something like this out? Either the bras were too big around her or she didn't fill them up. The training bras—yeah, like you could *train* them—weren't big enough anymore. They felt like strings pinching her in two. And some were so see-through and thin her nipples showed through her shirt. What good was that?

She shoved a plastic hanger onto the metal rack and grabbed another when the door opened and a woman walked in. Caroline paused with a frown, wondering why she hadn't seen her around. She'd bet *she* wouldn't need help from anyone.

Pretty, blond and put together, the lady had "I used to be a cheerleader" written all over her. Not that that was a bad thing, but they seemed to be a species of their own and completely *un*like her, the walking fashion disaster. Was she missing a gene?

The store manager called to the woman from where she was stocking a shelf near the register and repeated what she'd said to Caroline when she'd walked into the shop.

"No, thank you, I'm just looking."

Hey, maybe she'd done something right. That's what she'd said, too.

The blonde glanced around the store and headed toward the lingerie section, and Caroline went back to sorting through bras. Some she liked, some she hated and some, well, they looked like something Mandy wore even though it was only gym class.

The woman wound up at a rack near her.

Ask. She'd know what to buy…the manager would, too. But she couldn't. That would be way too mortifying. And only a moron would even *have* to ask what to get. Caroline glared at the stupid sizes and tried to make sense of them in comparison to herself. She stared at the cup, then down at her chest. Why had she thought this would be easy?

"I hate doing this, don't you?"

She glanced up, embarrassed. Had she been staring at her boobs or the bras when the woman asked her the question? "E-excuse me?"

"Shopping for things like these. Oh, that's lovely." She indicated the bra in Caroline's hand. "And look at that." She pointed out another. "I think that would be beautiful with your peaches-and-cream skin tone."

Peaches and cream? She'd always considered herself a polka-dotted mess, sort of like oatmeal with too much brown sugar in spots.

Caroline didn't acknowledge her comment, and looked at the bra instead. It was light blue with a little lace around the edge to make it pretty. Nothing sexy or skimpy but…that was okay. Until she had someone like Travis in her life, pretty would do. But should she pick up something for later? Just in case?

"I guess. The sizes are weird…aren't they?" She

waited for the woman to laugh. She shouldn't have said that and felt stupid because of it, but the woman didn't even crack a smile. Maybe it wasn't so stupid?

"Most definitely. I wore the wrong size for years until I saw this show on television where this woman told how to pick the right one."

"Really?" Why couldn't she have seen that?

"Oh, look at this one." The woman showed her a pretty tan bra with thin straps. "I love it. This would be perfect to wear under T-shirts. It's got a great liner." She leaned toward her and lowered her voice. "That way no one can see if you're *cold*."

The woman put the bra back where it came from, and Caroline tried to act casual while she moved to that side. She definitely needed one of those. Some mornings she got chilled going into school, and she'd noticed Travis looking at her even though he was supposed to be dating Mandy.

Travis was cute. *Way* cute. A senior, starting quarterback and a track star. If she could date, he'd be *the one*.

Irritated at her useless dreaming, she glanced at the woman again. "So, um, how did she say they should fit?"

The pretty blonde continued looking at the bras and lingerie sets while she went over the requirements, not making a big deal out of having to talk to an idiot like her while she shopped.

"Have you tried any on yet?"

"A few." What a humiliating experience that was.

"No luck, huh?"

"Not really." Caroline bit her lip and wondered if her dad would give her a lecture about talking to strangers. "You, um, think this is about the right size?" She felt her face getting hot and hated how easily she turned red when she got embarrassed. Mandy always made fun every time it happened in school. Especially in gym class. If only she could show Mandy and steal Travis away. Talk about payback.

Like Travis would date a loser who didn't even wear makeup.

"I think it's close." The woman paused in what she was doing, her head tilted to one side. "But if you really want my opinion—"

"I do! I mean—" Geez, Caroline, act like a grown-up! "I mean, sure." She shrugged. "Whatever."

"Well, I think this one might fit a bit better. Or this one. Maybe try this one, too?" she asked, picking out three bras from the rack. "You look like a B-cup to me. Maybe 34 B?"

"Maybe." How did she know? They'd just appeared.

And about time, too. Mandy had had boobs for two years now. *And wore a 34 D.*

"Tell you what—I've got some time to kill while my friends grocery shop." She leaned forward and made a face. "I *hate* grocery shopping so you'd be doing me a favor by not making me go over there. If you want, you can try them on and if you need other sizes while you're in the fitting room, I'd be happy to pass them over the top to you."

"You wouldn't mind?"

The woman smiled the way she imagined a mom would...should. Cheerleader or not, this lady was cool.

"No, hon. I wouldn't mind at all."

SKYLAR STARED UP at the cloud-spotted sky and tried to figure out why her mom liked being up there so much.

"Come on, it's your turn."

"Quit bugging me. I don't want to play." She ignored the way her cousin Maura's little girl pouted, and shifted in the rocking chair, noting the cute guy by the barn shoveling manure into the back of the truck. She'd seen him somewhere before. At school maybe?

"Who's that?" she asked Lexi, trying to act casual in case he looked their way. It took the little girl forever just to glance in the right direction without her having to point him out.

"That's just Marcus. Come on, Skylar, play with me now. Please?"

"No." Maura's husband, Jake, had seen her walking around by the horses and asked her to keep an eye on his kid so he could help his brother in the paddock. She'd wanted to say no, but like the first time she'd seen him a week ago when they'd arrived at the ranch, Jake had that *dad* way of looking at her and making her feel like she had to do what he asked.

She knew Jake and Maura had done a nice thing by inviting them to stay at the ranch until her mom found another fly-job, but she still didn't like it here. She missed the noise of the city. The stuff to do. Here there was nothing to do but sit and think about how bored she was.

"But I got the cards all set up," Lexi groused. "Please, please, *please?*"

"Play solitaire."

"Will you show me how?"

She slowly banged her head against the back of the rocker three times.

"Why're you doing that?"

"Because I don't want to play. Count the cards or something and leave me alone." After all, she was busy staring at *Marcus*.

"But Daddy said—"

Skylar grabbed the deck of cards out of the kid's hand. "Give me the rest of them."

"What are you gonna do?" Lexi asked suspiciously.

Smart kid. Skylar was tempted to teach her 52-card pickup, but hesitated. The kid was bored, too, and who could blame her?

She felt a prickling sensation and glanced up, meeting Marcus-the-shit-shoveler's gaze. He smiled and lifted his head in greeting before he leaned the shovel against the barn and climbed into the truck. Cute, maybe, but there wasn't enough showering in the world that would erase that smell. She wanted to hold her nose every time the wind blew a certain way.

"Skylar? Skylar, come on, give 'em back."

"Do you want to see a trick or not?" she demanded when the truck disappeared down the road.

Lexi nodded and quickly gathered up the rest of the cards she'd spread out on the porch floor. "Here."

Skylar rolled her eyes, unable to believe she had to play with a five-year-old when she was going to be fifteen in a few months. "Listen up and do what I tell you." She quickly shuffled and spread the cards. "Pick one, but don't show me."

It was a stupid trick. One her dad had shown her

when she was a kid. Something to keep *her* quiet
when she'd bugged him. Sudden tears stung her
eyes and she blinked. PMS sucked. Made her all
teary and emotional. Tears were for people who
couldn't fight back.

"I got one."

Skylar folded the cards in on themselves. "Now
put that one on top, but don't forget what it is."

"Okay."

Lexi did as ordered and Skylar gently bent the
tip with her nail so that she'd know which card
was the right one. She shuffled them again,
counted off the cards and then asked, "This it?"

Lexi's whole face lit up in surprise. Just like
hers probably had when her dad had performed
the trick for her. Over and over and over again
until he'd look at his watch and say he had to go.

Did he have a mistress back then, too? When
she was little? How many times had he cheated
on her mom?

"How'd you do that?"

Skylar shrugged, ignoring the memories
because she kind of liked how Lexi looked at her
as if she were someone important. She got out of
the chair and lowered herself onto the porch. "I
know a couple more. Want to see?"

"Yes, please."

Lexi reminded her of her used-to-be friend

Nicole's little sister. She'd been polite, too, even when Nic called Skylar names because her dad had screwed Nic's mom. Nic's little sister hadn't blamed her, but Nicole had.

"Watch," she ordered, her voice raspy. Who cared what Nic thought? She hadn't been all that great of a friend anyway. But it didn't keep Skylar from wondering how many of her friends' moms her dad had slept with. Was that why the moms liked it when she came over? Because they hoped to see her dad?

Skylar lost count and had to start over again. Lexi followed the movements of her hands, her head sliding back and forth with every card she dropped onto the porch.

"How come you wear so many rings? And how come you wear black all the time?"

"Because I like it."

"Aren't you hot?"

Skylar kept counting.

"Why do you paint a tear on your face?"

"It's symbolic."

"Oh… What's symbolic?"

"It means it means something."

"But what?"

Skylar tossed the cards down. "Why don't you go see if your dad is done yet?"

"Is it 'cause you don't have a dad?"

She sucked in a sharp breath and glared at the kid. So much for being polite. "Don't you know it's rude to say things like that to people?"

"Sorry."

"You don't sound it."

"I am," Lexi argued, her ponytail bobbing. "Really. I'm sorry." Big tears trickled down the kid's cheeks.

Skylar rolled her eyes. "Oh, give me a break. Don't be such a crybaby."

"I'm not!"

"Then why are you crying?"

"Because it's sad."

"*What*'s sad?" she demanded, her patience gone. *When* were her mom and Maura going to get home?

"You're sad," Lexi stated firmly. "Aren't you? When Grace first came here she was sad, too."

Grace was sad? Skylar remembered thinking how cool Grace Rowland had looked the first time she'd seen her. Maura was introducing them to everyone, and Grace had jogged up the road toward them like running five miles was no big deal. Tall and strong, her head high. Like one of those women you see on television, like Oprah or somebody.

"What was Grace sad about?"

Lexi frowned, her tears drying up now that the subject had changed. "Somebody mean hurt her and she had bad dreams. A *lot* of bad dreams. I heard her sometimes when I was supposed to be asleep." The little girl leaned over her crossed ankles and patted her hand. "Don't worry. We made Grace happy, and we'll make you happy, too."

"And if you can't?" Skylar challenged, just because.

"I don't know. But why would you want to be sad forever?"

"TAKE IT ALL AWAY. The clothes, the makeup—"

"If she gets desperate enough, she might steal to get it back," Grace murmured, interrupting Maura long enough to slide a warning look over her shoulder to where Rissa sat in the back. "Or she could finally come to terms with you regaining control. Her reaction to you doing something that drastic would be a crapshoot you'd need to prepare yourself for."

Rissa leaned back between the two car seats, careful not to jar them. The twins had fallen asleep two seconds after being strapped in, tired from their adventure in town.

Considering what had happened last year when Skylar had taken her credit card and shopped like only a teenager can, she didn't want to tempt Skylar to steal to get her things back. There had to be other options, other ways.

"Okay, she started wearing the makeup and clothes when?" Maura asked for the second time.

"Right after Larry died."

"And the professionals think it's based solely on her dad's death?" Grace added, her tone thoughtful.

Rissa nodded. "Because of the timing. But there's something else...I don't know what," she told them. "Something I can't put my finger on. It's sad and horrible and I ache for her, but...something's not right. Sky's always been a little more mature than the other kids. I honestly would've thought she'd handle Larry's death better given time...which makes me think something else happened, something she hasn't told me."

"And maybe in hiding it, she's hiding herself?"

Rissa glanced at Grace, confused. "I don't understand."

Maura and Grace exchanged a look.

"What?"

"Rissa, I love you, you know that," Maura told her firmly.

"And I've learned to love Grace, too. She's a great sister-in-law and a wonderful friend and...I hope you don't mind that I've told her a bit about you and Larry...that you had problems before he died and...such."

Rissa nodded hesitantly. She and Maura had

been close growing up. Inseparable when their fathers were stationed on the same military base, pen pals when they weren't. Maura had seen her through dating, her mom's death, flight training and childbirth—and a cheating husband. Nearly all of it handled through long-distance phone calls and e-mail. Maybe that was the key, though. Sitting there three feet from her cousin, it was a lot harder to talk about all the problems she faced.

"Are you upset with me?"

Maura only tried to help and she loved her for it. "Of course not. It's all history, and at this point, I'll take all the help and advice I can get." She looked to Grace. "But are you sure you want to get in on this?"

Grace laughed softly. "Trust me, we've all got skeletons and secrets hidden away in closets. Don't feel bad or embarrassed. I'd love to help if I can."

"Okay," Maura said, her tone stating she was taking them back to the subject at hand, "just remember that what we're about to say is based on the three of us sitting here, driving back to the ranch tossing ideas around about Skylar's behavior. Okay?"

She shrugged. "Okay."

"Grace?"

Grace shifted sideways to better see her. "So...what if Skylar is hiding herself?" she repeated. "You said her behavior changed with her dad's death?"

"Yes, at least—" She bit her lip, frowning. Trying to remember and think of what it was that bugged her about the days before the accident. "Near there. After she told me about Larry's affair, I have to admit…I'm a little blurry on some things. I was in a fog, hurt. It took everything I had to function and a lot of times I just went through the motions. The tension got to us all. Skylar especially, since she'd told on her dad. She became really quiet after that, moodier. She…she didn't talk to either of us nearly as much as she used to, and she spent a lot of time at her friends' houses. I don't think she liked living in our house then and I really can't blame her. It wasn't pleasant."

"But that could've been a combination of things. Teenage hormones, the affair, the problems she had with her friend—what was her name again?" Maura asked.

"Nicole. Nicole Denniston. Her mother was the, um, woman Skylar caught Larry with."

"Then Skylar's behavior technically changed after telling the truth about the affair, not the accident."

"I suppose…" she agreed. "But she didn't go Goth then. That wasn't until after I brought her home from the hospital. I thought she was asleep upstairs, and didn't find out until right before she came home looking like a monster with my credit card in her hand that she'd even gone out. I couldn't believe it. The funeral was the next day, too."

"Then whatever it was she felt, *feels*, whatever it was that drove her to stay out of the house and away from you and Larry was probably affected even more by Larry's death."

Maura hit the turn signal to pull off the road onto the long drive leading to the ranch.

"Or, maybe it's a bad case of survivor's guilt like the doctors have told you," Maura added softly. "Maybe she feels guilty because she lived through the accident and her dad died."

Grace nodded. "If you and Larry had a rough spot, got back together and made up, maybe Skylar thinks you'd be happier if he'd lived instead of her, and in her mind, she believes that girl died with Larry. It's been proven that teenagers are known to have a fixation with death at this stage of their lives."

The air left Rissa's lungs. "One of the shrinks mentioned that, and we discussed it in a session. Granted I did more talking than she did, but I think Skylar knows better than to think…I've told her so many times how happy and thankful I am she's okay."

"Then maybe it is a coincidence in timing."

Maura's tone was soothing. "You know, girls also want to find themselves at her age. Establish a 'look' and be trendy. Maybe the crash acted like a near-death thing and the change is based on that and nothing else. It's possible, right?"

"Maybe." But she doubted it. Skylar's behavior was more than establishing a look, and her head hurt thinking about all the possibilities. Why couldn't Skylar be easy to read like the sheriff's daughter back at the little shop? Blushing over bra sizes and embarrassing questions about how one should fit.

Self-reproach slammed into her. Her daughter had been the sole survivor of a major car accident. She shouldn't compare her to anyone else, no matter what.

"We're here. Look, Rissa, she's outside and not at your cabin brooding. That's a good sign, right?"

Rissa leaned forward to look out the windshield where Grace discreetly pointed. Skylar slouched by the paddock, Lexi at her side talking animatedly.

Maura drove the vehicle up to the bunkhouse and parked next to the large kitchen and dining area that had been added onto the building during the renovations. They'd unload the groceries into the multiple refrigerators and freezers, and wait for the delivery trucks to bring the rest of the requested specialty items later in the week.

"Mommy, Daddy asked Skylar to babysit me! She's fun!" Lexi cried the moment Maura opened the van door.

"Really? Well, thank you, Skylar. Lexi's very particular when it comes to who can babysit her. You must have a special knack."

Skylar shrugged and looked away. Embarrassed by the praise?

Rissa climbed out and tried to think of the last time she'd praised Skylar for something, but only remembered their arguments. Her breath lodged in her chest—how could she have forgotten how important positive reinforcement is?

"Whatever. She only cried a little when I pierced her belly button."

Shocked silence filled the air.

Lexi giggled. "*Mommmmy,* Skylar's teasing you! She got you good, didn't she?"

Maura laughed weakly and shot Rissa a rueful glance. "That she did."

"But can I?"

"Can you what?"

"Can I get a belly button ring like Skylar's?"

CHAPTER FOUR

JONAS WAS STILL LAUGHING at his deputy's joke when he entered the diner. Porter called out from the kitchen, and he raised a hand in reply. It was Saturday night and the diner was full. The ranch hands had been paid, and the small town overflowed with people looking for a little food and a lot of rowdy fun.

Two men were on duty all weekend to handle things, but Jonas often felt the need to pitch in a few extra hours in the evenings during the warm months since the ranch hands were more prone to leave the bunkhouses and venture into town. Usually things were fairly quiet, but he refused to be caught off guard.

"Ah, come on, sweetie, sit down with us. Ain't seen nothin' pretty in here in a long time. Lord knows Charlotte lost her waistline years ago eating Porter's food."

Jonas glanced toward the back of the diner where a new waitress stood with her back to him. His gaze narrowed. Why did she look familiar?

"Thanks, but no thanks. Here's your drinks and your bill. Bring it to the register when you're ready."

"I'm ready all right. What are you doing tonight after your shift?"

The waitress ignored the man and moved to another table. "Can I take your order?"

Rissa?

"Hey, I wasn't finished with you yet."

Ignoring the two newly emptied seats along the counter, Jonas walked over to where a booth had opened up near the hecklers.

"Sir, if you want to wait a minute I'll get that cleaned off for you."

"Take your time."

At the sound of his voice, she looked over her shoulder, her face flushing a dull burgundy when she spotted him. The crowd of cowboys quieted down, at least as much as a group of men could in the presence of a woman worthy of flirtation. Rissa Mathews was fresh blood in a community made up mostly of women already attached to someone. Word had probably spread like wildfire that she was a widow even with the Rowland name protectively associated with hers.

She returned to taking the table's order, ripped the slip off her pad of paper and hurried behind the counter to hand it to Porter. That done, she grabbed a tray from where they were stashed and headed back toward his booth.

Jonas ignored the dirty dishes stacked in the middle of the table. Restless, he picked up a menu to give his hands something to do even though he'd memorized the contents when he was eight or nine years old. It hadn't changed much since.

"Let me grab these for you." Rissa hurried to pile the dishes onto the tray and carried them to the counter before rushing back again to wipe the table down. "Sorry about that."

"No problem. But you'd better stop rushing around so hard or you'll be worn out long before the place clo—"

"Oh, yeah, now there's a view."

Rissa rolled her eyes, but didn't take the man to task. The comment had embarrassed her though because her cheeks reddened again.

Jonas focused on the group in the corner and adopted his sheriff's face. "That you, Ted? Surely not. You've got a daughter about her age, don't you? Can't help but make the comparison, almost like you're flirting with your little girl." He pursed his lips and shook his head. "There's somethin' not right about that."

The older ranch hand cursed and grabbed his

drink from the table, glowering when his younger buddies snickered at him. The group of men reverted to talking amongst themselves in low tones, but made no more comments even though Jonas saw them ogling Rissa every few minutes.

He couldn't blame them for looking. Dressed in snug jeans and a white T-shirt with an apron tied about her slim waist, she was a pretty sight.

"Thanks, but I can handle them."

"Let me guess, because you're from New York?"

"That's right," she countered without missing a beat, her eyes sparkling. "Ever hear anything about New York City women? We can kick butt and hail a taxi at the same time."

He smiled at her boast. "You're good to go then," he agreed. "But at least let me say thanks for earlier today. Caroline came out behind you grinning like she'd won the lottery."

"It was fun. She was thrilled when she figured out how things were supposed to fit."

"Visitors don't usually get jobs. Have you decided to stay?"

"Yes, well, no, not for long, but—" When he raised an eyebrow, she made a face and glanced around before she lowered her voice. "I am just visiting, but…I'm sort of in between jobs at the moment. The airline I flew for made some permanent layoffs and I was job-hunting when the accident occurred. Then I sold our house thinking we'd buy another wherever my new job took me, but I haven't had any luck yet. That's when Maura invited me to come help out at the ranch in exchange for one of the cabins. How could I refuse? It felt good to get away from everything, and I get to visit with her while I scatter resumes across the country."

If she attached a picture to them, she'd be hired a lot faster. Jonas nearly groaned at the thought. "Which airline was it?"

"You wouldn't have heard of it. It was small and privately owned. They mostly catered to high-paid executives and Wall Street types in the New York area."

The kind of men she preferred? What had her husband done for a living?

"Order up, Rissa! Ben, you need more coffee?"

"Be right there," she called. "What can I get you?"

"Turkey sandwich, no pickle or onion, and a water."

"Chips or fries?"

"Whatever fruit you've got. Porter'll know. He's used to me."

She scribbled the order down and took off toward the kitchen again, and it took everything in him not to follow her swaying hips like the other men present. He managed. Barely.

Jonas braced his elbows on the table and rubbed his hand against his mouth.

What was it that drew him to big-city girls?

THE WEEKEND PASSED in a blur of exhaustion for Rissa. Working at the ranch in the morning and the diner in the evening, she had little time for laundry, keeping the minuscule cabin picked up so that it wouldn't resemble a dorm room or spending time with Skylar. Not that her daughter seemed to mind.

After hearing all about the tricks Skylar had taught Lexi to keep her occupied, Maura had asked Skylar to babysit the kids—with Maura sticking close by just in case. Skylar hadn't looked thrilled by the idea, but the mention of cold, hard cash had her daughter nodding her agreement— and Rissa cringing because Skylar had finally agreed to get off her duff and do something to earn money. But did she have the heart to demand a portion of Skylar's small earnings to pay toward the debt Skylar owed her?

Rissa knew her cousin asked partly to help her out where Skylar was concerned, and she was grateful. With Skylar watching the kids under Maura's supervision on weekends, she could work at the diner and not worry, plus it freed Maura to do other things for brief periods of time.

Tonight she'd noticed the library was directly across the street from the diner. And three nights a week they didn't close until nine o'clock. She didn't like leaving Skylar unattended in a public place, but considering North Star held the equivalent population of the local mall back home, she figured a few hours in the library with her next door would be fine.

Rissa slowed to a stop outside Jake and Maura's newly built house. The lights were on in the kitchen, and inside she saw her daughter's dark head and pale skin. Her fingers tightened on the steering wheel. Was she putting too much pressure on Skylar to make amends for the thousand dollars? Maybe she should let the credit card thing drop?

No. Skylar had done wrong. She needed to be held accountable and work off the expensive charge, at least a large portion of it. Skylar was just lucky she hadn't reported the card stolen.

And the belly button ring?

She collapsed against the seat with a groan. Like it or not, she wasn't her military father who would've walked up to her and yanked it out by force.

"Stop worrying. Maura said that Skylar has been great with the kids."

Rissa started and glanced out her lowered window to see Grace walking toward her car. "What are you doing out here so late?"

The other woman laughed, the sound sheepish. "Maura called earlier to say she was working on a new dessert for our special guest and after thinking about it the last couple hours, I decided maybe I should taste-test it. What can I say, the chocolate is calling me."

Rissa laughed and shut off the engine. "Count me in," she said, getting out of the vehicle.

Grace's gaze narrowed on her face. "You look tired, Rissa. You can only burn the candle at both ends for so long. Trust me. I know you need the cash, but remember to take care of yourself. It's been a hard year for you, and a person can only do so much."

They fell into step side by side but when they reached the porch, Rissa paused.

"Something wrong?" Grace asked.

Rissa shook her head, watching Skylar through the window. Jake had walked into the room and handed Skylar a bottle, keeping another for himself. He plucked one of his sons into his arms and settled into a nearby chair, but Skylar sat there and her bemused expression slowly turned into a coaxing, gentle one replete with a fleeting smile when her charge spied the bottle and rolled onto his knees to crawl to her.

"See? She's coming around. Kids are great judges of character, and Lexi already thinks the world of her—the boys, too. Grief takes time, but she's getting better. Right there's the proof."

"Tell that to the school officials," she muttered drearily. "And the town. They've already condemned her. It's all over town how some vampire girl is beating up poor innocent victims."

"They'll forget once she settles down."

"Maybe." She brushed her hair away from her face, but the night breeze blew it right back again. "Grace…yesterday Maura mentioned you've taken quite a few classes to get your psychology degree?"

"I have, but not to practice or anything. They give me a better understanding of my patients and…I'm training to begin a women's support group for domestic violence and victims of violent crimes. This area doesn't have one."

"Wow. That's wonderful. I've volunteered to help out here and there with different causes, but never with something like that. I wouldn't know what to say, and I know I wouldn't know what to do if I was ever faced with that kind of situation."

Grace smiled, her gaze not quite meeting hers. "Yeah, well, time has proven to me that we're stronger than we think. With the right support system people can do more than they ever dreamed possible. They just need someone to—" she shrugged "—push them a little. Give them a shoulder when they need it or…just be a friend."

"Well, if I can help while I'm here, let me know, okay?"

Grace laughed softly. "Thanks for the offer, Rissa, but right now I think you've got enough going on."

"Ahh, yeah, probably so." She gave Grace a weary smile. "Um…Maura also mentioned you sometimes need help around the gym with your physical therapy sessions?"

"True, so how about I ask Skylar?"

"Pretty obvious, aren't I?"

Grace climbed the last two stair treads. "Yes, but I understand why. And it's not a problem at all. The extra pair of hands would help."

Rissa was humbled by her friend's quick acceptance. "I guess I didn't expect it to be this easy. In the past year, people have taken one look at her and immediately written her off as a lost cause."

"Not here. Rissa, you're not alone. That's what family—even extended family—is for," Grace murmured, the lights from the house revealing her warm expression. "I'm happy to try talking to her in the downtime between patients, but please remember I can't make any promises. I'm not an expert by any means."

"No, I—I don't expect any." Her gaze found Skylar again and she noted the way her daughter's face had softened now that she looked into the drowsy eyes of the baby staring up at her. She remembered holding Skylar the same way. "But maybe she'll talk to you…give you some clue… Grace, I'm getting desperate. I need to know what happened to my little girl."

Grace wrapped her arms around her and hugged her briefly. "I know you do. Just hang in there and remember you can talk to me and Maura anytime, all right?"

She nodded, said a quick prayer and thanked God above for her friends. Right now they were the glue holding her together.

TUESDAY EVENING Skylar glared at her mother. Two days of detention down, three to go.

It wasn't as bad as it could have been. Sitting there staring at the walls for two hours with the assistant coach watching her every move sucked, but both days *he'd* come by. Turned out Marcus-the-shit-shoveler was a football player.

"What am I going to *do* for five hours?"

"Homework?" Her mom turned onto the main road into town. "Use the time to get your grades up."

"Who cares what my grades are?"

"*I* do. And so did you at one point."

Her mom stopped at a red light, the first of six until they reached the diner. What kind of town only had *six* stoplights?

"Prove to me you can make A's like you used to."

"For what? What do I get out of it?"

Her mom muttered something under her breath. "Skylar, I'm not going to reward you for doing something you ought to already be doing."

"Just asking." She straightened the skull-and-crossbones ring on her right hand. "But I'm not sitting in the car for five hours."

"I don't expect you to," her mother said as she accelerated the second after the light turned green. "The library is directly across the street from the diner. You can stay there until it closes. I went inside Saturday evening on my break. There's a seating area in front of the windows to the left of the door. Plant yourself there and stay there, except to go to the bathroom. Read, listen to music. Play on the computers. I don't care, but *stay there.* When the library closes, come to the diner. It's pretty dead after eight o'clock so you can sit in a back booth until we close up."

"Your boss won't like it."

"He'll be fine if you behave yourself."

Skylar tapped the window with her rings. Should she tell her now? "I…got in trouble again today."

Her mom's head jerked toward her. "What?"

The second light turned red. *"Watch out!"*

The wreck flashed through her mind in an instant. Her dad driving, yelling at her. Cursing, swerving, weaving in and out of traffic trying to get there faster. Then he'd cut a delivery truck off and—

Her mom jerked the car to a stop at the last minute, but Skylar sat frozen, unable to catch her breath because the deafening sound of squealing tires and crunching metal filled her head, the horn blaring from where her dad lay slumped against it. Blood. His blood. All over everything.

If you'd only kept your stupid mouth shut.

"Skylar? Oh, honey, I scared you. I'm so—"

"I'm okay." She tried to swallow, but the lump in her throat wouldn't let her.

"You had a flashback, didn't you?"

The tenderness in her mom's voice brought tears to her eyes and she blinked, belatedly realizing her mom had put her hand over hers where she clenched the seat like a baby holding onto a blanket.

"I'm okay," she repeated, her voice sounding hoarse in her ears, unable to let go even though she told herself to.

"Yes, you are. You're fine and you're here, and I thank God for you every day."

She laughed weakly. "Don't overdo it." She unclenched her hand and pulled it from beneath her mom's, then slid her arms around her stomach and squeezed. She felt sick. Hot. Really dizzy. She leaned her head against the seat rest, stared straight ahead and tried to forget about everything but being in her mom's car right at that moment.

The light changed.

"Skylar—"

"It's green now. Go."

A horn honked behind them. Some people were idiots. Always in a hurry. She wanted to flip the jerk off because she felt like it, but thankfully the horn made her mom get the car going again.

"So…how did you get in trouble?"

The sick feeling was slowly fading, but now she had the shakes. Quivering inside like a puppy on its first car ride. God, she was a mess. "The stupid teachers don't like me."

"And you're completely innocent?"

Her mom's tone was soft, quiet, like she asked simply because she wanted to believe her. *Yeah, right.* "Me and a girl got into it, that's all."

"What girl? Who?"

She shrugged. "Mandy somebody. She's a bitch."

"Watch your language, Sky. That is not acceptable."

"Well, she is. And before you say it's my fault, what happened to the whole spiel about not making fun of people? I don't say stuff to her, not unless she says things to me first."

Her mom slid her a glance and pulled in to park right in front of the library. Geez, she really didn't trust her, did she? So much for using the excuse of getting something out of the car if she needed a break.

"What's your punishment?"

"Another week."

"*Skylar!*"

"It's not fair! She started it and she didn't get anything!"

"Were there any witnesses?"

"Only her friends. Look, just forget it, okay?"

"How can I when the drama never ends?" Her mom shook her head, her eyes sad when she looked at her. "What's next? Jail? Violent people lead violent lives. It's a simple fact. And eventually those people have to own up to what they've done."

"*She* started it!"

Her mom sighed and grabbed her purse and the apron she'd left on the backseat. "Maybe she did. But from the sound of things, *you* ended it."

Skylar sucked in a sharp breath. She'd ended it all right. Everything had happened because of her.

CAROLINE STARED at the new girl from school. Her dad would be picking her up soon and she needed to sit by the windows to see him when he drove up unless she wanted him getting out of the *police car* and coming in after her. Why couldn't he drive a normal car when he wasn't working?

everyone. She hadn't even blinked, but if Mr. Kline had said that to her, she knew she'd have bawled. Mandy really would've made fun then.

Caroline shifted in the uncomfortable chair and wished Skylar would smile or something. She should've gone outside to wait even though her dad told her not to because it wasn't safe. It wasn't like she was a kid who had to watch out for perverts or anything. Besides, who'd want her? She was ugly. Her mouth too big, her legs too short, her body too skinny and covered with ugly freckles. And how could she ever forget about the hair? She knew that somehow she was related to Carrot Top.

"I used to eat lunch with Mandy," she murmured, trying to make conversation, "but now I eat by myself. Maybe we could, I don't know, sit together tomorrow? If you want."

The girl stared at her, her black-lined eyes narrowed in suspicion. "Whatever."

Caroline smiled, then felt stupid. She was such a geek. Biting her lip, she looked down, hesitant. "My dad won't be here for a little bit. Want to help me find a name book?"

CHAPTER FIVE

JONAS HAD JUST sat down at one of the counter stools in the diner when his cell phone beeped at him. He checked the number and groaned. It had been a long day and all he wanted was to go home and spend some quiet time with Caroline before having to spend the following two or three evenings cleaning the house before Marilyn's next weekly visit.

Dave was supposed to come with her, but Jonas knew his ex-father-in-law would cancel like he always did. Other than a weekend visit here or there, Dave stayed in Helena and let Marilyn do her thing on her own. Jonas figured it was Dave's way of getting some peace and quiet himself once a week.

He flipped the phone open with a sigh. "Taggert."

"You at the diner, Sheriff?"

"Yeah, why?"

"Mrs. Keenan called. Said there's a disturbance at the library."

He turned to look out the windows of the diner.

A group of kids stood clustered inside the large windows, and from across the street, he spied Caroline's thick, curly mass of hair. "I'm on it."

Rissa came out from behind the swinging door with a takeout bag, but hesitated when she saw him. "What's wrong?"

Jonas slipped the phone back in its place. "A problem at the library with some kids. Hang on to that for me, will you? I'll be right back."

"The library?"

He nodded distractedly and headed for the door, made it across the street and inside the library before he realized Rissa had followed him into total chaos. A half dozen girls stood circled around two rolling on the floor. Both screeched, cursed and swore like pros.

"Break it up!" Jonas grabbed the spectators by their arms and pulled them out of the way until he got to the middle of the group. There he found some girl who looked like she'd come from an episode of *The Munsters* and Mandy Blake going at it like prizefighters. Just that morning he'd gotten a call from a concerned parent warning him there was a new girl at school who looked like a member of a cult, one who they felt needed to be closely watched. This was definitely her.

"Knock it off!" he roared when the girls kept swinging and screeching. A quick glance showed

Caroline standing quietly in the windowed alcove, her hands over her mouth in wide-eyed upset.

Jonas separated the girls and shook them to get their attention before he glowered at the rest of the group taking it all in. "Go home. *Now.*"

The girls began to disperse. They whispered amongst themselves and shot speculative glances over their shoulders.

Jonas gently shoved Mandy into one of the nearby chairs, the girl in black in the other. "What—"

"—*is going on?*" Rissa demanded hotly from behind him.

Jonas turned. Rissa looked primed for a fight herself due to the girls' antics, but when she noticed him staring at her, she bit her lip and a deep red flush crawled up her neck into her face.

"Rissa, go back to the diner. I'll take care of this and be there to get my food after I'm done talking to these two."

Her shoulders slumped slightly. "I can't do that."

Something about her expression warned him he wasn't going to like her answer to his next question. "Why not?"

She glared at the girl in black. "Because you're about to talk to my daughter and I want to hear what you have to say."

Jonas turned to stare down at the frightening face of the girl in black, and tried to put two and two together. Chalky white makeup covered her skin, her black lipstick and blush smeared. *Rissa's daughter?* "What's your name?"

"Skylar."

"How old are you?"

"Too young for you, perv."

Her smug look and cocky response had his hands clenching into fists.

"Skylar!" Rissa groaned softly. "She'll be fifteen in September."

Less than a year older than Caroline. He would've guessed her to be much older. His daughter was just beginning to develop, whereas Skylar Mathews had the body of a woman. Although covered by her black attire, the girl's generous breasts heaved with the aftermath of the fight.

He split his attention between the girls. "What happened?"

"I didn't do anything, Mr. Taggert."

"Dad—"

Mandy glared at his daughter, her chin lifted to a haughty angle. "Shut up, *Car-ly.*"

Carly? Jonas looked at Caroline and found her blushing furiously, her gaze glued to the floor.

"This is between freak-queen and me," Mandy continued bluntly.

"Watch your mouth," Rissa ordered Mandy.

"Girls your age should know better than to call people names."

Jonas held up a hand for silence. "What were you going to say?" he asked Caroline.

Instead of looking at him, his daughter glanced at Skylar, her eyes wide and questioning. Jonas almost missed the slight shake of Skylar's head. Unfortunately, Caroline heeded the warning and didn't speak.

"Girls, do I need to take you to the station to get to the bottom of this?"

"It was just an argument," Skylar muttered. "No big deal."

"She already has two weeks detention for fighting," Mandy volunteered.

The Blake girl gazed up at him, pretending innocence despite the nail scrapes down Skylar's arm and the bruises beginning to darken beneath the other girl's light skin.

"She's caused trouble since she got here. Just ask Principal Kline."

Jonas didn't like Mandy's attitude, but she was giving him needed information Skylar didn't refute. Nor did Rissa. Shaking his head, he glanced at Rissa, but saw she still glowered in the general direction of her daughter. He looked to Caroline next, but knew in an instant she wasn't about to say another word in front of the two girls.

What was it with females? Guys could beat each other senseless and get a beer right after, but females held a grudge for life.

He scrubbed a hand over his face. "That doesn't tell me what started this particular fight."

"She did." Mandy pointed a glossy, fake nail at Skylar. "She said nasty things about me and called me a bitch."

"Skylar, did you?"

Jonas heard the pain in Rissa's query and forced himself to ignore it. He'd known Mandy Blake since she was a kindergartner in the same class as Caroline, whereas Skylar—

He glanced at Rissa again. What was the deal? The girl couldn't drive, couldn't work. She couldn't have bought the makeup and weird clothes. Not without Rissa taking her to do so. *Allowing* it. How could Rissa look so normal and yet her daughter…

"I won't do it again, Mr. Taggert. All I want is for her to stay away from me and my friends. Right, Caroline?"

His daughter's face colored to yet a deeper shade of pink.

"I—I—"

The door to the library opened and Mandy's mother hurried inside. "What's going on? One of the girls called and said Mandy was attacked again."

Jonas prayed for the day to be over. "No one attacked anyone."

"You." Doreen pointed a finger at Skylar, and Jonas saw Rissa stiffen. If he didn't discharge the situation soon, another fight would take place—between the mothers.

"Doreen, nothing happened that I can't handle," he stated forcefully. "And before you pursue this further, I should warn you that if I have to, I'll take both girls to the station in the back of my cruiser. *Handcuffed.* Mandy caused quite a few bruises of her own as you can see."

Just as he figured, Mandy hurriedly shook her head at her mom, visibly horrified at the thought of being so humiliated. "Mom, no. The freak knows to leave me alone now."

"This is the third time she's come after Mandy, Jonas. *Do* something."

"I'll take care of it."

Doreen stepped closer to Skylar, her mouth flattened into a line of disdain. "Mandy says your father is dead, and all I can say is that it's a good thing he can't see you behave—"

Jonas rushed to step between Rissa and Doreen, vaguely conscious of the library door opening again. One of his deputies entered, along with Porter from across the street.

"How dare you say that to her!"

"Sheriff?"

"Rissa, what're you doin' over—"

"Why wouldn't I? Look at her! Not only does she look like a freak, she's violent and it's obvious where she gets it!"

"Being unique is better than looking like everyone else—and I sincerely doubt your daughter is all that innocent! Look at *her!*"

Jonas's head pounded harder. *"Enough!"* He glared at Rissa and had to fight back a smile when he saw her chin go up another notch. Her daughter might be…unusual, but Rissa was a protective mother. *If only Lea had been the same way toward Caroline.* "This ends now. Mandy, if I catch you and Skylar fighting again, I'll take you both in for inciting a public disturbance, understood?"

"But—"

"Understood?"

"Yes."

"Doreen, take Mandy home."

"Jonas, I insist you— What about that *child?*" Doreen never took her poisonous glare off Rissa.

"I'll handle it."

Mandy and Doreen shot them all killing stares before stalking out of the library.

"If she can leave, so can I," Skylar declared, her tone lacking one iota of remorse.

"Skylar, sit down and *shut up,*" Rissa ordered.

Porter cleared his throat. "I've got a business to run. Rissa, settle things here and go on home. It's slow tonight."

She closed her eyes briefly and nodded. "Thanks, Porter. I'll come in early this weekend and make it up."

The older man shook his head in bewilderment and left the library after taking a long, hard look at Skylar. Jonas felt the same way.

"Sheriff?"

"Go on back to work, Tomblin. I've got this covered."

The librarian had stood silent watching the whole unbelievable scene, and now the matronly Mrs. Keenan made herself scarce in the back of the library.

Rissa moved toward the chairs. "Skylar, *what* happened?"

"Nothing."

"Caroline?" he pressed, gentling his tone.

Once again his daughter glanced at the black-clad girl, her head down. "Nothing," she mumbled. "Mandy's just a spoiled brat. She wanted to sit here and when we wouldn't move, she started saying things she shouldn't have. That's all."

"Saying things is a lot different than throwing punches."

Caroline's nose turned red and her lower lip trembled with the threat of tears. Skylar stared blankly ahead, silent, a sneer on her face.

Jonas shook his head and looked for signs of drugs, but saw nothing. He turned to Rissa and his words stuck in his throat when he took in her vulnerable expression. Like Caroline, her eyes were bright with unshed tears. He found himself wanting to offer comfort, though not the fatherly kind he'd offer his daughter.

"One day, Sky? You couldn't make it *one day?*"

Caroline's head lifted at the raw, husky sound of Rissa's voice, and his daughter watched the exchange, biting her lip before she stepped forward. The moment she opened her mouth to speak, however, Skylar launched herself out of the chair.

"Arrest me, or I'm outta here."

He jerked a thumb toward the door. "You can go. But don't let it happen again or I will."

"Wait for me in the car," Rissa ordered, pulling a key from her pocket.

Skylar swiped it out of Rissa's hand. "What-*ever*."

"I'm going, too," Caroline added softly, glancing at him quickly before looking away. "I'll be outside, Dad, okay?"

He nodded. The library door closed behind the angry teen and his daughter, leaving him and Rissa alone. Silence stretched between them. Finally, Rissa sighed. "Thank you for not—thank you. It seems I owe you again."

"Has she ever threatened you?"

"*No*. And thanks for the vote of confidence." She laughed wearily, the sound lacking all traces of humor. "You're like them, aren't you? After one look, you think you know everything there is to know about her."

"I know what I saw and heard when I pulled her and Mandy apart, and that's enough to have me wondering why you've put up with it. Why you're *putting* up with it." Jonas rubbed his neck. "Rissa, from one single parent to another—that girl is out of control."

Her chin raised, her cornflower blue eyes filled with upset. "'That girl' witnessed her father's death firsthand. You're the sheriff, Jonas, have *you* ever seen a gory accident?"

He nodded slowly, reluctantly.

"Then you have an idea of what she's seen, what she's been through. She had to watch it all. She *heard* what they said and did when they cut her dad out of the vehicle to get to her. When I got to the hospital she was covered in blood—*his* blood. If that's not enough for you to have a little compassion, I don't know what is."

"I'm sorry about your husband, and that Skylar

had to go through that, but it doesn't excuse what just happened. Her behavior—"

"She's not the only teenager out of control. What about the other girl?"

"You're making excuses. Yes, Mandy is at fault, too, but Rissa, you strike me as a levelheaded woman. Are you really going to stand there and talk up Skylar's behavior and attitude in an attempt to pass it off as *normal?*"

"I'm *saying* I'm not perfect," she bit out, her voice low, shaking, "and while I would love nothing more than to be able to compare my angry, self-destructing daughter to your quiet, sweet Caroline, I can't. I don't have a magic wand to make her better. If I did, I'd use it!"

"I don't want you to compare them," he countered, feeling guilty that he had done just that. "I'm simply suggesting—" Jonas broke off, unsure of what to say. Was he really going to offer advice? How could he when he was out of his element with Caroline and the simple matter of bras?

"Well?" Rissa said impatiently. "Let's hear it. Tell me how to understand her. How many kids would be okay after watching their father bleed to death all over them? Would Caroline? Do you think I *like* the change in Skylar? She wasn't like this before!"

"Maybe not. Maybe you can't control her

attitude or change the past, but you can control what you buy her to wear."

She laughed, the sound high-pitched, full of pain and anger and fear, emotions he knew too well.

"What's so funny?"

Rissa smirked and wiped away an errant tear before it could fall from her lashes. Shaking her head, she turned on her heel and stalked toward the door, her long strides eating up the distance. "Nothing. That's just *really* funny coming from someone who obviously hasn't seen what his daughter bought the other day in the form of underwear."

"GET IN THE CABIN and stay there."

Skylar didn't move. Her mom got out and slammed the door hard enough to rock the car, and she wanted to ask where she was going, but figured she already knew. By tomorrow Grace and Maura and their husbands would be giving her those looks, the kind older people gave kids.

Her mom disappeared into the trees between their cabin and the ranch house without a backward glance, but she didn't expect anything else. The order to stay in the cabin was the first words her mom had said to her since the library. She didn't know how Carly's dad already knew her mom, but it was obvious that he'd liked her up until he realized they were a package deal.

She snorted. At least she didn't have to worry about them hooking up. Not now anyway. Besides, she wasn't staying in this loser town any longer than she had to.

"You gonna sit there all night, or get out?"

Skylar glanced into the side mirror and smothered a groan. "What business is it of yours?"

The poop-scooper sat atop a horse, slowly making his way closer. When he got a good look at her face, he shook his head. *"Again?"*

Skylar abruptly shoved her door open and smirked when the horse jerked in surprise and he had to hurry to calm it. She probably did look stupid just sitting there, but at least she wasn't wearing a dumb T-shirt that read *Save a horse, ride a cowboy.*

"You and Mandy get into it again, or was it some other enemy?"

"Do I look like I want to talk to you?"

Marcus nudged the horse with his heels. "Fine, but you'd better go put some ice on your cheek."

He sounded like he cared, but she knew better. Marcus was one of them. "It was courtesy of your friend, Mandy." Even though her cheek hadn't hurt that much before, it did now that he'd mentioned it.

"Guess your mom's pretty ticked at you, huh? I saw her storm off after she pulled in."

Skylar grabbed her backpack from the rear seat. "You could say that." She remembered how her mom had taken on Mrs. Blake, and almost smiled. Until she thought of how Carly's dad had looked after her mom had claimed her for a daughter. Was that why her mom was so mad? Because she'd embarrassed her in front of him?

Had to be. It wasn't like it was her first fight.

"You wanna tell me what happened?"

She shouldered the bag with a wince. Another bruise? Gym would be fun. "Why, so you can run to Mandy and tell her what I said?"

"I wouldn't do that."

"Yeah, right."

"Look, just ignore Mandy and she'll move on. By letting her get to you, you're giving her power. Ignore her and she'll find someone else to pick on."

She didn't acknowledge his words. Instead she headed for the porch steps and hoped he didn't see how stiff she walked.

"Skylar?"

"What?" God, she hurt.

"Mandy's in a mood over the end of school and summer. She's after everybody."

"Is that supposed to make it okay?"

The saddle creaked when he shifted. "She has to spend most of every summer with her dad in

Washington. I just thought you might want to know she'll be gone soon."

She gripped the porch rail, the muscles in her leg pulling painfully because one of Mandy's wanna-bes had either stepped on her or kicked her during the fight. "Yeah, well, so will I. I can't wait to get out of here and go somewhere where the jocks don't smell like horseshit."

The words left her mouth before she could stop them. She made it to the top step and paused, but by the time she had the nerve to turn around and say, "Marcus, I'm sor—" he was gone.

Cursing and not caring who heard, she let herself into the cabin. She'd been a latch-key kid for as long as she could remember, but she always hated coming home alone. It was too quiet.

Sniffling, she grabbed hold of the banister rail leading up to her room and began the long climb. Her cheek hurt with every beat of her heart, but she didn't feel like getting ice or a wet rag. Besides it was nothing compared to how badly she felt about telling Marcus he smelled. *Why* couldn't she ever keep her mouth shut? When would she learn?

Skylar eased onto her bed and took her boots off, every pull shooting pain through her sore body. But she figured she deserved the pain after causing so much of it. Deserved it for what she'd done.

Half an hour later she was lying on the bed in the same position when the phone rang. Skylar ignored it. But when the phone kept blaring, she rolled her eyes and snatched it up. "What?"

Silence.

She snorted. Great, that was all she needed. Prank calls from Mandy and her group of losers. Would Marcus join in after what she'd said? She started to slam the phone back on the base when she heard a noise on the other end. "Who is this?"

"It's me," came a choked whisper, "I wanted to say thank y-you." A sniffle sounded. "Sk-Skylar, I'm so *sorry*."

"Forget about it."

"But—" Carly's voice broke and Skylar pictured her crying like a baby. The way she'd been the first time she'd seen her last week in the bathroom.

"You're letting her get to you again. Mandy's a bitch. Forget about her. Ignore her and she loses her power." Skylar winced when she realized she'd used Marcus's words.

She'd apologize later. Tomorrow. *If he talked to her again.*

"I don't mean to cry or—or… Every time I stand there and hear her say those horrible things about me, I think she'll stop, but then she doesn't, and everybody laughs and—"

"I'm not laughing."

"I'm going to make her stop," Carly promised thickly. "I *am*. Before I'm through, Mandy will be the one crying. She'll see."

Skylar stilled, not liking the way Carly said that. "What are you going to do?"

"I'm—I've got to go."

"She's a *loser*, Carly. I'm your friend now, and I'll be a better one," Skylar bragged, sick to her stomach at the way the girl sounded. Sort of desperate and sad and broken. "What do you mean about making Mandy stop… *Carly?*"

"I don't know yet, but just *some*thing! Something that'll make her realize I can be popular, too. Something that'll really shut her up and show her."

"Like what? What're you gonna do? You've got something in mind or you wouldn't have said that."

"Dad's home," Carly said in a rush, her voice lowering to a whisper. "I've got to go."

"Carly, come on. Don't do anything stupid. Promise me you—"

"No," she said hoarsely. "I'm tired of Mandy laughing at me and telling me what a loser I am. She thinks she's so hot, but she's *not*. She's going to regret making fun of me because I'm going to show her how wrong she is, and prove I can do what I want."

"Let me take care of Mandy, okay? Forget about her, and don't do something stupid."

A click sounded on the line like lightning had snapped somewhere. Skylar looked outside and saw dark clouds in the distance. Great. A freakin' storm. She hated storms. It reminded her of the accident. It had been storming then, too.

Air left her lungs in a rush. She turned away from the window, and wished her mom would come home. Wished she hadn't been so mean to the only other person who'd been nice to her. Had Marcus gone to the barn or was he still out there, her words the last he'd hear?

"But, Skylar—"

"Keep your mouth shut, Carly. I mean it. You don't say or do *any*thing, you hear me? You'll regret it if you do…. Trust me."

"I'M TELLING YOU I heard them. No mistake, Rissa. Your daughter threatened mine on the phone last night. Told her to keep her mouth shut or she'd regret it."

Rissa slumped forward against one of the many tables scattered about the large informal dining area and leaned her head in her hand, wishing she could go back to searching the Internet for pilot jobs as she'd been doing before Jonas had shown up demanding they talk.

A few of the ranch guests visiting before the summer rush sat by the large stone fireplace lining the wall, talking amongst themselves and waiting for breakfast to be served. A family of four crowded around a table in the corner playing Go Fish, the father in a wheelchair, his young daughter in his lap giggling because every time he discarded, the man blew a raspberry into the little girl's neck.

"What did Caroline say?"

Jonas wrapped his fingers around the coffee cup in front of him. "First she said I should call her *Carly,* a name your daughter apparently found in a book—and that I was wrong," he muttered. "She says they're friends."

"Then are you sure—" His eyebrows rose in response, and Rissa nodded. "Okay…you're sure. But I don't get it. Skylar said this Mandy person makes fun of people all the time so I could see Skylar getting into it with her, but with *Caroline?*"

"I know what I heard." Jonas sipped his coffee and swallowed. "It has to have something to do with the incident at the library last night, but I couldn't get anything out of Caroline. I get information out of criminals, but not my thirteen-year-old," he muttered with disgust.

"Teenagers are tougher than criminals," she offered wearily, trying to lighten the mood and give herself time to take it all in, "too many burgeoning hormones interfering with brain power."

Jonas winced, but smiled. The move made him appear more boyish, his rugged countenance more attractive.

"Rissa, I know no parent wants to think of their child as abusive—"

"*Abusive?*" Rissa was taken aback by her train of thought versus his.

"Bullying," he quickly corrected. "But this has got to stop. *Now.* I don't want to find myself arresting Skylar, but I will if I have to."

She stared at him, hurt even though she told herself she had no reason to be. Hadn't she warned Skylar herself that violence led nowhere? She'd lost it at the library and screeched at Jonas in anger, but he wasn't the bad guy. The compassion in his eyes, the way he'd stared at her when he'd pulled her over and then let her go with a warning. Much as she hated to admit it, he was right.

"I'm pretty good at first impressions, and you seem like a very nice woman—"

"She is," Maura stated firmly from a few feet away. Her cousin moved toward them and set two large plates of food down on the table. "But if you're going to discuss such heavy topics this early in the morning, I suggest you do it on a full stomach."

"Good advice," Jonas said with a smile of thanks.

"Thank you, Maura." Rissa stared down at the colorful eggs peppered with seasonings, a few red and green peppers, and a little cheese. Her stomach rolled, and it was everything she could do to wait until Maura turned her back to them before she pushed the plate away.

What must Maura think? It was barely seven o'clock in the morning, and here she sat across the table with Jonas Taggert in full uniform discussing her daughter, who'd come home from the *library* scraped, scratched and bruised.

"Oh, wow. I haven't had anything this good since—ever."

Like it or not—like *him* or not—she laughed softly. "Maura's cooking is phenomenal."

Jonas swallowed the bite in his mouth, his expression troubled. "Rissa, I know this can't be easy for you—it isn't easy for me—but…there's no good way to say this."

"What?"

"I've told Caroline to stay away from Skylar. And I'd appreciate it if you'd tell Skylar the same thing. I think it would be best."

Rissa's hopes that Caroline would soften Skylar's Goth-girl edges disintegrated. "Don't you think that's a bit drastic?"

"She *threatened* her, Rissa, and she has to be taken to task for it."

Jonas stared at her, his solemn gaze direct, intense, that of a concerned father. A man who knew trouble, saw it on a daily basis and recognized it in her daughter.

"Rissa, if there was another way—"

"I understand," she murmured. "As soon as I find a full-time job, we'll be leaving North Star anyway so...hopefully we'll be out of your hair soon."

Jonas scowled at her words. Because she'd said they were leaving?

Wishful thinking.

"HE SAID HE DOESN'T want me to talk to you, but I don't care." Carly leaned against the locker next to her friend's and tried to look cool. "I didn't know she was your mom. She's really pretty. And nice. She, um, helped me the other day at a store."

Skylar grabbed her math book out of her locker and shut the door with a snap. "Just remember what I said. What if he'd heard you instead of me?"

"Guess I was stupid to say it out loud."

"You're not stupid, Carly. Stupid is quitting the Quiz Bowl. Why'd you do that? You said you liked it."

She shrugged, head down. "Mandy says only geeks are in Quiz Bowl."

"Mandy also thinks it's okay everybody knows she gives her boyfriend head."

Carly wrinkled her nose, but didn't comment. She might not know how to pick out the right bra, but she knew about sex. Most things, anyway. And what she didn't know, she was rapidly learning. Soon she'd know all the stuff needed to put her plan into place and show Mandy once and for all.

"Travis *is* really cute. The best-looking guy in school."

"Who cares? He'll want her to do more soon if she isn't already."

Carly caught her breath and focused on Skylar's words. "You sound like you… *Have* you?"

The bell rang, announcing third period.

Skylar wouldn't look at her. "See you at lunch." She walked away, chains clanging together with every step.

Carly stared after her, uncaring that she might be a little late. The teachers wouldn't yell at her. She never got in trouble because she was always on time, always the one they called on when they got tired of hearing the wrong answer and needed the right one.

A few students hurried to class and she watched them, wondering, frowning when she saw Kimmie Boyd pause long enough to kiss Randy Spears. *French kiss.*

Was she the only one who *hadn't* messed around with a boy?

Mandy and the other girls she knew were already dating, now Skylar acted like she knew what was what. Who else? Other girls her age went to boy-girl parties. Mandy had even gone to an overnight one once at her cousin's house in Helena, and had come home laughing and bragging about what all she'd done with a boy while her cousin's parents were right upstairs.

She shoved herself off the locker and walked down the hall, her head down. She had to do something. *Soon.* Otherwise she'd never fit in, and with four years of high school ahead of her—well, the thought of it being like the last year gave her the shivers and scared her way more than the thought of having sex.

Getting a guy's attention would take a lot of work. Makeup, hair, clothes. She needed it all. But her birthday was coming up and if that were the *only* thing she asked for, the odds were that she'd get it. Maybe then she could turn herself from boring, plain Caroline into fun and daring *Carly*. That would be so awesome.

She hurried down the hall toward class, a smile on her lips when she envisioned it all in her mind.

Then Mandy would be the one crying because she'd have Travis.

CHAPTER SIX

RISSA SPENT THE REST of the day in a fog, torn between anger and depression. Jonas didn't want their daughters hanging around together, and while she could understand why he wouldn't want his precious Caroline with her teenaged Vampira, she'd already imagined the girl bringing Skylar back to her.

She moved into the rental cabin's bathroom and began taking her frustration out on the wheelchair-accessible, roll-in shower, scrubbing until her elbow and shoulder ached. Of all the—

"Must've been some meeting you had with Jonas. What'd she do this time?" Maura asked from behind her.

Rissa jumped, not having heard her cousin enter the bathroom, much less the cabin.

"Sorry. I thought you heard me."

Laughing weakly, she shook her head and shifted onto her hip, sitting on the floor outside the enclosure. "It's not your fault. My nerves are shot lately. Plus I was too busy imagining what it would be like bashing Sheriff Taggert over the head with the toilet brush."

"Ouch."

She gave her cousin a sour look. "Did you ever have one of those days when you wished you'd never gotten out of bed because things just keep getting worse and worse?"

Maura walked over to the toilet and lowered the seat before sitting down. "Spill it. What'd he say?"

"Wait!" Grace called, hurrying into the bathroom. "I just finished my last session." She laughed softly and sent Rissa a sympathetic look. "You'd just have to repeat it all again."

Smiling wearily at the two women who had fast become her very best friends, she told them of Jonas's demand. "What am I supposed to do? Skylar finally befriends someone and look what happens."

"Try not to worry about it too much," Grace told her. "If the girls are true friends, they won't listen to him."

"Yeah," Maura agreed. "They'll talk at school and be fine."

"Until Jonas finds out."

Grace frowned. "Maybe he'll come around after he gets tired of listening to Caroline complain about not spending time with Skylar."

"And if they do talk at school and Skylar drags Caroline into one of her messes?"

"Cross that bridge when you come to it," Maura declared firmly. "What else can you do? Worrying won't get you anywhere."

"What I'm wondering is how Skylar took it?" Grace questioned, her expression contemplative. "Did she go ballistic?"

Rissa nodded. "How'd you guess? She ranted and raved, but beneath it all there was something in her face, something that reminded me of how she used to be. She wasn't indifferent, and the news hurt. I could see it."

"Then maybe this will make Skylar straighten up," Maura added, her tone cheery but forced. "That way they can hang around together."

"Maybe." Rissa got to her knees and turned on the shower to rinse it. "Did Seth or Jake say anything?" She could only imagine how wonderful it must've looked to have the sheriff on the ranch's doorstep at dawn. She paused in what she was doing and caught Maura and Grace exchanging a glance. "What?"

"Nothing." Grace tilted her head to one side and leaned against the wall behind her. "Really. All they said was that they hoped everything was all right."

"But?"

Maura was the weaker of the two and couldn't hold her gaze. "I, um, think they might be a bit concerned with the California guests coming, but don't worry," Maura continued when Rissa groaned, "everything will work out."

"We'll help you keep an eye on Skylar," Grace added. "Between the three of us and the guys, she'll be fine."

Uh-huh. She wasn't so sure. "They have every right to be concerned, you know." Rissa fought back tears, something she'd done a lot of over the last year where Skylar was concerned. "I shouldn't have come," she told them thickly. "I should've just rented an apartment and stayed in New York until I found another job. Maybe it would've helped if I wouldn't have packed her up and taken her away from everything familiar."

"No one should handle something like this alone."

"Exactly. Rissa, please don't think that. You needed a break from it all, and so does Skylar." Maura smiled, but it lacked her typical sparkle, and revealed her trepidation and worry. "We're glad you came to visit. You were so frazzled after Larry's death. All the arrangements, the bills, selling the house…I know how badly you want to get back into the air, but you need to get back on your feet first. I'm sure you could've done it on your own, but it'll happen a lot faster with people around who care about you and love you. You're very welcome here for as long as you want to stay. Right, Grace?"

"Absolutely." Grace kneeled down onto the floor next to her, her hand on Rissa's shoulder. "Do *not* feel pressured to leave. The cabin is yours for as long as you need it. We love having you here."

"Actually, Grace and I hoped you might look for a permanent job nearby. Close enough that you could come visit regularly and rely on us when you need help with Skylar."

She was humbled by their generosity, over-whelmed by their friendship. "I, um, already tried," she admitted softly, the disappointment she'd felt at not having any luck crowding her already strained emotions. "The Helena airport isn't hiring, and the few guys hangared there aren't willing to let me rent their planes for charters because of the insurance hassles."

"What if you opened up your own charter business?" Grace suggested. "North Star certainly doesn't have anything like that, and there's definitely a need. The guy coming in from California would probably have welcomed a quicker route than driving from Helena. And we've had several requests for aerial tours since the mobility of our guests is always a problem. Maybe you could focus on them, or take fishermen up to Seth's special spot?"

Rissa heard the excitement in Grace's tone and wished she felt it within herself. "It's a good idea, but I don't have the key piece of equipment needed, and no bank is going to give me a loan with all the debt over my head right now." She tried to smile, but knew she failed when Grace patted her shoulder again, and Maura's expression became even more despondent. "Look, the ideas are great, and I appreciate them, but the fact is, I can't hold up financially much longer if we don't get that check and…I promised Skylar we wouldn't stay long, only until we either got the check or I found a job flying."

"Maybe she'll come around."

She gave Maura a dubious look. "I doubt it. Believe me, she'll hold me to moving again, and Skylar is definitely a deciding factor even if everything else fell into place. She needs counseling and right now, I do still have some control even if Jonas Taggert doesn't think so. I have to get her help, and the last thing I want to do is antagonize her even more by not keeping my promise."

GUILT WAS A pain in the rear, but even though Jonas knew he was right in telling Caroline to stay away from Skylar Mathews, the expression on Rissa's face after he'd made his request had haunted him all day. She'd looked stricken, hurt, her eyes revealing her pain and anger that he'd demand such a thing.

He walked into the kitchen and swore when he

saw the pan of spaghetti on the stove top snapping and popping, smoke beginning to curl toward the ceiling. He automatically reached for the handle and swore again when heat blistered his thumb. Belatedly, he grabbed a pot holder and managed to pull the pot from the burner about the same time he heard Caroline's footsteps on the kitchen floor.

"Dad?" She gasped. "Oh, *no!*"

His daughter rushed forward to help, but he waved her back. "I got it."

"I only left for a minute—"

"This doesn't happen in a minute's time, Caro."

"But—"

He turned on her, frustration riding him. "We've talked about this. If you're cooking something here alone, you aren't to leave it. *Ever.* Not without turning it off first."

"I'm sorry!"

"You could've burnt the house down with you in it!"

"I *know!* I guess I got distracted and—"

"By what?" He stuck his throbbing thumb under the faucet and blasted the cold water, glancing at her and seeing her face color. "The computer? You're spending way too much time online. What happened to getting outside and playing?"

"I'm not a little girl anymore, Dad, playing is for kids."

"Fine. Then why aren't you doing whatever it is young girls do when they get together? Instead of surfing the net, call Mandy or one of the other girls you used to hang out with. Invite them over for popcorn and movies."

"Mandy's got a date—"

A *date?*

"And how come you always told me not to judge people, but you're judging Skylar?" Caroline frowned darkly. "If I invite someone over, I want to invite *her.* She's nice."

Needing a breather, he shut the water off and opened the freezer instead, reaching inside for an ice cube. The frozen cubes stuck to his wet hand and he wound up with five instead of one, the skin of his palm rapidly going numb and burning from exposure. What a lousy day.

"No way. Believe it or not, I feel bad for asking you to stay away from Skylar, but what I *see* is that she's out of control. Rissa's nice, and maybe Skylar is, too," he said reluctantly, "but until she straightens up and stays out of trouble, you are to stay far away from her." His gaze narrowed. "Does this mean you talked to her at school today after I specifically told you not to?" She didn't answer. *"Caroline?"*

"A little!" She clenched her hands into fists and crossed her arms over her chest. "Dad, I can't be rude! I see her in the hall, we have a couple classes together—"

"Seeing her in class and nodding or saying hi is one thing, spending time with her is another. Don't be rude," he instructed, "but don't seek out her company, either. *I mean it*. I'm only doing what I think is best for you."

"Even though you're wrong?"

"If Skylar behaves in the next month or so," he offered, "*maybe* I'll change my mind. Fair enough?" Her glare spoke volumes. "Look, sweetheart…I'm sorry for yelling at you about the spaghetti. Especially since I've burnt way more than my share of our meals." Jonas forced a smile. "Truce? How 'bout we stop arguing, and you and I figure out what we're doing for dinner?"

His daughter remained silent a long moment then gave him a measured look before stepping close to the stove, her shoulders slumped, her nose wrinkling. "I didn't know spaghetti would do that."

More than willing to have a quiet hour or two before having to face the world again, Jonas laughed gruffly. "Yeah, well, had you asked, I could've confirmed it without this experiment." He nudged her arm with his now dripping hand and smiled at her soft giggle when the cold water from the melting ice cubes slid down her arm. "Tell me, what had you in your room instead of watching over our dinner?"

She whirled away and practically danced to the bar jutting out from the wall. "I figured out what I want for my birthday."

Jonas noticed the teen magazines scattered across the top. "Yeah? What's the verdict? How much is this going to set me back?"

She began stacking them into a neat pile, and unease thickened in his gut. "Caroline?"

"Carly," she insisted, sliding him a glance over her shoulder. "Caroline is too old-fashioned. I want to be called Carly from now on, remember?"

Jonas groaned inwardly and stared down at the magazine on top of the rest, cringing. A scantily clad blonde stared back. He lifted his hand to indicate the stack, his burn forgotten. "What are all those for?"

"Me."

He raised an eyebrow and waited, his insides twisted into knots. His daughter's chin lifted, a sure sign of battle.

"For my birthday I want a…a makeover."

Jonas fought the urge to sit down. "A *what?*"

Her eyes widened in a you-heard-me-and-I-can't-believe-you're-making-me-repeat-myself look of irritation. "A *makeover*. You know, like on TV? A couple new outfits, a new hairstyle and—" she paused long enough to gulp nervously "—makeup."

He'd started shaking his head before she'd

finished the word *hairstyle*. "You don't need makeup. You're beautiful the way you are."

"And you're my dad and you have to say that."

"Caroline—"

"Carly!"

Jonas walked to the closest barstool and sat down, his knees weak. He was a cop, a single dad. What did he know about makeovers?

His gaze caught on the magazine. The blonde stared at the camera with a sultry look that would make any father cringe, her belly button ring sparkling. "Is this because of Skylar? Caro— *Carly,* you can't want to look like her."

He glared at the belly ring. Skylar had one of those piercings. He'd seen it when he'd pulled her and Mandy Blake apart and Skylar's shirt had ridden up.

A put-out sigh sounded behind him. "Can you imagine me with black hair? Dad, I want this because I'm fourteen—going to *high school*— and I'm tired of looking like a little kid."

"You are—" Jonas wisely stopped himself short of finishing his statement "—uh…fourteen," he muttered instead. But since when did fourteen equal twenty-one?

"Please? It's the *only* thing I want for my birthday."

Jonas turned, seeing the excitement and hope in

her eyes, and felt as if he'd been slammed by a Mack truck. He rubbed a hand over his mouth, his jaw, wondering how he was going to survive the next few years if this was his reaction to a birthday request. What about boyfriends? College? Dear Lord, help him…*sex?*

"Sure you don't want a TV or something? What about one of those iPod things? I've seen a lot of kids at the high school with those hanging out of their ears."

"*Daaaaaad.*"

He shoved himself to his feet and staggered back to the stove. The spaghetti-mush resembled his legs at the moment. "I'll think about it."

Caroline—*Carly*—squealed.

"I *didn't* say yes."

Thin freckled arms slid around his waist from behind and her hands clasped over his stomach. When had she started painting her nails? Dark purple was a far cry from little girl pink.

"But you will! Thank you, Daddy! *Thank you!*"

Daddy, huh? This called for backup—only he didn't have anyone to call.

"LOOK, IT'S FREAKY FRIDAY," a male voice called from somewhere behind her.

Skylar shoved all her books into her locker and grabbed her iPod to take with her to detention. She ignored the caustic laughter that followed the insult and turned in time to see Mandy, Travis and their sports jock buddies walking shoulder to shoulder and taking up the entire hallway. All were dressed in track shorts and T-shirts, with hundred-and-fifty-dollar shoes on their feet. She had shoes like that.

Mandy gave her a smug grin. "Better hurry, you don't want to be late for *de-ten-tion.*"

The group snickered and continued on their way, but when Skylar began to raise her hand to flip them off, she saw Carly watching her, the girl's big, sad eyes taking in her every move.

"They're all jerks," Carly said, coming up to stand beside her.

In a mood after a week of nasty comments and glares, and still really sore, Skylar slammed her locker shut, taking out her frustration that way. "If you think that then why do you like them so much?"

Carly's face glowed hot pink, the color making her freckles stand out. "I don't."

"Yeah, right. You stare at them all the time, talk about them, and moon over Travis. I don't get it, not after the way they've treated you."

"They don't treat you any better."

"But *I* expect it from them. You take it and ask for more."

"Do not."

"Do, too."

"Is there a problem here? Mathews, you want another week?"

"It's okay, coach. We're just talking," Carly said.

"Caroline?"

Skylar heard Carly stifle a low groan and turned to find an older woman staring at her in horror. A hand fluttered to her chest when she got a good look, and Skylar fought the urge to scream "Boo!" for shock effect. Hadn't anyone ever taught *her* it was rude to stare?

"Mathews, detention starts in four minutes. If you're late—"

"I'll be there."

The assistant football coach glowered at her before turning on his heel and stalking away.

"Um, hi, grandma. What are you doing here?"

The woman turned her head toward Carly, but didn't take her eyes off Skylar, like she was afraid she'd jump her or something.

"I—I came to pick you up, dear. I thought we might do the grocery shopping together this week."

"Oh. Oh, um, Grandma, this is Skylar. Skylar, my grandma, Mrs. Wells."

The woman nodded once. "Skylar. What a unique…name."

"Thanks. It's nice to—"

"Caroline, I believe it's time to go."

"But, Grandma—"

"*Now,* Caroline." The woman gave Skylar a terse smile. "We wouldn't want to keep Skylar. As we heard, she has somewhere to be." Mrs. Wells turned and began walking away, her old woman shoes squeaking along the tile floor.

Carly released a huff, her shoulders hunched. "I'm sorry."

"She's going to tell your dad you were talking to me, you know."

"I know."

"Caroline?"

Carly rolled her eyes but automatically began walking toward her grandma, looking over her shoulder. "See you Monday."

"Yeah." Monday. Detention again. "'Bye, Carly." Skylar fell into step behind them, trying to walk "light" so her boots didn't make so much noise.

"Why did she call you Carly?"

"It's my nickname."

"I don't like it. Your name is Caroline and it's a perfectly good name. Why are you hanging around the hallways with someone like that unchaperoned?"

"Why would I need a chaperone? Grandma, she's my friend."

"You should not have friends spending time in detention."

"You sound like Dad."

"So your father has already warned you about that girl? Why haven't you listened to him?"

"*Grandma.*"

"Wait until your father gets home. We're going to have a nice long chat about this. I *knew* something was wrong when you stopped spending time with Mandy Blake. Now, *she's* a sweet girl. You could learn a thing or two from her, Caroline. I'll bet she isn't on her way to detention right now."

Skylar made it to the classroom where the assistant coach waited, Carly and her grandmother's conversation fading until she couldn't hear.

The coach looked up with a smirk and pointed to his watch. "You almost earned another day, Mathews. Take a seat."

JONAS EXPERIENCED a strong sense of déjà vu when he entered his house Friday evening. He'd taken two steps down the hall when Caroline—*Carly*—flew out of the kitchen, her face bright red with obvious fury. Groaning inwardly, he braced himself. "What now?"

Marilyn appeared in the kitchen doorway. "You will not walk away from me, young woman—Jonas! Thank goodness, you're home! I called Dave and asked that he leave work to come talk to you and his granddaughter, but he hasn't returned my call. Now that you're here, I'll do it myself."

His daughter rolled her eyes and crossed her arms over her chest. "Dad—"

"Talk to us about what?"

"I stopped by school to pick her up today, Jonas, and caught her talking to the most frightful creature!"

His gaze narrowed on Caroline. "And why was that when we *have* talked about it?"

"Skylar's my friend, and *she* was rude to her!" Caroline glared at her grandmother, but glanced at him every second or so.

"Caro, you were told to stay away from Skylar. Had you followed instructions your grandmother wouldn't be upset."

"She's *always* upset."

Marilyn sucked in a sharp, indignant breath. "Caroline Elizabeth—"

"Carly!"

"Watch it," Jonas warned, moving closer to where Caroline stood. "You might be upset, but you'll *not* speak to your grandmother in that tone. Ever. Show her respect."

"But, Dad— *Oooh,* what's the use! You don't understand anything!" With that she turned on her heel and ran down the hall. A second later a door slammed shut.

"Jonas, you have *got* to do something."

Jonas took hold of Marilyn's elbow and steered her out of the hall, back into the kitchen. "I know, Marilyn. She's having some growing pains."

"Ha! She's rapidly on her way to becoming that—that Skylar person I saw today. You actually *agreed* to give her a makeover for her birthday? I do not approve. Jonas, have you *seen* that girl? Dave will die, *I'll* die," she stressed, "if I see our sweet Caroline dressed like a—a—"

"That's not the look she wants," he countered wearily. "Do you think I'd agree if that were the case?"

"I honestly don't know what to expect from you anymore."

He stared at her, angry that she dared give him such a hard time when it was her daughter that had abandoned them. *Lea* deserved the tongue-lashing, not him.

"Something must be done immediately. It must be stopped!"

"I'll talk to her."

"She needs more than a talking to or she'll wind up—"

Jonas bit out a curse beneath his breath. "I'm not in the mood for a lecture, Marilyn. At Caroline's age your daughter was not only wearing makeup, she pranced around in bikinis in front of audiences all over the state in the name of beauty pageants! Whether or not I agree to let Carly wear a *little* makeup is up to me."

Marilyn's shocked expression turned slightly remorseful, a little ill. She nodded shakily and turned away. "We realized Lea did too much too soon, and I—I'm mostly at fault for that."

"Marilyn—"

"Let me finish, please." She hesitated a long moment. "Jonas, I can't change the past or how I raised my daughter, but I'm older and wiser now. So much wiser. And I think it's time I took more of a role where Caroline is concerned."

A ten-ton brick lodged in his stomach, weighing him down and stealing his breath. She'd worn the same look last summer when she'd asked to extend Caroline's one week of summer vacation at her house in Helena to two weeks. Now she wanted more?

"You can't deny Caroline is coming to an age where she needs a feminine touch. A role model she sees daily rather than weekly."

"She has female role models. Her teachers, the—"

"A steadying influence then," Marilyn interjected. "Someone she can talk to, confide in, someone who'll help her through these awkward years she faces." Her mouth pulled down at the corners, the heavy lines on her face deepening. "You're the sheriff. What are you going to do when you find Caroline drunk at a party? In the backseat of a car with a boy?"

"What are you getting at?" Jonas tried to remind himself how much of a help his ex-mother-in-law had been since Lea's desertion. "She has more sense than that."

The older woman gave him a dubious look. "Like my Lea did with you?"

Jonas ground his teeth together until pain shot up the side of his head. "I wasn't a saint, but neither was Lea. I wasn't the one to introduce her to those things, Marilyn. Or her... I wasn't her first boyfriend."

Cheeks blazing, Marilyn raised her head. "But part of your appeal was your reputation. Fun-loving, charming. She told me how you'd come out of your shell once you had a bit of alcohol inside you. What if Caroline is the same way?"

He muffled a groan. "She wants a little makeup, that's all."

Marilyn shook her head. "That's the beginning," she countered. "Jonas, last summer we talked about Caroline staying with us for two weeks—why not let her stay all summer?"

"Three *months*?"

She nodded, her gaze on his. "She needs me.

I know she needs me. I think it's obvious to you, too. Caroline will have a better time of it if she has a woman to get her through these teenage upsets. Someone who sees and understands the mistakes made in the past. Jonas, she's only going to get worse."

"She's a good kid."

"She has been, yes. Here lately, however, things have changed. Let me take her this summer and maybe when you see the changes in her behavior, you'll reconsider letting her move in with me and Dave permanently."

Jonas turned away from her and moved to the French doors leading off the patio. He'd known it was coming, knew she'd ask again. But was his automatic denial in his daughter's best interests? Would she be better off with her grandparents?

Maybe so. Marilyn and Dave were smart, they wouldn't make the same mistakes with Caroline like they had with Lea—but would they go to the opposite extreme instead? He'd seen examples of that already. The plain clothes Marilyn chose for Caroline that even he knew weren't in style, and her attitude. Whatever happened to middle ground?

"I know how much you love her, Jonas. And I know you want what's best for her. You've done everything a single man can when it comes to raising a daughter alone, but surely you can see it's time and…"

Marilyn's words droned on, but he remained lost in his thoughts, the past. Rethinking decisions, choices. He saw all right.

Maybe it would be best.

"Jonas? Jonas, are you listening to me?"

"I'll think about it," he promised huskily. "I'll…talk to Carly and see what she thinks."

His ex-mother-in-law *tsked.* "Right there is your answer, Jonas. Her name is Caroline, not Carly—"

"It's simply a nickname she likes."

"Yes, well, what will be next? Adults need to make the decisions, Jonas, not children. That was something I learned the hard way. Now is the time to be firm, to regain control while you still can. You don't want her turning out like that Skylar person."

"I'M NOT GOING," Carly whispered, carefully tiptoeing back to her room. Her hands shook, and she was cold and sick. "They can't make me go and even if they try, they can't make me stay."

Could they? She sat on her bed only to hop right back up and pace the room. Her dad needed her. She might not be pretty, but she was smart and she helped out a lot.

When she wasn't burning dinner.

But that was an accident. Dad knew that. She'd

gotten distracted reading the posts in the chat room and forgotten about the stupid spaghetti. It happened. Dad said himself he'd burned his share of their meals but—

He was sending her away. His "I'll think about it" almost always meant yes. But she hated Grandma's house. Everything was perfect and all she ever heard was "Don't touch" or "Don't make a mess."

He couldn't send her away. He couldn't!

Carly stopped where she stood, frozen, gasping for breath because tears choked her. Her dad didn't want her anymore.

Just like her mom.

Wiping away the stupid tears, she opened the window, breathed deep and tried hard not to cry. She should leave. Run away and make her dad realize how much he'd miss her. How much he needed her.

Before she could have second thoughts, she swung her leg over the sill and slipped to the ground.

CHAPTER SEVEN

RISSA PAUSED, a plate of steak and potatoes in her hand, and watched while Caroline Taggert slid into the booth opposite her daughter. "That can't be good."

"Pardon?"

She smiled weakly at the older man waiting expectantly for his dinner, and shook her head. "Nothing, just talking to myself," she murmured, setting the plate down. "Here you go. Enjoy." Rissa started to move away when she noticed the man's ball cap, a naval aviator insignia embroidered on the bill. Since she'd spent yet another afternoon scouring Internet job sites for pilot positions, she had to comment. "Nice hat. Navy, huh?"

The man peppered his food, his expression sad. "Reminder of better days gone by."

Rissa glanced at the girls again, saw they'd leaned in close to talk and would no doubt hate her if she interrupted them. She focused on the old man. Two canes were propped against the seat beside him, and a discreet glance down showed his painfully distorted legs. "My dad was career military, an air force pilot. Now he can tell some stories."

He glanced up at her, his expression measuring. Like he wanted to talk, but not very many people took the time to listen.

"You fly?"

"Only way to travel. My dad didn't have any sons so he resorted to teaching me."

Her comment earned a smiling nod of approval. "Good for you. Most folks don't appreciate what it's like up there, and they get tired of hearing about things they don't understand."

She winked at him. "Well, I'm not most folks," she said, tucking the food tray beneath her arm to hold out her hand. "So if you want to reminisce, you let me know. I'm Rissa Mathews."

"Ben," the old man murmured gruffly, accepting her hand. "Ben Whitefeather."

She raised an eyebrow and shot him a look, waiting expectantly.

The old man's shoulders squared. "Commander Ben Whitefeather, U.S. Navy, retired."

"There you go," she said, smiling. "Nice to meet you, Commander."

The old man nodded, his expression warm. "What's a pilot doing playing waitress to Porter? No wings?"

She laughed softly at his bluntness, and nodded. "No wings. The company I worked for folded, and after some…personal stuff, my cousin invited me out to visit until I'm airborne again."

"Who's your cousin?"

"Maura Rowland?"

Another smile of approval. "My grandson works for Seth. Name's Marcus. If you haven't met him, you will sometime. He's there after school most days and on weekends. The Rowlands are good people."

"I think so, too. But I am still looking for a pilot job if you hear of anything. I can't wait to get in the air again."

Ben nodded his understanding. "Nothing like it. Got a Bell Jet Ranger rusting on its rails. Should've sold it years ago, but can't bring myself to part with the old girl," he murmured sadly, making Rissa wonder what kind of shape his helicopter was in.

He glanced over his shoulder toward the kitchen. "If Porter will give you a break, you come back and sit with me. I'll tell you stories like nothin' your daddy *ever* experienced."

"I'll do that," she promised. "Who knows, maybe I'll even tell you a few of my own. But right now I've gotta run. Enjoy that steak before it gets cold."

Walking away from the commander's booth, Rissa's smile faded when she spied the girls again. Was Caroline upset? She headed in their direction only to stop short when a customer asked for a refill. Irritated and yet knowing she ought to be grateful for customers who'd leave tips, she retrieved the coffeepot and spent the next ten minutes going table to table topping off the cups and retrieving desserts from the displays and food from the counter as Porter put them up. The last delivery placed her close enough to the girls to catch a glimpse of Caroline's face.

Oh, boy. What had Skylar done now? Was Jonas right? If Sky had taken to picking on girls like Caroline Taggert then she'd—

Before her silent rant could continue, her mouth dropped in awed surprise when she saw Skylar console Jonas's daughter, Skylar's black-rimmed gaze soft with concern. This was the girl she remembered, the one she'd raised. Kind, compassionate. Caring of others. And despite the fact she'd told Jonas she'd do her best to keep Skylar away from Carly, she absolutely refused to send Caroline home. She'd come there after all. It wasn't as if Skylar had sought her out.

The Friday night dinner crowd kept her busy. She waited on more ranch hands than she'd known existed, turned down three marriage proposals and seven requests for a date. But other than checking on Ben to see if he needed refills, and keeping a close watch to make sure the girls didn't leave, she didn't get a moment's rest.

The girls continued to sit and talk, and what she saw warmed her heart and gave her hope for the future. Skylar passed Caroline napkins to dry her tears, and listened intently. All the things a friend did in times of trouble.

Just like Skylar had done for her.

Distracted, she had to take an order twice before she got it right, the image across the diner disturbing her because of the memories it evoked of Larry's betrayal. Skylar had caught *her* in tears more than once, offered her tissues and sat with her, listened to her, more friend than daughter. Their roles reversed in a way she shouldn't have allowed to happen. She should've shielded Skylar from the pain she'd experienced, not created more upset and tension by putting Skylar in the middle.

Another customer requested coffee, and Rissa grabbed the pot. She'd made up her mind. Somehow, someway, she had to change Jonas's mind about keeping the girls apart. Really, what did men know about the power of female friendships?

Coffee poured, Rissa grabbed a couple of the old-fashioned glasses from beneath the counter and made two chocolate malts. The girls leaned toward one another, but sprang apart when Skylar saw her coming.

One look at Caroline's face had Rissa's stomach doing flip-flops much like it had when she'd first taken flying lessons. Whatever it was that had brought Caroline there, it wasn't good.

"I—I'm sorry, Mrs. Mathews. I know I'm supposed to s-stay away but—"

"Call me Rissa." She set the malts on the table. "And I understand what it's like to need a friend to talk to." She smiled gently and pushed the malts closer to them both. "I've also discovered that whatever the problem, chocolate helps. Enjoy."

The girls exchanged a look and then reached for their glasses.

"Thanks, Mrs.— Rissa. You can call me Carly," she murmured in a low voice, head down. "I like it better, but Caroline is okay, too."

So eager to please. "Caroline is a beautiful name, but Carly is more modern. If you like it better, of course I'll call you that." She glanced at Skylar, not really expecting much, but hoping all the same.

"Um…it's good. Thanks."

Rissa's heart stopped momentarily at the sincerity in her daughter's voice. Oh, yeah, Caroline— *Carly*—was a godsend. "Well, I'd better get back to work. Would you two like anything else before I go?"

Carly bit her lip and about that time, Rissa heard the sound of someone's stomach growl loudly.

"Maybe some fries?" Carly asked hesitantly. "I only have a dollar."

"Don't worry about it. How about a cheeseburger, too? My treat."

The girl gave her a bashful glance. "A cheeseburger sounds good."

"Skylar?"

"No…thanks."

Two *thanks* in the space of five minutes? She wanted to rub her hands together. "A cheeseburger and fries coming up."

JONAS CLOSED the front door and stomped through the house, angry at Marilyn and himself. His mother-in-law gave new meaning to the word *interfering*.

He stalked into the kitchen, forgetting Marilyn had done her thing and cleaned up while they'd— or rather *she*—had continued to discuss his daughter's future, her behavior, her grades, everything, while he'd sat there praying his beeper would go off allowing him to escape.

Jonas glared at the sparkling kitchen, but couldn't be grateful at the sight. Instead he felt hemmed in, inadequate. The kitchen was a symbol of perfection that he was far from reaching when it came to being a dad.

He ran his hands over his head and glanced behind him down the hall. Marilyn was furious with him for not forcing *Carly* out of her room and to the dinner table. And even more incensed when she went to Caroline's bedroom to say goodbye and found it locked, the girl inside ignoring her.

Jonas closed the distance in a matter of seconds and rapped on his daughter's door. "Hey, you hungry? She's gone, you can come out now."

Nothing.

"Come on, Caro. You've got to eat. If you don't want your grandmother's cooking, how 'bout we go out and talk? Just us."

Still nothing.

"Open the door, hon, or I'm going to." He reached out and grabbed the knob. Still locked. "Caro? I'm getting the key."

Swearing, Jonas headed for the junk drawer in the kitchen, glad to find the peculiarly shaped key right off.

She'd fallen asleep with her headphones on. That was it. Had to be. His little girl wasn't one to play games and he couldn't blame her for wanting to avoid Marilyn's ongoing litany when he'd wanted to run for the hills himself.

He quickly opened the door, but—

Jonas blinked, stared at the open bedroom window and the curtain blowing in the breeze, and wondered what had happened to change his little girl from a sweet kid to a teenager sneaking out of the house.

Then he knew.

Ten minutes later Jonas burst into the diner. He zeroed in on Skylar's dark form, and headed toward the back booth. The girl watched him approach, unmoving, but instead of the guilt he expected to see, her expression was one of teen attitude and anger. Slumped in the opposite seat was Caroline.

"Caroline, what are y—" He stopped when he realized she'd been crying. Not a few tears, either, but the kind of crying that caused major, albeit temporary, damage. Her face was red and splotchy, her eyes swollen and bloodshot. Her nose running despite the mound of used napkins littering the table.

"I'll be around."

"Skylar, no, please—"

"You can do it," Skylar said, giving his daughter a firm look. The girl proceeded to scoot over along the bench seat and got to her feet, chains clinking. She glared at him before stalking away, her boots thudding against the old black-and-white checked floor.

Jonas lowered himself into the booth, only then noticing Rissa's presence nearby, her expression concerned.

His inadequacy as a parent returned, but he shoved those thoughts away for now. Rissa was the last person with the right to judge him. "Sneaking out?"

His daughter fiddled with the straw in her malt. "I'm sorry," she whispered, her voice low and husky with renewed tears. "But I couldn't stand to stay there anymore."

Couldn't stand to stay there? "Why?" he demanded even though he already knew. He grimaced. "You heard, didn't you?"

"That you want to send me away? Yeah."

"Caro, it's not like that."

Her forehead wrinkled in a deep frown and she grabbed a fresh napkin when a tear slipped down her face. "You said you'd think about it, and I know what that means." She blinked at him, her expression hopeless.

Conscious of the curious looks shot their way by the other customers, Jonas wiped a hand over his mouth and fought the need to stand up and pace, tell them all to mind their own business and their own kids, and leave him and his alone.

Instead he opted for false calm, pulling on every ounce of restraint he managed to maintain.

"Sweetheart, the last thing I want is for you to leave, but it's obvious to everyone I'm struggling to keep my head above water where you're concerned, so yeah, I agreed to *consider* it. Maybe it's a good idea."

"It's *not!*"

"Are you sure? Something's changed with you. One minute you're hugging me and calling me daddy and the next—" his voice lowered "—*you're sneaking out of the house.* Caroline—"

"*Carly,*" she cried with a wail. "And I said I was sorry! I didn't want to sneak out, but I don't want to live with Grandma and—you can't make me! I won't go and if you send me anyway I'll—I'll—"

"What?" Jonas growled tightly. He looked away long enough to regain some measure of control only to notice once more that they had the attention of every late-night patron. A door on the left opened and Skylar exited the bathroom. The girl took one look at his daughter's quivering form and glared at him before shaking her head and stomping over to an empty seat at the counter.

Jonas glowered at her profile, at those still staring, and resettled himself after they hastily looked away. "You'll do what I tell you to do," he informed her. "Whatever the decision, it'll be made with your best interests at heart, and you'll do it."

"Daddy, *please.*"

"It would only be for a couple of months. When summer is over—"

"She won't let me come back. You *know* she won't. She wants me to live with her and Grandpa. She's said it often enough since Mom left. She said it tonight! Dad, please, I don't want to go."

Jonas fought his fury, his frustration. All he wanted was to be a good dad—his daughter deserved nothing less. "Your grades have gone up and down all year, you're not hanging out with Mandy or any of your friends anymore."

"Skylar—"

"Your grandmother is worried, and so am I."

"I'll do better! My grades only dropped a little—"

"I found the F, Caro. And the C. They were on your desk."

Her cheeks paled, the red splotches all the more noticeable. "I wasn't hiding them, I left them out to show them to you," she said defensively. "Honest. Dad, the subjects are harder since I started the advanced program, but my *bad* grades are better than their *good* grades. Just ask the teacher."

"All I want is for you to do the best you can. You know that, sweetheart, but lately it seems to me like you're more interested in makeovers and clothes and hanging out on the computer. That isn't doing your best."

"That's because…"

Her lashes lifted and Jonas found himself staring into beautiful eyes that were so filled with pain and upset and confusion, his stomach clenched into a hard knot of unease.

"Dad…I'm… The other girls are dating and stuff and—"

"You're not old enough to date."

"They have boyfriends—"

"They're too young."

"They go to dances, and do cool stuff." She bit her lip and sniffled. "I'm just trying to fit in and if I make the highest grade each time—"

"Do not tell me you're dumbing yourself down because of the other kids," he commanded darkly, incredulous. "*Are* you?"

"They don't like it when I do better than they do," she hurried to explain, "and…the end of year dance at the high school is coming up. All the eighth graders are invited since they'll be freshmen. Everyone is going and a lot of the boys are asking girls, and I thought maybe if I didn't make them feel bad…"

Someone would ask her? He shook his head, unable to take it all in. "Let me get this straight. You want me to reward your sneaking out and spending time with a girl you were specifically told to avoid by letting you go to this dance if a boy asks you—*because* you've pretended to be less intelligent? No, Caro. Absolutely not."

She stared down at the half-empty malt. "I knew you'd say that. You always say that."

"With good reason. Now, about your grandmother's request that you spend the sum—"

"Dad, please, I'm sorry I snuck out and I promise I'll do better in school. I'll turn in all the extra credit assignments and bring my grades up. There's still time! And—and I'll do more around the house. I'll do whatever you want, but, *please*, don't send me away."

Her choked plea tore his heart in two. What was the right decision? His hands trembled and Jonas clasped them together, swallowing, forcing himself to forge ahead.

"This isn't only about grades and Skylar. And you do plenty around the house now. Honey, what about this makeover thing? Your grandmother made a good point tonight when she said you need a woman's touch with stuff like that. She can give it to you."

Her expression went from heartbroken to bright in a split second. "Rissa can help me. She—she helped me in The Blooming Rose and she'll do it again, I know she will."

"No, absolutely not. *No*," he repeated when his daughter opened her mouth to argue. "Honey, Rissa Mathews has her own—" *problems* "—life. She doesn't know us, and probably doesn't want to considering I asked her daughter to stay away from you."

"But she likes me. I *know* Rissa would help, Dad. Please?"

Jonas wanted to groan when Rissa's head turned in their direction. She'd heard Caroline say her name, and now she walked their way.

"Do you need something, Carly?"

She'd gotten the name thing, too?

"Yes, I want a—"

"*Caro.*"

"Makeover, and since Dad doesn't know *any*thing about women—"

He winced at the truth of her statement, conscious of Rissa's amused glance.

"He wants Grandma to help me, but I want you. Will you? Please?"

"Oh." Rissa shifted uncomfortably. "Um… Well…" She glanced at him.

"Caroline, *drop it*."

"Please say you'll help me, Rissa."

Rissa took an instinctive step back, staring dazedly between Jonas and his daughter. Carly's expectant, hopeful expression broke her heart.

Then her gaze fastened on Jonas's much more reserved one, making her wish she'd never walked over to their table.

The man looked carved from stone, angry and upset that his daughter wouldn't listen to his warnings to hush. He wanted her to say no. *She* wanted to say no, but just when she was about to, she made the mistake of glancing at Carly again and couldn't form the words.

"Caro, I've already told you. Rissa has her own life. She works here and at the ranch, and her daughter—"

Jonas broke off and Rissa waited, dared him to voice his true thoughts where Skylar was concerned. "Yes?"

He cleared his throat, not making eye contact. "Skylar obviously needs any time Rissa has left over," he told Carly. "Besides I haven't decided yet if you'll even *get* a makeover for your birthday. Not after this stunt. It just proved to me that you're too young."

In other words, he didn't want his daughter to resemble hers?

Rissa smirked. Jonas was probably beside himself right now, picturing his daughter's gorgeous red-gold hair dyed black. He was fighting a losing battle whether he knew it or not.

"She's old enough for a little makeup," she

heard herself blurt. So much for giving it time and thought. She ignored Jonas's put-out glare. "Lip gloss, mascara, a little blush. What's the harm? She's beautiful the way she is, but what woman doesn't want to look her best?"

"She's not a woman."

"*Dad!*" Carly looked at Rissa, her intelligent gaze full of hope. "See?" Her head swung back toward her father. "Not that long ago *women* my age were preparing for marriage."

"And they lived to the ripe old age of twenty-five. Drop it, Caroline. We're not doing this here."

"Dad—"

"Carly, hon, why don't you and Skylar go grab the dishes from that table over there. The tray is on the counter, and you can put them in the sink in back, okay? I'd like to talk to your dad alone for a sec."

"That's not—"

"Okay!"

Jonas's daughter scrambled out of the booth and Rissa took her place, well aware the last thing he wanted to do was talk to her.

"Rissa, I know you're trying to help, but right now I'd appreciate it if you'd—"

"What? Your plan—or should I say *demand*—for them to stay away from each other isn't working. The fact she came here to find Skylar proves they're still talking at school." She dropped her voice to a convincing pitch. "Come on, Jonas, short of locking her up in your jail cell, what are you going to do? And why? They just want to be friends."

The muscles in Jonas's jaw worked while he contemplated her words. The poor man wouldn't have any teeth left if he kept at it.

"Look, I understand why you want Carly to stay away from Skylar. I'm not blind nor do I have my head in the ground when it comes to my daughter's behavior or appearance. *But*, Carly sees something in Skylar she likes, something she trusts, and it's the same something I was very afraid was lost forever after the accident. I've already told you we won't be here long. North Star is a transition for us, Jonas. I'm looking for a job and don't know where we'll end up, but until then, why can't they hang out?"

"She snuck out tonight," he grumbled, "to see *your* daughter. Skylar probably put her up to it."

"Sky's been here all night and not talked to a single soul until Carly showed up, and I'm *grateful* she did. Otherwise I wouldn't have seen that deep down Skylar still exists."

His gaze shifted to focus on a spot over her shoulder and Rissa glanced back at the counter and saw the girls whispering, trying to appear nonchalant even though they repeatedly looked toward the booth where she and Jonas sat.

She turned back to him and chose her words carefully. "When Carly came in here tonight, *she* went to Skylar. Skylar listened to her and calmed her down *despite* Carly crying her heart out."

"I could tell she'd been crying hard," he admitted, color creeping up his neck into his face, "but a few tears do not change the facts."

"Jonas, come on. They're friends. You're worried about what you overheard on the phone, and I don't know what they discussed, but I think you're wrong. Skylar took care of her, was kind and compassionate and you *can't* take that away from them or me," she snapped, unable to suppress her anger any longer. "Not when I've waited a year and gone through *hell* watching my daughter distance herself from everyone. I've already made too many mistakes where Skylar is concerned, but I won't knowingly make another. Not about this. So long as they stay out of trouble, what could it hurt for them to spend time together? Hopefully it'll only be a matter of months, weeks if you're lucky."

Jonas was quiet a long moment, frowning unhappily at his clasped hands. "The makeover—"

She laughed softly, thoroughly enjoying his discomfort. "You might as well give up because it's going to happen whether you're ready or not. She's right, too." When he raised his head and his gaze met hers, she shrugged. "Sorry, but she is. Most girls *are* already wearing a bit of makeup by now. Would you rather she snuck it to school and loaded it on there because she doesn't know how to apply it, or show her the right way from the beginning?"

Jonas went back to studying his callused hands. "Skylar isn't... She's—"

"Not the ideal friend. I get it. So does Carly, I think. But I didn't hear her say she wanted to look like Skylar, just that she simply wants the chance to do something other girls her age are doing."

"Does this mean you'll help?"

Rissa stomped down a surge of premature joy. "With some conditions, sure."

"Do I need to guess?" he mumbled, blatantly irritated.

"Letting them be friends is non-negotiable."

Jonas swore softly, his expression torn. "How can you two be so different?" He didn't give her a chance to answer. "Will she stay out of trouble?"

"There's only one way to find out, but nobody ever said peer pressure couldn't be positive." She tilted her head to the side, trying to smile in spite of the fear running through her that he'd still say no. "What do you say? You help me, I help you?"

Jonas stared at her, then slowly nodded. "Deal."

Rissa grinned and held out her hand. His much

bigger palm swallowed hers. "To friends helping friends and…single parents surviving teenagers."

Her words brought a smile to his lips. Rissa fought the urge to free her hand so she could smooth her fingers over them. Her gaze met his and time stilled. Neither of them moved, and it took Porter banging his pots in the kitchen to snap her out of Jonas's hypnotic pull. Blinking, she tore her hand away and straightened. Handsome or not, she wasn't interested. She didn't have time to be interested.

"Um…girls?" Not making eye contact, she got out of the booth and stood beside the table while the girls slid in opposite Jonas. Carly couldn't hide her enthusiasm, whereas Skylar appeared battle-ready.

"Rissa and I have come to an agreement of sorts."

"About the makeover?" Carly swung her head back and forth between them, her gaze searching for clues.

"Rissa's agreed to help us out—"

"Rissa, *thank you!*"

"But," Jonas added firmly, "there are conditions."

"Here we go," Skylar drawled sarcastically, slouching in the seat. "We have to stay away from each other, right?"

"Wrong," he countered without a blink. "But as far as catches go, we don't consider this unreasonable or—"

"Just say it already."

"*Skylar.*"

Her daughter shut her mouth and slumped again, doom and gloom in her expression while she glared at Jonas.

"The catch is that *you*, Skylar, have to stay out of trouble."

Fear swamped Rissa when she watched Carly glance at Skylar in trepidation. Didn't she think Skylar could do it?

"But…Dad, Skylar—"

"No *buts*. Either she stays out of trouble, or Rissa and I will go to the school and insist on their help in keeping you two apart. No classes together, different lunch schedules, the works."

Rissa smothered her instinctive protest. They hadn't discussed *that*.

"You want to be friends, fine—but it means you *both* put your schoolwork first, and you behave in a responsible, respectable way. No more fighting, no more detention—no exceptions."

Neither girl said anything for a long moment. Carly bit her lip nervously and peeked at Skylar from beneath her lashes, but Skylar simply sat there and glared at Jonas, her expression full of anger and hatred that he was handing down yet more demands.

"Sky…what do you say?"

"Come on, Skylar, please? Say yes. We can do this together."

The sneer reappeared and while it was obvious Skylar didn't like Jonas's terms, she shrugged. "Whatever. So long as Mandy stays out of my face, fine."

Jonas leaned forward over the table, his expression grim. "That's not good enough."

Rissa glared at him. What did he want? For her to sign it in blood? "Jonas, I think—"

"After what I heard the other day at the library, I realize Mandy Blake is no angel, but I think your mom will agree that part of growing up and becoming an adult is being able to handle yourself in tough situations. Doing the right thing sometimes means *walking away* from a fight and ignoring the insults being slung at you."

"Dad, Mandy—"

"I said whatever. I'll do it, just drop the whole good cop, bad cop routine already."

Rissa brought her hand to her mouth to cover her gasp of relief. *Thank God.* Jonas's tough love tactic had worked. She'd hoped, prayed, Skylar would accept, but she'd honestly thought her daughter would tell Jonas where he could stick his demands.

"Sure you're not agreeing because it's what your mother and I want to hear?"

"Like I'd do it for that," Skylar snorted. "You got an ego or what?"

"Skylar tells it like it is, Dad. She's not two-faced like Mandy."

The admiration in Carly's tone reinforced Rissa's flagging spirits. Despite the attitude she was presently giving Jonas, somewhere in her Goth-girl teen a nice girl stayed hidden. Carly saw her. Had touched her. *Now if only she could.*

"But…what about Grandma? Do I have to go live with her this summer?"

All three of them looked to Jonas for the answer, and for the first time since he'd entered the diner, Rissa saw his expression soften.

"Two weeks, that's all. *Unless* you two do something that makes me think your spending the summer there would be a better solution. Understood?"

Carly quickly nodded, Skylar rolled her eyes and Jonas frowned across the table at them all, clearly unhappy with the compromise.

Rissa sighed. Why did she get the feeling things were going to get worse before they got better?

CHAPTER EIGHT

RISSA HAD EXPECTED Jonas and Carly to leave the diner after coming to the agreement, however, Jonas stayed and ordered dinner. Forty-five minutes later she grabbed her keys and purse from atop the counter and followed them out the door. "G'night, Porter! See you tomorrow!"

"Be careful driving home," Porter called from the kitchen before coming out to lock the door behind them. "See you tomorrow."

Outside the girls stood huddled beneath a streetlight, whispering back and forth.

"We'll walk you to your car."

Rissa stared up into his tense features and smiled gently. He was worried about his daughter, something she understood well. "It's okay, we'll be fine."

Hands tucked in his pockets, he scanned the nearly abandoned surroundings. "Might not be New York, but there is crime here, too, Rissa. Better safe than sorry."

Imagine that, chivalry wasn't dead after all. Feeling inordinately awkward and still acutely conscious of whatever had passed between them when they'd shaken hands, Rissa walked down the street toward the alley. Jonas shortened his longer strides to stay at her side, the girls up ahead of them.

How long had it been since a man had looked out for her? Larry had opened doors and done the look-at-me-I'm-a-gentleman thing when needed, but more often than not, she'd fended for herself. A practice learned from working in a field where the majority of pilots were male. Walking with Jonas was nice even if he still scowled every few moments at his thoughts.

Head down, she sidestepped to avoid a puddle. Jonas gently snagged her arm and held it, slowing her to allow the girls to get a little farther ahead of them.

"Caroline is different around her," he murmured, his gaze fastened on the girls. "More talkative and…outgoing."

The streetlight allowed her to notice the way little lines were beginning to creep out from the corners of his eyes, the way his jaw was strong and blunt. Jonas was a man's man. Raw. Big-boned and muscular, and the complete opposite of Larry. Her husband had been softer, more polished. *Slick* her dad often said. Her father had never particularly liked Larry, something she now understood.

Sensing this was the sheriff's way of making amends, she nodded. "I think they bring out the best of each other. Skylar…softens, seems more relaxed. Not so angry." She caught the slight smirk he couldn't hide. "Don't believe me if you like, but I know it's true. That's why I think it's so important to nurture this friendship of theirs instead of ending it."

Jonas didn't comment, and Rissa turned her attention back to putting one foot in front of the other. She was so tired. Convincing Jonas to give Skylar a chance had taken the last of her energy reserve. All she wanted was her comfortable pajamas and bed.

Moments later they caught up with the girls at her car and Rissa covered her yawn with her left hand and unlocked the door with her right. "Thanks," she murmured. "For everything."

His gaze slid to where Skylar and Carly stood on the other side of the car discussing a movie soon to be released, and stepping closer, Jonas lowered his head toward hers. "Rissa," he asserted, his voice pitched low, "I have nothing against you personally, it's just—"

"It would look badly if your position and image were somehow compromised by the antics of two teenaged girls?"

His surprised expression told all. "Yeah, that's right."

"Then we'll think positive that it won't be an issue, and pray for the best. Deal?"

"Deal." He opened her door for her. "Drive safe."

She mumbled her thanks and slid behind the wheel, sticking the key in the ignition before she leaned over to unlock Skylar's door. That done, she tossed her purse and apron off her lap into the back and twisted the key. The lights and the radio came on, but nothing else. Hitting the button to turn off the sound, she tried starting it again. And again. Nothing.

"Don't worry," she said with a strained laugh, "it always starts."

Jonas raised a skeptical eyebrow. "Doesn't sound like it's going to tonight."

She twisted the key again. *Come on.* It had been a long week, a long year. She couldn't deal with anything else right now.

"Mom, give it up. The thing's finally died."

No. No way, it couldn't have. How would she get to work? How would she pick up Skylar from school? Drive to an interview when she finally landed one? She couldn't borrow from Maura and Jake or the ranch any more than she already had. It wasn't right.

Overwhelmed, she said a silent prayer and tried

again. Nothing. Unable to cope, she reared back and hit the steering wheel with her palm. She didn't need this on top of everything else. It wasn't fair. It wasn't—

Skylar said something to Carly and the girl laughed. When Carly responded, Skylar's startling burst of laughter echoed off the buildings and into the car where she sat.

A strangled sob caught in her throat. Sudden. Out of nowhere. Uncontrollable. She quickly clamped a hand over her mouth, but it was too late. Jonas heard. He leaned down, into the car, one hand on the open door, the other on the roof, his gaze intense and concerned and taking in every detail of her face. With a single look he understood exactly what he saw. It was all there in his gaze. In the expression that said he related to her present state. Even sympathized.

It was his sympathy that had tears flooding her eyes faster than she could blink them away. Oh, please. She could *not* have a meltdown here. Not in front of—

"Come on," Jonas ordered softly. He reached into the car and grasped her elbow, gently but firmly pulling her out. He ignored her averted eyes and tug of protest. "Rissa, let's go. We'll give you a ride home, and tomorrow I'll get Spencer over at the garage to take a look at your car."

"I'll do it myself," she said, her voice choked.

"Fine. But let's go. Skylar, get your things and your mom's. Caro, lock up the car."

"Okay, Dad."

Giving in, Rissa allowed Jonas to pull her ahead of the girls, thankful he either didn't hear or else ignored Skylar's mumbling complaints about Jonas giving her orders.

They retraced their steps back down the alley, Rissa acutely conscious of Jonas's presence at her side. When they were far enough away from the girls that they wouldn't be seen, he grabbed her hand and pressed something soft into her palm. A handkerchief? What kind of man carried one of those in this day and age? She said as much to him and a husky laugh filled the air.

"I've learned it pays to have one ready. You never know when you'll need it. Better now?"

She sniffled, but nodded. Jonas opened the police cruiser's passenger door and she got inside, hurrying to pat her face dry before the girls caught up and noticed the waterworks.

The first few minutes of the drive proved awkward. Silent, there was a distinct tension between them. In the backseat the girls whispered nonstop, seemingly oblivious, and for that she was grateful. Then the town's few streetlights faded and Rissa found herself staring out the window, up at the star-studded Montana sky.

It never failed to amaze her. How could something be so big? The expanse of twinkling lights never looked the same, and she wished with all her heart to be up there right now. Night-vision goggles in place, the wind, the steady drone of the engine, the power and control and freedom she felt while she skimmed the treetops and soared. That's what she needed to de-stress.

Settling more comfortably into the seat, her thoughts drifted, back to happier days when Skylar resembled her and everyone commented on how sweet she was. Larry was conspicuously absent, but it hadn't mattered, not after a while. She and Skylar had only grown closer as a result.

Too close, she realized. When had she crossed the line? She'd had few women friends to talk to because they'd always come on to Larry, feeling that they knew him since he was in their homes via television nearly every day of their lives.

She should've known he'd eventually give in to temptation. The signs were there, but she'd purposely ignored them, and made up for the lack of female companionship with Skylar's company. Shared too much with the daughter she'd treated more like a sister.

The car bounced, startling her, and Rissa

realized despite her jumbled memories and erratic thoughts she'd actually dozed off. Jonas had turned onto the long driveway leading to the ranch, and she glanced at him, even more embarrassed.

He drove up to the main building without comment, reminding her he didn't know which cabin they lived in. Thankfully, none of the cabins were that far and, tired as she was, she didn't have far to walk.

Jonas pulled to a stop and the girls scrambled out of the backseat saying something about retrieving a CD for Carly to borrow. In a flash, they disappeared into the stand of woods separating the main area from what was once Seth Rowland's first wife's art studio.

"Rissa—"

"I'm sorry," she said before he could say more. "I'm...embarrassed. First my car... I can't believe I fell asleep."

"Don't be. You were out before we got to the city limits, a sure indication that you're exhausted. Everyone is emotional when they're worn out. I'm just glad you trust me enough that you could rest. A lot of people can't sleep when someone else is driving."

His comment stopped her cold. *Trust him?*

Maybe. But only because he understood what it was like to be a single parent. Understood how hard it was to cope with the physical and emotional demands. But trust intimated more. A lot more.

Rissa shook her head at herself, at the craziness of her thoughts. She had enough problems without adding into the mix romantic fantasies about a man who couldn't stand her daughter.

"Rissa, what happened back there? Why the tears?"

She fiddled with the handkerchief in her hand. The girls were so different. How could she make him understand? "Skylar laughed." His blank stare brought a weary smile. "Yeah, I know, it's silly, but I—I couldn't help it. Skylar laughed, and…it's been such a long time since I've heard the sound of real laughter from her. Derision, sarcasm, snorting, I hear those daily, but not laughter." Rissa opened the car door and shifted to get out, uneasy with her convoluted emotions when it came to the handsome sheriff.

Maybe she trusted him a little. He was the sheriff, after all, a man whose profession garnered trust. But it was more than that and she knew it. Jonas appealed to her as a woman, and yet he held a power over her and her daughter she didn't like, even though she'd allowed it, *encouraged it*. At this point all she could do was deal with the consequences.

"Rissa, wait. How long?"

The car's dim interior lights played over his

features, made them harsh and hard and shadowy. She ignored the part of her that wanted to stay with him and slid out of the car. "A year."

Jonas turned the cruiser off and got out as well. They slammed the car doors shut about the same time, and she watched warily while he walked to the front of the vehicle and waited for her. She opened the door to the backseat, but one glance proved the girls had already gathered up her purse and apron. She shut the door, hesitant.

The night surrounded them. Horses snuffled in the paddock, and a breeze laced with the smell of horses and hay and the slightest citrusy tinge of the sheriff's cologne lifted the bangs framing her face. In that moment, she no longer saw the creased uniform, or the overly protective father wanting to keep his daughter a child. She simply saw a sexy man who was…a man. The kind some lucky woman could count on, be able to lean on in times of trouble. Strong and hard and very, very likeable.

Unless her daughter screwed up.

And that was why she moved away from him even though she wanted to step closer, why she headed toward the cabin before she did something more embarrassing than she already had.

Skylar's behavior over the last year ended all the outrageous thoughts creating havoc in her head.

Thoughts that maybe, possibly, her interest in Jonas might be more.

"Rissa?"

The sound of her name on his lips brought her out of her stupor. "Thanks for the ride, Jonas. I've got to…I've got to go." She lifted a hand and brushed her hair back from her mouth when the wind blew it over her lips. "Good night. I'll send Carly right back."

She set out down the driveway toward the path leading to her cabin, and her heart skipped a beat when Jonas fell into step beside her once again. She looked at him in surprise. Jonas smiled, his teeth flashing white in the darkness. Not a polished grin like Larry had performed for the news cameras every night, but a friendly, charming smile that didn't last long enough.

Shaking her head at herself, she left the driveway and entered the shadows of the pines. The ranch house, cabins and bunkhouse all had large utility lights illuminating the grounds, but they didn't penetrate the trail separating her cabin from the rest. Darkness enveloped her, them, a haven of calm quiet.

Her steps slowed. The pine scent soothed her, made her feel protected. She paused, not sure why, simply unable to take another step. Then Jonas was there.

Heat scorched her in all the places he touched. His chest to her back. His hands slowly smoothing up her arms, the moist heat of his breath caressing her temple.

After the day, Rissa knew she was on overload because she couldn't catch her breath, couldn't move. The awareness there that she was way too tired, truly exhausted, if she considered being held by him a solution to anything. Yet still she wanted—

"You okay?"

She nodded and her mouth parted to draw in more air. She wasn't a masochist who wanted more pain. Under the circumstances, how stupid would she be if she let Jonas get to her?

"You're trembling..." His voice lowered, became husky. "Rissa?"

The thin material of her T-shirt was no barrier against his furnace-like warmth, his strength. It took everything she had not to lean against him. Every ounce of stubborn pride she possessed to keep from turning around and attempting to lose herself in him if only for a while.

"Tell me."

His breath hit her ear, his mouth so close that if she turned her head, rose on her toes... "I...I just need a moment before I go...inside."

His hands tightened on her arms. "Rissa—tell me what I'm missing. Tell me how Skylar used to be."

Memories bombarded her, painful jabs of what once was. She moved her head and gently hit his chin, his lips her temple. She closed her eyes. "I don't know if I can."

His palms slid, turning her in his arms. She raised her hands, but wasn't sure why. To protest? To wrap around his neck? They wound up trapped between them, resting on his chest. The touch deepened the intimacy, and she knew she should protest the familiarity. Pull away. But she didn't. He felt too good. She needed it too much.

"Tell me."

She had to break the chaos and form order in her thoughts, focus on what he asked rather than how he made her feel. "Blond hair," she blurted suddenly, her voice a hoarse whisper. "She had long, gorgeous blond hair. Beautiful blue eyes." Tilting her head, she looked at him, seeing her own doubts and worries reflected in the glimmer of his eyes.

"She wears contacts?"

She nodded weakly. "For two years now. Who knew they came in black?" Rissa shook her head, the warmth of his hands comforting like nothing else had in ages. "She was a—a straight A student. A cheerleader. She played volleyball and softball, took dance classes. Heaven forbid if I got home late and we missed a session." A harsh laugh erupted from her before she could stop it, more than a bit bitter about all she'd lost. "Picture her in a leotard and toe shoes," she murmured, "on stage in full costume. She danced the lead in *The Nutcracker* the winter before Larry's death."

The pine trees blocked most of the moonlight overhead, but the beams of light breaking through allowed her to see him. See the muscle working in his jaw while he digested her words, the heat in his gaze they both tried to deny.

"Why the tears when you got in the car?" Jonas lifted a hand and stroked his knuckles over her cheek. "It was more than her laughing."

She nodded slowly, compelled to tell him. "It was...you," she admitted simply. "The girls. I'm tired and frazzled, and everything crashed down on me with Sky's laugh and I couldn't—" She rubbed one of his shirt buttons with her thumb, each stroke somehow soothing, normal. She needed normal. "Because I *knew* with one wrong move, you'd go back to demanding the girls stay away from each other again, and it *hurt* knowing her laughter could disappear in a heartbeat should she anger you."

Jonas inhaled roughly and stared over her head toward the cabin. She turned and could see over her shoulder the light on in Skylar's loft bedroom, two images moving back and forth behind the lace curtain.

"What do you want me to do?"

Rissa turned back to him in surprise. "Do?"

"Tell me what you expect in regard to them. Help me understand them because I'm out of my element here."

She fell for him a little in that moment. With those words of compromise, she saw hope, the ability to meet halfway even if they didn't always agree. "Just give them a chance. Let them talk and help each other without judging everything Skylar does or making no attempt to hide the fact you're ready to jump in and whisk Carly away at the first sign of a problem."

He stared down at her a long while, his gaze probing, seeking answers she wasn't sure she had. Then his hands smoothed up her back and reminded her that she'd stood there all that time in his arms, leaning against his broad chest, and it didn't matter because he felt good, right.

The thought had barely registered when Jonas lowered his head and pressed his mouth against hers, and even though her brain immediately told her to end it, that kissing him was a mistake, the warning was ignored. Her lips parted and let him inside, and her heart slammed against her ribs going full throttle. Heat poured through her, filled her, elicited a moan Jonas returned after one of his callused hands slid back down to settle on her hips and nudge her closer against him.

The world tilted, the heavy pine boughs above their heads becoming blurred. Jonas didn't kiss her lightly or with hesitation, but like a man starving, one responding to the answering call of her body. His lips pulled at hers, his tongue nudged and played, swept aside everything but him.

His hands roamed her. Slid over her hips, her waist, slipped beneath her T-shirt and stroked. The abrasive pads of his fingertips rasped over her skin like the finest sand, caressing, warming, creating another ache deep within her. An ache too long ignored and forcibly buried due to a marriage in trouble and a cheating husband. She gripped his shirt with her hands and matched him kiss for kiss, unable to help herself, to stop, needing to press closer in order to better feel his body, hot and hard against her. A simple kiss that wasn't simple at all because with every stroke of his tongue, his hands, she wanted more.

Jonas released a low groan and abruptly raised his head, his hands jerking out from beneath her shirt. Bereft, Rissa buried her face in the material covering his chest, desperate for the moment to last a bit longer.

"Dad? Can I spend the night with Skylar?"

Rissa tensed, praying the night sky and the

shadows hid her red face and what they'd been doing. Thank goodness Jonas had heard Carly's approach because she'd been oblivious to everything but him. She inhaled and slowly stepped back, hoping to not attract Carly's attention.

"Please? I can ride back to town in the morning when Rissa checks on her car."

"Caro, that's not—"

"We'll behave, I promise. Please?"

"It's fine," Rissa murmured, clearing her throat when her voice emerged husky and full of lingering desire. "She's very welcome to stay."

"You're exhausted," he reminded gently, "and she's in trouble for sneaking out... Now's probably not the best time."

"But things are better after our talk, aren't they, Dad? We'll be quiet and let Rissa sleep... she's already agreed!" Carly pointed out hopefully. "Please?"

Rissa tried to smile and thought she must have managed when Jonas's gaze slid to her lips in a visible caress, one glittering with enough heat and desire to singe her. "Y-yes, I did. It—it's fine, let her stay, Jonas."

He continued to watch her, his gaze searching, appraising. Warm with gratitude and hot with longing all at the same time.

"You can stay."

"*Yes!* Thanks, Dad! Thank you, Rissa!"

Carly's running footsteps faded away to nothing and they were alone again. Seconds passed and then the screen door opened and closed with a gentle slam.

Jonas closed the distance once more, a sexy smile curling the corners of his mouth. Rissa's rapidly beating heart had finally started to slow from the kiss and near discovery, but now it increased again, her response surprising. She'd never experienced this type of knee-jerk reaction, and wet her lips, more than ready for a second chance to lose herself in his kiss. But instead of kissing her mouth, he lowered his head and oh-so-slowly brushed his lips against her forehead. "Good night, Rissa. Make them go to bed and try to get some sleep, all right?"

"Jonas?"

His gaze met hers, dark and sensual. Very, very hungry. But wary as well. She recognized all those emotions because she felt them herself.

"Sweet dreams...I'll see you tomorrow."

CHAPTER NINE

"HAND ME THAT pair of pliers." Rissa stretched her hand out, but didn't get the requested tool. What she got was a disgusted sigh from Maura that carried to where she lay beneath her car.

She'd called Maura's house early that morning to find out who to call to tow her car. But Jake and one of the other men were ready to go to the supply store in town, so they tossed in a tow chain and, two hours later, had left her car parked in the open area by the bunkhouse.

"Maura?"

"I'm looking. How on earth do you tell what's what?"

Rissa scooted on her back and butt until she could see more than Maura's sandaled feet. "You're such a girly-girl," she teased, her mood light despite spending the night tossing and turning due to her dreams of Jonas. R-rated dreams that made her cheeks warm just thinking about them. "It's there by your right foot," she laughed, watching her cousin's movements from her under-the-car view. "Your other right. Are you *sure* you should be handling hot appliances?"

"Ha-ha." Maura grabbed them up and slapped the pliers into her hand surgeon-style. "I might be a girly-girl, but at least my mama never had to drag me under a faucet to get the grease out of my hair."

"Hey, you can't blame me. We'd nearly finished rebuilding that Mustang."

"It was prom night and your date was *waiting!*"

"Girls, are you going to argue all day or prove to the men around here that cooking and cleaning aren't all we're good for?" Grace squatted down and then lowered herself even more to look under the jacked-up car. "You've put our reputations on the line," Grace informed her with a grin. "By working out in the open like this, bets are being made that it won't start when you're done."

"Maura better go raid her cookie jar then." She scooted back into position and put the pliers to use, Grace and Maura at her feet. "And it's Seth's fault I'm here. Jake told him I planned to work on it myself, and Seth told him not to tow it to the cabin," she complained. "He said when I gave up, it would be easier for the garage to tow the car from here. You've got one egotistical man on your hands."

Grace laughed. "Don't I know it. Humbling him is half the fun though, so don't let me down."

"She done yet?" Seth called, amusement strong in his voice.

Grace chuckled. "Just a little while longer, boys."

Boys? Rissa turned her head and spotted several of the ranch hands and even some of the male guests in a shady spot on Seth's back porch.

"Taken roost is more like it," she muttered.

"So," Grace said casually, "rumor has it some woman was seen kissing the sheriff here last night."

The statement surprised Rissa so badly she raised up, banged her head on the car suspended above her and bit back a gasp. Apparently she'd lifted and lowered her feet in the process as well because she heard the rumblings of male laughter from the peanut gallery.

"Are you okay?" Maura asked quickly.

She rubbed the spot and winced. "Yeah."

"Are you the woman?" Grace queried next.

"Uh...what was that?" She used the pliers to bang on the underside of the car. "I can't hear you!" Rissa glared at their feet. They were fishing, that's all. No one was around last night when Jonas had brought them home. No way could anyone have seen them except Carly, and she hadn't because she would've said something.

Maura dropped down beside Grace until she and Grace both stared at her, witnessing her wide-eyed shock.

Rissa pointedly ignored them and went back to work. "Who started this nasty rumor?"

"The same guy who has the rocking chair's view from the porch," Grace informed her. "Seth was checking on a mare about to foal, and witnessed it all. Said this kiss was so hot, he almost needed a cold shower when it was over."

Maura's mouth fell open. "With *Greasy Rissy?*"

"Hey!" Rissa nudged Maura with her foot and watched smugly while her cousin scrambled for balance.

"She not only looks guilty, she *acts* guilty," Maura declared knowingly.

"Seems that way, doesn't it?" Grace agreed with a raised eyebrow.

The sound of a car driving up to the ranch distracted her tormentors, and Rissa got back to work. She fixed the only problem she'd been able to find, and smirked. Maura should've spent less time teasing and more time getting her cookie jar money.

Multiple feet headed her way, most of them boots, some sneakers and a few old-man loafers along with several wheels, walkers and canes. She watched their progress from beneath the car, making sure everything was in place. When all was exactly as it should be, she began her forward butt-scoot again. "Just in time to eat your words, boys."

"What the— *Rissa?*"

She froze when she heard Jonas's familiar voice, then continued crawling out from under the vehicle until she squinted up at him and smiled. "Uh…hi."

"Hi yourself," he ventured, his gaze moving over her from head to toe and lingering on a few spots in between.

"Jonas, I believe you've met my cousin, Greasy— Ha! You missed again! Sheriff, doesn't that count as attempted assault?"

The men laughed at their antics and Rissa's playful glare.

Chuckling, Jonas stepped forward with his hand outstretched, but Rissa shook her head and crooked a grime-coated finger at Maura, who immediately backed away.

"No way."

"Girly-girl."

Jonas watched Rissa's every move while she got to her feet and wiped her hands on a towel she pulled from her waistband. The sight of her reminded him of the pin-up calendar posted in Spencer's garage.

She was dressed in army-issue shorts and a camouflaged, sleeveless shirt with worn sneakers on her feet. But it was the smudges on her cheek, nose, forehead and left breast that made him want to kiss those spots and more.

"What are you waiting for?" a man demanded. "Let's hear it, honey."

Rissa scowled and Jonas heard her say something about a cookie jar to Maura when she walked by. Seth's wife bit her lip nervously and due to the talk and dollar bills being exchanged when he drove up, he couldn't help but think Grace and Seth had a bet going as well, one of a more personal nature.

Rumors of their battles when Grace first came to the ranch to help Seth recover from his back injury were now legendary, and it was said that Grace had conned Seth into therapy the first time by betting he couldn't beat her at arm wrestling. Jonas wasn't so sure he believed the rumors. Seth was a big man and heavily muscled. No way could Grace have taken him on and won.

Rissa had finished cleaning her hands and opened her car door, but now she hesitated and glanced at him with a small smile. "Would you start it for me? The seats aren't spotless, but they're better than I am at the moment."

"Don't let her cheat, Sheriff!"

Smiling, Jonas moved forward and folded himself into the small car. To draw out the suspense, he fumbled to adjust the seat and give himself more room. "Here we go." One twist of the key and the car started right up to a chorus of groans, cheers and whistles.

Rissa grinned. "Gentlemen, let this go to show you that you should never underestimate the abilities of a woman."

The men groaned. Still smiling, Jonas cut the engine and lifted his head in a nod at Jake's wave goodbye. Rissa thanked the few who'd supported her and laughed at their comments. Once everyone began to wander away, Jonas got out— every second that passed a battle not to blurt out what he'd come to say before he gave in and kissed her again.

"Thanks, I—" She caught him eyeing her rear and flushed. "I'm a mess. Sorry."

"You're beautiful." She was, too. Success had put a rosy blush on her cheeks and made her eyes sparkle. Look in a way that had him wondering if this was what she'd look like after making love. The thought sent heat shooting straight to his groin. "Uh, *ahem*, I, um, have to admit I didn't expect to see you under your car when I drove up. I didn't realize you're a Jane-of-all-trades."

"A girl's gotta have some hobbies. I didn't even break a nail." She flashed him her dirty hand, wriggling her fingers at him and grinning. "Better scrub good before I go in to the diner tonight, huh?" Her smile held, then slowly dimmed. "What's wrong?"

"Wrong?"

She tilted her head to one side, her gaze shrewd. "I was supposed to bring Carly home tonight, and yet you're here and you look like a man with a problem on his mind."

He glanced around to make sure no one was nearby, and spotted Jake on the kitchen's covered porch getting ready to ring the bell for lunch. Soon they'd be surrounded. "Rissa, we need to talk."

"About? Ah…I see." She didn't look at him.

"No, you don't see." Conscious of Jake watching, he took her elbow in hand and pulled her around the side of the building, then on to the back until they couldn't be seen by prying eyes.

"You think last night was a mistake," she said bluntly, her tone…hurt? "Do you regret letting Carly and Skylar be friends, too?"

Jonas pressed her against the side of the building and held her in place with his hands against the wall by her shoulders. "Listen to me first before you start arguing their case, all right?"

She didn't like the idea and wanted to protest, he could see it in her face, but she managed to hold her words. He leaned low and nudged her chin up a notch when she tried to avoid looking him in the eyes. "Rissa, the kiss wasn't a mistake—" his voice lowered as heat raised his blood to the boiling point "—and I can't wait to kiss you again. But," he added quickly when she opened her mouth to speak, "Caroline is struggling to figure out who she is right now, torn between being a girl and a woman. I'm interested in you, Rissa, I can't deny it. But I—*we* have to look at this from all the angles. If Caroline continues to distance herself from her friends because she's latched onto Skylar, and then you leave, what then? It's not just the two of us we're dealing with."

She stared at him, her lower lip caught between her teeth. "I—I hadn't thought of that. What the—the impact of them being friends now would mean later when…"

"Then you see that it could hurt both of them?" He waited for her nod. Lifting one hand off the wall, he snagged a tendril of her hair stuck to a smudge on her cheek and tucked it behind her ear. "And you'll understand why I'm going to encourage Carly to see her other friends, to go out with them with or without Skylar so that she'll have others to lean on when you…when you leave?"

"Yeah, I understand." She blinked. "You'd better—"

"I'm not done." He smoothed his finger over her lips, tracing their shape, feeling their texture and softness. "I'd like us—Rissa, despite the fact that you're going to leave soon, I'd very much like to see where things take us while you're here."

"Things?"

"The kiss and…whatever happens next."

Her gaze narrowed on his. "Then why do you look so upset by it all?"

Unable to help himself, he leaned low and gave her a slow kiss that had him hard in an instant. Unlike last night, she didn't hesitate. Rissa parted her lips and stroked her tongue to his, raised her hands to his chest then seemingly remembered their condition and chose not to touch.

Jonas slid his hand up to her head and held it gently so she wouldn't hit it against the wall behind her when he took the kiss deeper, exploring her. The suppleness of her mouth, the silky feel of her cheek under his thumb, the scent of her, combined with the murky tinge of grease.

Unable to withstand any more, he pulled away even though he wanted nothing more than to slip his hands beneath her clothes. Once he regained control, he stroked her face again, watching her, liking how his kiss had left her visibly dazed.

"That," he breathed, desire still thick in his voice, "is what I want to explore while you're here. I want to spend time with you, Rissa. Do things, watch a movie—whatever. But while I'm not at all sure how we'd manage it, the problem you sensed in me earlier is…how you're going to feel when I ask you to see me without letting the girls know?"

Jonas stared down at her, watched her face for every sign or hint of unease. He knew he was asking a lot. But the protective father in him had to do what he could to shield Caroline from the past repeating itself, even if it was at the risk of his own heart. He didn't know Rissa, but he wanted to. Her willingness to help a girl she didn't know and her fierce defense of her troubled daughter moved him. He admired the woman who'd packed up and headed cross-country in the hopes of a better life and wore her strength and determination proudly so that few saw the vulnerability beneath. He saw it—the tears, the hard work, the exhaustion. The laughter.

"If this is too much to ask, I understand. Say the word and I'll leave you alone." He didn't know how, but he'd do it. And he almost wished she had more strength than he did so that she'd protect them all by sending him away.

Rissa lifted a hand to her face and rubbed, making another smudge. "I do understand what you mean, what you're saying," she clarified. "I honestly hadn't thought what the future would bring other than a new job in a new town, another move."

He waited, not wanting to pressure her in any way. Not liking her words, but glad she was being honest.

She swallowed, lifted her long lashes to stare up at him, her eyes wide and bright and scared, but brave. "Seth saw us. Last night, he saw us. Grace and Maura know—"

"They won't say anything. Especially if you ask them not to."

"That's true. But if we do this—whatever this is," she whispered, "it has to be slow, Jonas. I'm coming off a bad marriage, and like you, I don't want my daughter hurt in any way. I won't be able to separate myself or not get angry if you and Skylar get into it. I'll need time to see how you two do…together, and…go slow."

"We'll take it slow," he promised, relieved she'd brought it up first. Slow was good for him, a bad marriage common ground between them. "In case the girls need to be separated." For the first time he hoped that didn't happen.

"I'm not an actress, Jonas, and I can't lie at all."

That was a bad thing? "Good."

"But Skylar—she would *not* understand," she said with a groan. "And should she ever ask me, I want to be able to say we're…*friends*. That way I'm not lying."

"Caroline, too. She—" *would get her hopes up* "—wouldn't understand, either. And we are friends, aren't we? No matter what the girls do?"

She swallowed again. "I suppose so. I mean, yes, we are— Jonas, I know you only want what's best for them. We both do."

"Then we both understand each other. Now will my *friend* give me one more kiss before I have to go back to work?"

She smiled, and that was all the encouragement he needed.

TWO MORE DAYS. All she had to do was make it two more days. Then no more detention, and only four lousy weeks of school left.

Skylar leaned forward in the chair and glared at Marcus. Unlike the other jocks, he seemed to prefer his broken-in cowboy boots to sneakers when he wasn't on the field.

A cream-colored Stetson sat pushed back on his head and highlighted his sun-darkened complexion and American Indian heritage, and the navy blue T-shirt he wore brought out the blue of his eyes. Stupid hat or not, boys just didn't look like him in New York.

She glanced down at the paper she doodled on and was mortified to see she'd written his name in curly letters. *So not going to happen.* Especially after what she'd said to him.

Marcus might be cute and all, but she couldn't forget for a second that he was buddies with Travis and Mandy, and while he was nice when they weren't around, he probably acted just like them when they were. All that mumbo jumbo he'd spouted during the end-of-year assembly about always looking at a person's inner spirit instead of the outer shell was for show. It had to be.

Idiot, of course it was. The assembly was a joke, the speech class teacher's way of showing off. Marcus had written the speech a long time ago, before she'd moved to *Loser*ville. Her mom had to find a job soon. That or score some big tips when the people from California came. It was only a matter of days now, and Maura had said the whole ranch had been rented out. There'd have to be lots of tips there, right? Maybe then they could get the heck out of Dodge.

Marcus glanced her way, and Skylar's heart thudded hard in her chest. Oh, yeah, he was a hottie. She looked down and determinedly colored over his name, reminding herself that guys were jerks and treated females like the crap Marcus shoveled.

"Mathews, time's up. You going to sit there all day or are you going to let me go home and get some dinner?" the coach asked abruptly.

Feeling her face heat, she glanced at the clock and realized she'd stayed five minutes later than needed. Embarrassed, she grabbed her bag from the floor and shoved her notebook inside, not paying any attention to the coach when he hurried from the room.

"You need a ride to the ranch?"

Her head jerked up and she stared at Marcus, dragging her bag over one shoulder. "No thanks…. Look, about the other day—"

"Suppose your mom wouldn't like it, you riding with some guy she doesn't know and hanging out."

Hanging out? "I wouldn't care if she didn't like it, I do what I want. Look, I was really mad the other day after the fight and…I shouldn't have said what I did."

He shrugged. "Yeah, well, it's probably true half the time. Mandy's caught me in town after a day's work and said the same."

God, she so didn't want to be compared to that bitch. She walked to the door, aware he was watching her. "Yeah, well, I shouldn't have said it. Sorry, okay?" Turning, she walked out of the room—and right into Mandy in her cheerleading outfit, her cronies two steps behind.

"Hey! Watch it, loser."

"Mandy, lay off." Marcus now stood beside her.

"You're kidding me, right?" Mandy's expression darkened to pure hate. "She tried to run me down. Did you see that?"

The girls behind her nodded.

"She did not. Give it a rest already."

Skylar glanced back and forth between them. He was taking up for her? In front of them?

"Girls!" the coach called from down the hall.

"I'm not spending the evening here. You got a problem, take it off school grounds." The coach glared at Skylar as if she'd started it all. *Of course.*

Skylar ignored Mandy and after a last glance at Marcus, headed down the hall toward the coach and the main doors.

"She is such a freak show."

"Mandy, you're so right."

"I'll say."

"Bet the rumors about her are true," Mandy said snidely. "I heard she went crazy after her dad died in a wreck. I mean, look at her, who'd wear that if they weren't crazy?"

Skylar stiffened, paused midstep and almost turned around. But then she remembered Marcus's comment about Mandy, remembered Marcus still stood there watching. She glanced over her shoulder. Yeah, still there. She couldn't go back and bash Mandy's face in with him watching her like that, like he'd be disappointed if she did. So she forced her feet to keep moving and with every step it got easier. Yeah...she'd be the adult since Mandy wasn't up to the challenge.

And because she didn't want Marcus looking at her the way everybody else did.

ANOTHER WEEK *closer to summer vacation.*

That was Jonas's first thought when he made his

way into the house. A handful of bills awaited him on the hall table, but it was the muted sound of comfortable soles that had him turning to face Marilyn—and wish he'd put in some overtime. *Not again.*

"Have you come to a decision?"

One look at her face told him the conversation wouldn't go well. "Two weeks, Marilyn. That's all she'll stay this summer."

Marilyn put her hands on her hips, an exasperated expression on her face. "You're making a mistake, Jonas. She came home in a horrible mood and talked back *again!* She ignored my requests to spend time with me and went straight to her room to get on the computer. I drive all this way and she wants to study? It's Friday!"

Jonas glanced down the hall and noted his daughter's door was cracked open, her five-foot shadow blocking the light of the lower half. He stepped forward and tugged Marilyn with him into the kitchen. Once there Jonas released her and turned to stare out the window over the sink.

"Jonas, I know the thought of letting Caroline go can't be easy, but we both know it would be for the best. Your schedule is atrocious and Caroline's attitude is a reflection of that. She needs stability."

"By changing yet another aspect of her life?" His hands gripped the counter tight. "I've already told her she doesn't have to spend the summer, and I'm not going to be pushed by you into changing my decision."

"*Well*...if that's how you— I—I'm not feeling very well today," she said abruptly. "So I—I think I'll let you and Caroline handle things here this week. I wouldn't want—" she sniffled loudly "—I wouldn't want to stay and—and upset either of you."

Jonas's knuckles turned white, and even though he knew she waited for him to protest, to make it up to her the way he and Carly always did, he refused to feel guilty. The time had come.

"I'll just go...gather up my things."

"Marilyn?"

"Yes?"

Her tone was so eager, so needy, he cringed. "Give Dave my best and tell him when he gets some time off to come by and I'll take him to that fishing spot I told him about out at the Second Chance."

"That's all you have to say?"

He didn't turn. "You expected something else?"

She harrumphed. "You just wait, Jonas. You'll come to your senses when Caroline continues to misbehave. Until then, maybe it would be best if I stayed away. You'll see you're *not* handling her and things here as well as you seem to think. You'll see you *can't*."

Again she waited. He didn't move, didn't protest

or make any attempts to apologize. Finally Marilyn gave up and grabbed her purse and keys from the table, the time it took her to walk to the front door three times the norm. Jonas stayed where he was until he heard her car start and drive away.

Taking a deep breath, he walked down the hall to Carly's room. "Caro?"

"I'm sorry, Dad. I didn't mean to be so grouchy with Grandma. I have a stomachache and don't feel good, but I'll apologize later for being rude."

"Were you rude?"

She hesitated. "Some. She wanted me to practice piano, and got mad when I wanted to lie down. I told her I sucked at piano and her lessons didn't work."

He tried to keep his laughter out of his voice. Musical she wasn't. "Want me to bring you something? Maybe some crackers and ginger ale?" He thought he heard a sniffle.

"No, thank you."

"I think I'll order us some dinner from the diner. You want anything special?"

"No, I'm not hungry.... Dad? I love you."

The weight on his shoulders pressed down a bit more. Was he doing the right thing? "I love you, too, sweetheart."

"If I feel better later, can I go to Skylar's tomorrow?"

The question had him frowning. "Are you sure nothing's wrong? Do you need a doctor?"

"No, I'm okay. But I'd like to go see them— since it's okay now. I got an A today," she added hastily. "It'll bring my B in world history up to a solid A and that's without the extra credit. It'll give me an A plus."

Jonas chuckled softly, relieved. "That's my girl. I knew you could do it. And yeah, kiddo, you can go if Rissa says it's okay. Tell you what," he drawled, wanting the excuse just to hear her voice, "how 'bout I call and talk to her for you?"

"RISSA SAID she's really proud of me and Skylar."

"Is that right?" Jonas asked a week later, looking up from the paperwork he'd brought home with him so he could spend some extra time with his little girl. Marilyn's comment about his schedule had gotten to him, and he'd exchanged his office desk for the kitchen table.

"Rissa said if we keep it up, maybe we could do something special together this summer. You know, like go somewhere overnight or something, like a minivacation."

Jonas set the pen aside and stared at Carly. If she began another sentence with the words "Rissa said" he'd—

"Rissa said she asked Maura where to go for my

haircut and Maura gave her the name of a great place in Helena. She said she'd call and get the cost and then help me come up with a budget to spend the money you said I could have for my birthday."

"Why not go somewhere here?" he asked, wondering if his daughter's excited chatter was just that—excitement over her soon-to-be makeover—or the start of a deepening appreciation of Skylar's mom. Either way, it worried him. Him getting his heart broken was one thing, his daughter's heart was another.

"Rissa said she'd work Friday night at the diner and then come get me Saturday to go shopping if that was okay with you?"

"Shopping for what?"

"*Daaad!*" When he smiled, she grinned. "Anyway, before Rissa dropped me off to go to the diner, she also said Grace asked if I might be able to work at the ranch for the summer helping Skylar babysit the kids that come with their parents. She said we'd be chaperoned and we'd even get *paid!* So can I? It would be my first job."

A job? "I don't know, sweetheart. That sounds like a big responsibility." And it would mean spending even more time with Skylar when he was trying to get her to see her other friends.

"Please, Dad? I really want to and…"

"What?" he asked suspiciously.

"It would mean I wouldn't be a problem to you all summer since I'd be somewhere working. And chaperoned," she added, repeating herself and dangling the word like a prize. "And I wouldn't...I hoped I wouldn't have to go to Grandma's, at least not for long."

So that was it. Jonas got up from the table and walked over to where she stood mixing up a salad for dinner. He took her shoulders in his hands and gently swung her around. "Caro—"

"Please, please, *please* don't say no! Dad, I want to do this. It's job experience and—and I'd be earning money for college!"

"You'll also be limiting your exposure to your other friends by tying yourself down like that when the fact is, Skylar and Rissa plan on leaving soon. Rissa told me herself they're not staying here permanently."

"But—" She blinked rapidly. "Then shouldn't I spend as much time as possible with them while they're here?"

Jonas frowned at her alternate thinking. After Lea's betrayal he'd felt the compulsion to distance himself from people, to guard his emotions, but Caroline didn't feel that need. Thank God.

"You'll be hurt when they leave."

Her chin lowered. "I won't like it," she agreed softly, "but Skylar's already my friend. I'd like to see her as much as I can before she moves—*especially* if she's moving."

"Your grandmother will be more upset than she is now." Was he really using Marilyn as an excuse?

"I know, but…maybe if I still go stay with her a week and do the ballet thing, she'll be happier."

"Not two weeks?"

Carly bit her lip. "I got so bored last time it was *awful*."

He chuckled and pulled her close for a hug, sighing. "Okay, then. You can take the job."

"*Yes!* Rissa said you'd be reasonable and do what you thought was best."

Jonas stared down into his daughter's soft gray eyes and smiled. "She did, huh?" He tugged on her ponytail, curious even though he told himself not to be, wondering if he'd agreed for his daughter's sake or his own because it would give him a legitimate reason to visit the ranch without drawing too much notice or gossip. Why was he setting himself up for a fall? "So, what else did Rissa say? Anything about me I need to know?"

CHAPTER TEN

RISSA HAD NEVER given much thought to the saying "time flies" but since Jonas had tugged her behind the bunkhouse and kissed her, well, it had. New guests had arrived at the ranch to stay each week, and the number of occupied cabins continued to increase, which meant she spent more time cleaning.

Jonas had come to see her at the diner the two days she'd worked, and at closing time reappeared to walk her to her car "for her safety," leaving her breathless from kisses that would start slow and leave her quivering the entire drive home. How could she feel that way for a man she'd only met weeks ago?

Jonas was tender and kind, a good man. Almost too good. And that scared her *why*?

The phone rang, interrupting her confused thoughts. She spritzed her hair once more before tossing the hair spray aside and hurrying over to the portable phone. "Hello?"

"Are you decent?"

His husky voice sent an immediate surge of heat curling through her body. "Yes."

"Too bad."

Rissa dropped down onto the couch and grabbed a pillow to hold. "What about you?"

"Sadly, yeah. Looks like I'm going to stay that way, too. Are you headed to work?"

"Soon, why?"

A gusty sigh came over the line. "I need another favor and before you say anything, I'm aware of the fact I seem to be relying on you more and more and…"

"And?" she asked, holding her breath.

"And I hope you don't mind. If you need something, all you have to do is ask. I'm more than willing to help you if I can."

"I'll remember that. So…what do you need?"

"I've got to work tonight."

"Oh, no."

"Yeah. Carly invited you over for cake and ice cream, right?"

"She did, and she'll be so disappointed."

"I know, but it can't be helped unless…"

"Maybe I could set things up for when you get home?" she volunteered, unable to disappoint Carly—or deny her need to see him again. "I'm sure Charlotte wouldn't mind covering for me since we switched earlier this week. She seems to like hanging around Porter. Their banter has become a little more intense lately."

"Those two have been fighting it for years."

"It's settled then. The girls can hang out at the diner until I'm off, and afterward we'll go pick up the supplies and make a cake. It'll give us something to do to kill the time and it's cheaper than buying one since you've got her big shopping spree coming up tomorrow."

He groaned, but didn't comment on the reminder. "You really don't mind?"

"No. But you might have to think of some way to make it up to me."

"Ah," he drawled softly, a smile lacing his words, "now there's something to look forward to."

LATER THAT EVENING, Rissa pulled into Jonas's driveway. "Looks like you have a visitor," she told Carly.

An older woman stood on the porch watering what looked to be a newly purchased flowerpot.

"Um, that's my grandma."

"Crap," Skylar muttered, "this'll be good."

Rissa's good mood evaporated with her daughter's words. Like her, Skylar and Carly had both been in decent moods all evening, the three of them looking forward to some fun time. Now their faces revealed their worry and that caused hers to skyrocket.

"Hey, Carly, duck down. Maybe we can turn around and drive away," Skylar said hurriedly. "Like we're lost or something."

"Why?" Rissa asked, forcibly maintaining a smile, but wanting to do just what her daughter suggested. "Too late, she's looking this way."

The woman continued to stare, a frown puckering her forehead. She set the watering container down and stepped off the porch.

"Here we go."

"But, Mom—"

"Hello, may I help— *Caroline?*" The woman's sharp gaze skidded from Carly getting out of the backseat to Skylar to her. "Oh. Well, thank you for bringing Caroline home. I'm sure in the future she'll do better about not missing the bus. Right, Caroline?"

"I didn't miss the bus. Grandma, this is Rissa Mathews, and you've met Skylar. Rissa, this is my grandma, Marilyn Wells."

"Nice to meet you."

Mrs. Wells said nothing in return.

"Rissa and Skylar are here for my birthday, Grandma. We're making my cake so it'll be ready when Dad gets off work."

The woman grew two inches before Rissa's eyes.

"You mean your father agreed to let—"

Her hand lifted in Skylar's direction, and Rissa raised an eyebrow, smiling tightly. "Yes?"

Marilyn's mouth worked, but she continued to flounder. "He didn't say anything to me about this."

"We didn't know you were coming," Carly murmured, staring at her feet after flashing Rissa a quick yet leery glance. "You know, after your fight."

"Don't be insubordinate," Mrs. Wells told Carly. "And as for you hanging out with—with your friend, I believe you were specifically told not to, and until I know differently, your father's orders are to be obeyed. Now, go into the house and wait for me."

Carly sucked in a sharp breath and tears flooded her eyes. "Grandma, no! I *am* allowed to be friends with Skylar and—and—"

Rissa stepped close to Carly and wrapped her arm around the girl's shoulder. "Carly, how about you and Skylar take the groceries into the house, please? Maybe get started on the pizza mix?"

"Okay."

"I'll not have Caroline alone with that—"

"My daughter has a name," she informed the woman, her voice deliberately low and controlled for the girls' sakes. "You obviously know it, now I'm asking you to please use it."

Carly and Skylar had slowly walked to the porch, but gone no farther. "Girls, inside, please."

"Don't you tell my granddaughter what to do! Who do you think you are?"

"She's Dad's girlfriend!" Carly called loudly from the porch, drawing a gasp from both women.

Rissa stared at Carly in wide-eyed horror, but that was nothing compared to Skylar's expression. Her daughter shut down before her eyes, her glare deadly.

"You're dating the cop?"

She opened her mouth to comment when Marilyn shrieked in outrage.

"He's *married!*"

"No, he's not," Carly countered from the porch. "You're lying, Grandma! Dad's divorced!"

"That is *enough,* Caroline!" Marilyn turned back to glare at Rissa. "This is your doing, isn't it? She's changed from a sweet, obedient little girl into a—a monster like—"

Her words were cut off by the powerful sound of Jonas's police cruiser pulling into the drive. Within seconds Jonas was there beside them, and Rissa couldn't help but be relieved by his presence.

"Jonas, I insist you tell this woman and her daughter to leave. You aren't in high school or college, and it's unacceptable that you're behaving this way in front of my granddaughter!"

Rissa watched Jonas stare at Marilyn, his gaze moving to where the girls still stood side by side on the porch and finally to her. She waited, knowing from experience that this was it.

When she'd confronted Larry about his mistress and ordered him to end things, he'd hesitated and she'd known then their marriage could never be repaired. The same was true of Jonas. Maybe they weren't anything more than friends yet, but friends didn't share the chemistry they did. She knew where it would eventually lead and when it did, there would be no denying her heart's involvement. But if he sent them away now, she'd know where she stood in his life. It would prove to her she was someone Jonas used to help him out, a single dad's crutch and nothing more.

He shifted uncomfortably. "Rissa, I'm sorry—"

Marilyn lifted her chin in triumph.

"—that my ex-mother-in-law feels she owns and controls our lives. She doesn't. And I'd like you and Skylar to stay and continue our plans for the evening like I asked you to. If you wouldn't mind?"

The older woman sucked in a sharp breath, her hand flying to her chest. "How dare you! How dare you choose them over me after everything I've done for you!"

Jonas didn't take his eyes off Marilyn. "Rissa, would you take the girls inside? I'd like to talk to Carly's grandmother alone."

"Her name is *Caroline*."

"Sure," she mumbled, her legs shaky from the confrontation. She wasn't a coward when it came to standing up for herself, but this wasn't about Marilyn Wells. This was about her and Jonas and—

She wrapped her arms around the girls and herded them inside the house, unable to keep from smiling to herself. For such a rotten beginning to an evening, Jonas's words had sent her feelings for him soaring.

"WHAT DO YOU THINK they're saying?" Carly glanced at Rissa from beneath her lashes and saw Skylar's mom quickly smooth the worry from her face.

"I think they're discussing you, and us, and her role as your grandmother," Rissa murmured.

"So are you dating the cop?" Skylar glared at her mom.

Carly frowned. "Why are you calling him 'the cop'? And wouldn't it be great if they were dating?"

"Uh, let me think—Nuh-o!"

"Carly, why did you say that?" Rissa asked softly.

She reached down and grabbed the pizza pan from the cabinet. "I couldn't help it. Grandma makes me so mad sometimes. She thinks if she says something often enough then we have to do it, and I thought...I don't know, I guess if she believed you were Dad's girlfriend, she'd go away and leave us alone."

"So are you?" Skylar asked again.

"Dating Jonas? No."

Disappointment filled Carly. "Why not? You're friends, right?"

"Yes, we are."

"*Just* friends?" Skylar's glare turned vicious.

"I guess I should've just said that. It wouldn't have mattered because Grandma wouldn't have liked that, either."

"She's a witch."

"*Skylar.*"

"Well, she is." Skylar nudged her. "You know I know your grandma can be okay some of the time, right? I mean, everybody can be a witch sometimes, even Mom."

"Gee, thanks. I'll take that, but only because you didn't say 'all the time' and the same goes for you, too."

Carly laughed and wished she had a mom like Rissa, wished Rissa really was dating her dad. Maybe he'd be happier and…Grandma really would leave them alone and not complain so much about everything they did. "Do you guys fight a lot?"

Rissa and Skylar exchanged a glance.

"That was rude. Guess I shouldn't have asked, huh?"

"No, hon, it's not that. It's just recently Skylar

and I do fight a lot more than we used to. But, no matter how much we fight, I love her and I hope she knows it. The same is true with your grandmother, I'm sure."

Skylar didn't say anything and Rissa looked a little sad. Why didn't Skylar see how great her mom was?

Her dad entered the house, and all three of them left the gooey pizza dough and met him in the hall.

"What happened with Grandma?" Her dad smiled that smile of his that meant everything was going to be all right, but she'd learned a long time ago to look into his eyes for the truth. What she saw there told a different story than the smile. "Does she hate us?"

He opened his arms and even though Rissa and Skylar stood behind her watching, she hugged him because he looked like he needed it.

"No, sweetheart. She's simply not thrilled that you and I have made new friends."

"Does this mean I get out of going to the ballet?"

He chuckled, the sound rumbling under her ear. "'Fraid not. In fact, she's more determined than ever that you need to spend time with her this summer. But only the one week. She wanted two like I'd told her before, but I made it clear you can't stay longer because of your job at the ranch. She didn't like it, but even your Grandpa Dave is a big believer in kids holding summer jobs. He'll back us up."

She squeezed him tight. "Thank you. I really didn't want to tell her."

He kissed the top of her head and let her go. "What are dads for?"

She let him go and turned around, surprised when she saw Skylar scowling at them. She wondered if Skylar was upset because she'd lost *her* dad.

"Are you staying for pizza?" Rissa asked. "We'll need to speed it up if you want to eat before you go back to work."

Carly tried not to think about how sad she'd be if her dad died. Her mom wasn't around anymore, but at least she wasn't dead. Her grandma got cards and letters from her sometimes. She did, too. On her birthday and at Christmas. But there was never a return address so she could write back.

"No, I need to get back to work."

She glanced up and caught her breath at the look her dad gave Skylar's mom. No way. Was she right? But why would they hide?

Oh, she *really* hoped she was right! How cool would that be to get a mom like her? And a sister! Skylar already understood her and—*didn't want Rissa to date her dad.* But why?

"When I remembered what day it was, I figured I'd better come by because there was a chance

Marilyn might show even though she wasn't supposed to."

"Well, thank you. For taking care of…things."

"Want to walk me out?"

"Sure."

"Caroline, behave. I'll see you later."

"'Bye, Dad."

Her dad glanced at Skylar and nodded, but Skylar just glared back at him. How rude.

Instead of going out the front door, her dad left through the garage door instead, Rissa following behind him.

"I need to get some tools for work," he explained while he unlocked and opened the door, but there was something in his eyes, that look again.

Carly watched them go and as soon as the door shut behind them, she glanced at Skylar. "Did you *see* that?"

Skylar ignored her and continued to glare at the door, her mouth twisted into an ugly sneer. She shoved herself off the wall where she leaned and headed back to the kitchen, but when she passed the garage door, she raised her middle finger.

"Skylar!" She giggled. "Why'd you do that for?"

JONAS SHUT THE DOOR behind him and Rissa, and held it closed in case curious minds decided to follow them. With his other hand, he beckoned

Rissa close and snagged an arm around her waist to pull her against him. He buried his nose in her fragrant hair. "You smell so good," he sighed, the tension draining from him now that she was near. That was *not* a good sign. Carly wasn't the only one he reminded on a near daily basis that Rissa and Skylar would soon be gone, but right now he couldn't think about it. "I'm sorry, Rissa."

"For what?" she murmured. "You can't control other people, and you defended our presence here quite admirably."

He pulled away far enough to kiss her forehead, her cheek, skimmed lower to kiss her mouth. Rissa opened for him and wrapped her arms tight around his back. He liked the feel of her hands on him, the way her breasts pressed high on his stomach. She fit him perfectly. Too perfectly.

"Mmm, I think I heard a giggle."

"Don't worry about it, I've got the door."

With that bit of news, her arms tightened even more and Rissa flashed him a brief smile, one of awareness and desire. She wanted more? God knew he wanted her to feel what he did. In the past week he hadn't stopped thinking about her, how she laughed, the way she moved. Smiled. Tasted.

Rissa held on to him for balance and raised to her tiptoes, kissing him like there weren't two teenagers on the other side of the door, before she pulled away and seductively wiped her lip gloss from his lips with her thumb. Jonas nipped at her, making no attempt to hide the effect she had on him. One kiss and he wanted to press her against the wall. Taking things slow had never been so torturous.

She looked a bit shaky herself when she pushed him away. "Go to work," she whispered huskily, "or I won't be able to face the girls. We'll be here when you get home."

Jonas smiled, liking the sound of that way too much, and let himself forget for a moment that it wouldn't always be true.

JONAS SPENT the next day on edge. When he'd gotten home from work Rissa and the girls had been curled up on the couch surrounded by teen magazines. The baked cake had been covered and put away since Carly wanted to wait and celebrate after she received her makeover.

The rest of the evening his daughter had talked nonstop about clothes and hair and makeup, and Rissa had silently teased him when he continually failed to follow along. She seemed to know it was because of her and the kiss in the garage.

Jonas frowned and hit his turn signal to head down the street toward his house. The more Carly had talked and laughed and the more tension between him and Rissa had risen, the quieter

Skylar had become. She'd glared at him, sent her mother looks that would've withered most anything, and Rissa either didn't notice or chose to ignore Skylar's expressions. With the girls always present, he didn't have a chance to ask if Skylar had said anything about Carly's claim. Marilyn had certainly pointed it out in her upset before leaving, but he'd quickly informed her the topic wasn't up for discussion.

No doubt Skylar and Marilyn were both worried about what would happen if he and Rissa hooked up. Skylar would be his stepdaughter and her image *was* a problem so—

Stepdaughter?

He shook his head at his thoughts. He was getting way too serious about a temporary woman.

Jonas stopped the car and got out, making his way to the door with no small amount of dread. The makeover and his daughter's new look and attitude, Rissa and Skylar—things were changing and not necessarily for the better. But like a boulder rolling down a hill, there was no way to stop his feelings now that they'd begun. And they'd started the first time he'd seen her, cemented the second time when she'd smiled at him outside The Blooming Rose.

Before his hand could land on the knob, the door swung open and Rissa's smiling face had him forgetting all about his worries. At least until she said, "Brace yourself," with a sympathetic yet amused expression and stepped to the side.

Framed in the hallway behind her stood his baby girl, no longer a baby at all.

Carly's normally curly hair was board-straight and teased the sides of her delicate face. A lightly made-up face that brought out the gray of her eyes in startling detail, left her freckles to be seen— *thank God*—and made her lips shine with a bit of sparkle. Her cheeks held just a hint of color, and her long lashes were darkened, her eyes looking bigger than ever.

She wore a thin, stretchy shirt the color of bronze, snug jeans with embroidery and sparkles along the legs, and a wide belt dangled from her slim hips. Brown, low-heeled shoes added to her height, and overall the look was perfectly decent, but definitely more grown-up and different than anything she'd worn in the past.

"Well?" Carly asked, turning around slowly, posing with her hands on her hips, a too grown-up expression on her face. "What do you think? Do you like it?"

He had to clear his throat twice before he could speak. "You look…beautiful. Absolutely amazing." And more like her mother than he'd ever noticed her resembling.

"Are you going to come in and join us?" Rissa teased.

The laughter and understanding in her eyes cut through the terror sliding through his overprotective dad-cop bloodstream. Once the boys saw his little girl looking like that—

Rissa took hold of his arm and tugged him into the house before closing the door behind him.

"I only went a little over the budget, but I'll pay you back with my allowance and job money. We bought two more pairs of jeans, a few shorts and we found a bunch of tops on sale to mix and match."

"That's...great."

Rissa covered her mouth with her hand, but it did nothing to hide the smile in her eyes. "Carly, I think your dad needs some time to adjust. Why don't you and Skylar go hang your new clothes up in your room while he unwinds a bit? I'll get him some food and then we'll cut that cake and celebrate."

Carly took off down the hall without a word of protest, and Skylar's dark shadow detached from a wall and followed. Until then, Jonas hadn't even seen her.

"Come on. You look like someone sucker punched you."

"I feel that way, too," he admitted honestly, following Rissa and enjoying the sway of her hips while she led the way to the kitchen where a grilled chicken salad waited. "It's not much, but I found it in your fridge and figured when you saw her, you could use the food to keep your strength up."

That brought out a resigned chuckle. "Thanks for planning ahead." He sat down at the bar. "I still can't believe the difference."

"Amazing, isn't it? A few highlights, a little wax and she definitely doesn't look like a little girl anymore."

Wax? Jonas poured himself a glass of iced tea and shoveled a bite of chicken into his mouth while Rissa told him all about his daughter's makeover and where they'd shopped per Maura's urging. Before long the food was gone and the girls were back, Skylar's scowl in place.

"Is it time for cake?" Carly grinned, her excitement visible.

Jonas grabbed the camera and snapped some pictures. Carly with her purple cake and fourteen candles plus one for luck, Rissa and Skylar beside her. Skylar and Carly together, the older girl unsmiling.

Rissa held out her hand for the camera, and Jonas gave it to her before stepping to his daughter's side. That led to Carly asking Skylar to take a picture of the three of them. Rissa glanced at him nervously.

"Can't," Skylar muttered, holding the camera Carly had shoved toward her. "It's out of film."

Rissa quickly cut the cake and Jonas sipped his coffee, liking the chatter and laughter filling his kitchen. Amazed at the difference in his daughter. She was so at ease with them.

"Dad, we need a digital camera so we can take more pictures," his daughter complained before adding, "Hey, I know what we can do! Can we go to the movies?"

"Tonight? Caro, I've had a long couple days."

She bit her lip. "Actually, I meant me and Skylar...by ourselves. *Please,* Dad? It's my birthday!"

"Yesterday was your birthday. What, you want a birthday *weekend?*"

She giggled. "Of course!"

Jonas glanced at Rissa, who shrugged and mouthed, "up to you." "Okay. But the early show which means we've got to leave now."

"If you want to drop them off, I'll stay and clean up," Rissa offered.

Jonas noted Skylar didn't look thrilled at the prospect of going anywhere with him, but she didn't protest. Good thing because he figured it was a test of sorts.

After they piled into his cruiser, Jonas tried to make conversation with Skylar, but the girl was rude in the extreme, either glaring at him, rolling her eyes or sneering at him in response. Finally he gave up and they made it across town to the old theater in no time, but per his daughter's embarrassed request, he dropped them off at a nearby corner and then kept them in sight while they walked the block and purchased their tickets.

A group of teens crowded around a bench out front and they said something when the girls walked by. Jonas couldn't hear what it was, but from the look on Skylar's face it wasn't good. The heavily made-up teen kept walking, though, and in that moment, Jonas saw that she was truly trying to stick to the terms of their agreement. Which meant he had to be willing to overlook her rude attitude and behavior whenever possible. She was Rissa's daughter, and if he wanted a relationship with Rissa, he had to come to terms with Skylar for as long as they stayed in North Star.

He saw Skylar turn and search the parking lot until her gaze locked on the cruiser where he sat a ways away. From there he could see her smirk, but she trudged her way into the building without pause. Carly followed after her, but at a slower pace, smiling nonstop, obviously enjoying the response to her new look.

Jonas stayed a bit longer to make sure there wasn't any trouble either inside or out, that no calls to dispatch were made. By the time he put the car into gear and drove home, nearly forty minutes had passed. He locked the door behind him, set his watch alarm so he wouldn't forget the girls, and found Rissa in the kitchen, drying the dishes and reading the newspaper at the same time.

"Hey, you're back."

"I'm back." Something in his tone must have warned her about his thoughts because she wet her lips and smiled shyly.

Stepping closer, he watched her gaze become soft yet wary, seductive. She shook her head, her expression torn, and Jonas wondered if her mind tried to warn her body what was coming. His certainly had, not that it had worked.

The image of Rissa scooting out from beneath her car flashed through his head. She might be a city girl, but she wasn't the high-maintenance kind like Lea. Maybe they could find a place on the outskirts of North Star, closer to Helena and the airport. Surely one of the airlines there would be hiring flight attendants eventually? A compromise of sorts that would satisfy them both?

And Skylar?

"Jonas, I—"

"What?"

"That's just it." She groaned softly. "I don't know. When you're around I—I'm happy and sad and—" she glared at him "—horny. It's not fair!"

His heart in his throat, he pulled her into his

arms, the dishtowel trapped between them. "Horny, huh? I'll use anything to my advantage."

"Why doesn't that surprise me?"

He chuckled at her disgruntled tone. "Would it help to know I feel the same way? I can't allow myself to think about you when I'm at work because I wind up having to do everything twice."

"Really?" A smile curled the corners of her full lips, but her expression remained hesitant. "Then I'm not the only one driving myself nuts thinking of all the reasons we shouldn't be together? What we're risking…?"

"Not by a long shot."

"But here we are."

He pressed a kiss to her forehead, right between her eyes. "Here we are." Another to her cheek. "Alone." Another. "Very, very alone… Hear that?" She shook her head. "Exactly."

Closing her eyes, Rissa swallowed audibly. "Jonas, I don't know if… If I let myself," she whispered, "I think—I—I…"

His feelings exactly.

"And I can't." Her voice lowered. "I *can't*, Jonas. Skylar shot us death glares all evening if we even smiled at the same time. I can't believe she willingly left us alone." She shook her head again. "She must've really wanted to see that movie."

He lowered his head until his mouth was

directly over hers, their breaths mingling. A moment passed, and he gave her every opportunity to pull away. To do what he couldn't.

She moaned softly and raised herself on tiptoe, pressed her mouth to his, her eyes open, her need, her hesitation, there for him to see. One kiss turned into two, her lashes lowered at five, and then Jonas lifted her up onto the counter and settled himself between her spread legs.

CHAPTER ELEVEN

"JONAS... WAIT," she murmured, holding him off with her hands at his shoulders. "We said we'd do this slow, but— Have you ever heard of speed dating?"

He shook his head with a muttered no and Rissa laughed, the sound flowing over his skin like erotic music. "It's a quick way of getting to know one another, there's an article about it in the newspaper."

"Is that right?" he asked against her mouth.

"Mmm. Want to try?"

"Do I have to stop kissing you?"

Her breath tickled his ear when she laughed. "What's your...favorite color?"

"Green."

"Mine's blue," she whispered, her hands falling to the buttons of his shirt. She undid three and yanked, forcing Jonas to stop and pull his uniform shirt from his pants, willing to play along so long as he got to play with her. "Favorite food?"

He pressed a kiss to the spot below her ear. "I love fried chicken."

"Shrimp with lobster sauce," she murmured, tilting her head back to give him better access. "We need to eat healthier."

Buttons undone, her hands slid over his chest, lingering on his pecs and making Jonas glad he'd kept in shape. His gaze narrowed, liking how she seemed to have gotten a little dazed while touching him. He knew the feeling. She was so beautiful.

"Country music," he countered, dispensing with the "what's your favorite' part of the question and *not* liking it that her hands were causing him to want to forget slow and easy and go for quick and satisfying.

"Classic rock and roll."

"I can deal with that." His hands slipped under her T-shirt and he grinned when she gasped. Jonas tugged the material over her head and let it drop to the floor, then covered the cups of her bra with his hands, kissing her deeply. "Mysteries."

"Huh? Oh, um…romances. Really gushy, emotional ones."

"Rain storms." He trailed his lips down her neck to her shoulder, biting gently. She stiffened in his arms and gasped out his name, the sound accompanied by a breathy moan.

"B-blue skies."

"Long winter nights, a blazing fire."

"Got—got me there."

"Small towns."

"Anywhere with an airstrip."

"Fly-fishing."

"Flying."

He paused, more than a little dazed, and pulled away. "Flying? You like being a flight attendant so much it's your favorite hobby?"

She nipped his chin, soothing the little bite with a stroke of her tongue, and laughed up at him. "One, I *never* said I was a flight attendant. I said, I worked for an airline. And two, if you haven't already figured it out, I'm a pilot. I'm certified roto and fixed wing, and I don't 'like flying,' I *love* flying."

Jonas chuckled, unable to hide his amazement. "A pilot and a mechanic to boot," he murmured. "You are one amazing woman."

"Thank you," she drawled seductively, her hands smoothing over his chest. "You're not so bad yourself."

"I take it you learned on planes?" He ran his hand down her hip and scooted her closer so that her breasts met his chest.

She nodded. "My dad was career military. Said I couldn't…fly them until I could repair, um, repair them if needed. Or at—*oh*—least, um, know if someone didn't do their…job."

"Anything you can't do?" He paid close attention to the tender spot in the curve of her neck, wanting to hear her moan again.

"I'm a lousy shot."

"Got'cha covered there," he murmured, palming her side and following the length of her bra to unfasten the back. "No worries."

She moaned when his thumb rubbed.

"Movies," he ordered, the breathless quality of her voice jacking his desire up even more. *"Quigley Down Under."*

"Mmm…too many." She tightened her thighs around his hips, the move making them both hold their breath for a moment.

Jonas raised his head from his exploration and he stared deeply into her eyes, willing her not to look away. "Marriage," he challenged next.

Only the raspy, quickened sound of their breathing filled the silence. "Forever," she whispered, unblinking, but looking sad. Because of him and Carly? Skylar? Because she liked to fly? Whatever the reason, surely they could find some middle ground? Their connection was powerful. Too powerful to set aside for technical difficulties. Wasn't it?

Inordinately hopeful that he could—*would*—change her mind about leaving, Jonas gripped her hips and lifted her off the counter. Rissa gasped at the move, but locked her arms and legs around his back and pressed her mouth to his while he carried her into the living room and lowered her onto the oversized leather couch he favored. He followed her down and pinned her beneath him, loving the way she arched into his touch, realizing he loved her even though he knew he ought to know better.

Jonas laced his fingers gently into her hair until he found the clasp holding it in its bouncy ponytail and released the catch. Dropping it beside the couch, he fingered the silky length of blond hair and used it to guide her mouth back to his.

"This is crazy," she murmured against his lips, "you know it is." Rissa turned her face into the palm he used to caress her soft skin and squirmed beneath him. "We could wind up ruining a perfectly good friendship."

"We could," he agreed, leaning low to kiss her parted lips, drawn to the taste of her more than he'd been drawn to any woman in his life. "Or we could make it even better."

"But like you said…if we leave—"

He latched onto the word. "If?"

She blinked, confusion spreading across her features. "I mean when," she said with a quick shake to her head. "*When* we leave…I don't want it to be with regrets or…or pain. For the girls or…us."

The words hung there between them, the air thick with desire and need. Anticipation. What if he told her he loved her? Would it make a difference? It was then that his watch alarm began beeping.

"What is that? Your beeper?"

Jonas smothered a groan. "The girls. I set my watch to remind me to go pick them up."

"You needed a reminder?" she teased, the barest hint of relief in her eyes.

He held back the words he wanted to say, and nodded. "I had a feeling once we were alone I'd be distracted."

He stared down at her, the moment gone even though he was still hard and hungry for her.

"You'd—you'd better go get them."

"Rissa?"

"Timing is everything, Jonas. And who knows? Maybe this…the girls are our reality check."

MONDAYS SUCK. Especially since she'd spent the last two periods watching Carly make an idiot out of herself. A little makeup and a new do and her friend thought she was a supermodel or something.

"Hey, did you see what happened back in class?"

Skylar grabbed her notebook and rolled her eyes. "You mean how jerk-wad said a few words to you and then leaned over the desk to look down your shirt? Yeah."

Carly laughed. "He did not…did he? Shut up! *Really?*" She leaned closer and whispered, "My new bras fit better and make me look bigger." She grinned. "Travis noticed?"

Skylar slammed the locker door closed and flipped the dial on her lock. "Carly, I know you really wanted a makeover, but you've gotta realize jerks like Travis don't change. He might flirt and stuff, but it doesn't mean anything and you're crazy if you think it does."

"Says who?" Carly demanded. "Maybe he's starting to like me."

Skylar tilted her head sideways and stared. "You can't be serious. Considering what happened to you this year, you've got a *huge* ego to think it would all disappear overnight."

"I do not!"

"Oh, yeah? What's the test on in world history tomorrow?"

She stared at her blankly. "There's a test?"

Skylar snorted. "See? All you've done today is check your hair and your makeup and look around to see if anybody's looking at you. Just like you did at the movies the other night."

"It's because it's different and I like my new look. Everybody's talking about me and saying how pretty I am, and it's…nice."

"That's fine, but you don't have to—"

"Hey, Carly. You wanna have lunch with us today?" Randy Spears stood a few feet away, a stupid grin on his face. "Me and the guys found room for you at our table."

"Really? Oh, well…"

Skylar waited, her gaze narrowed while she watched Carly blush and stammer. Randy stepped closer, ignored Skylar entirely, and leaned on the lockers between them, effectively cutting her out of the discussion. *Jerk-wad Number Two.*

"Come on. Come sit with us. You can't go to all the trouble to look this hot and sit at the loser table. Besides, I know a guy who really wants to get to know you."

"Who?"

Randy looked around and then leaned closer to Carly. "Trav."

Skylar turned on her heel and walked away. Whatever Carly's answer was, she didn't want to hear it.

LATER THAT EVENING Rissa dropped down onto the couch beside her daughter. "What's wrong? Something happen in school today?"

"No."

"Did you get in trouble again?"

"*Noo-o.*"

Skylar shoved herself up into the corner of the couch away from her, flipping channels rapidly. She finally settled on a pop rock station. That was one of the things that had always given Rissa hope. Skylar might look like a Marilyn Manson groupie, but she didn't listen to that type of music. Instead she seemed to prefer contemporary artists and rock groups like Alanis Morissette and Evanescence. Even Kelly Clarkson, the common theme being love gone bad.

Had Skylar liked a boy back in New York? Before her dad's death when everything changed?

"I thought I'd have to unglue the telephone from your ear this evening. You and Carly talk every night when you get home from school—why not tonight?"

A shrug was her answer.

"O-kay." Rissa stood and headed toward the kitchen only to pause. "Sky…when we moved, was there anyone you liked or—or someone special you didn't want to leave behind?"

Skylar stilled. "No. Why are you asking?" She shot to a sitting position and glared. "This isn't about Carly's dad, is it?"

"This is about you. I just wondered—"

"Because you're dating him?"

"Skylar—"

"*Are* you?"

"We're friends." Their last evening together lent truth to her words. They were friends because, honestly, they weren't anything else. "You and Carly spend so much time together, how can we not be friends?"

"You promised! You said we'd only stay a little while!"

"And I'm asking because you and Carly have gotten so close. You're doing much better in school. I thought you might've changed your mind, that's all."

Skylar slumped back down on the couch. "I haven't changed my mind. I don't want to stay."

Wishing she'd never brought it up in the first place, Rissa sighed and fixed herself a glass of iced tea. She left Skylar to stare blankly at the gyrating figures, and stepped out on the porch, seating herself in the swing. Rissa leaned her head back against the wood slats and moaned.

"That sounded kind of disturbing. What's up?"

She raised her lashes and smiled weakly at her cousin. "Where are the boys?"

"Asleep. Jake's keeping an eye on them. What's wrong?"

"Everything."

Maura leaned against the porch post at the bottom of the steps. "I didn't see you much yesterday since I was doing inventory, but Grace watched the kids for us Saturday night. Jake and I drove into town and took in a movie. Strangely, we saw the girls, but not you and Jonas." She raised a questioning eyebrow. "What did you do while they were there?" One look at her face had Maura's expression turning to one of slack-jawed glee. "You *did?*"

"We didn't," she corrected hurriedly, glancing at the window. She hurried off the porch and away from the house, conscious of Maura hot on her heels.

"Well?"

"We…messed around a bit."

"I *knew* it!"

"Nothing happened," she insisted. "Seriously. Nothing except… Oh, Maura, I'm so confused."

"What's the problem? He's certainly hot enough."

"His being hot is part of the problem. When I think of Larry and his running around…"

Maura linked her arm in hers and pulled her toward one of the newly constructed paths. "Jonas is nothing like Larry, at least not now. After the divorce he might have accepted some of the offers tossed at him, but they weren't anything serious."

"How can you be sure? Larry—"

"You and Larry weren't happy for a *long* time before he died. It's only natural for you to be leery of Jonas or any man. It's hard to get back in the swing of things."

"And Skylar?" she asked. "He hates how she looks, her attitude and just now when I questioned Skylar about something, she bit my head off because she assumed I asked because of him."

"Did you?"

Rissa groaned. "Sort of, but—I just asked if maybe she'd changed her mind about staying here because she's doing better in school and has Carly as a friend. She flat-out refused and threw the promise in my face."

"Think she's afraid he'll try to take over? You know, ban the hair and makeup and all that stuff?"

"All I know is that she hates him, he doesn't particularly care for her and yet I'm in the middle and can't get Jonas out of my head."

"And that's a bad thing?"

"Of course, it is! Maura, you and Jake have helped me out when I needed it most, but North Star is the last place I think I'd be happy staying permanently." She paused when Maura made a face. "What?"

Her cousin frowned. "Nothing, you just remind me of myself because I used to think that, too. When Seth was injured, I gave up my dream of cooking in a five-star restaurant to help out, and I *hated* it. But it was necessary. I couldn't expect

Jake to go it alone, especially not after everything Seth had done for us in regard to Lexi when we were both still in school."

"But what about that five-star restaurant? Seth's well and now he has Grace, and you're still here. What about *your* dreams?"

"That's just it. I'm here because I want to be here," Maura insisted softly. "Dreams change. I'm cooking, but I'm also raising a family, and I feel very lucky to be able to do both. I've managed to find balance when it honestly wasn't something I was looking for. And I'm smart enough to appreciate the hand God played in *not* giving me what I thought I wanted."

Rissa blinked at her, the words churning in her head. "What changed your mind? Was there something specific?"

Her cousin looked around them and Rissa followed her gaze, taking in the tall pines and trees newly green with spring, the rocks and grasses and early blooming wildflowers, and absolutely breathtaking clear blue sky overhead. Each day here was different, changing, always beautiful. Ready to be explored. New skies for a new life? But how would she get up there from here?

"I can't think of any one thing. It simply became home. My priorities changed. Suddenly I couldn't see myself working for some demanding restaurant owner who liked to yell. Here I'm in charge of my kitchen, cook what I want and still get to play with my kids and be home with my husband. It's the best of both worlds."

Rissa stilled, happy for her cousin, sad for herself. She wanted that, too. She wanted to regain Skylar's confidence. Have a home, more children. Play time free of hassle or work responsibilities. How would she have that in the future when beginning a new job was always a challenge? Her flight skills would be tested and debated simply because she was new to the crew and a woman to boot. She'd get all the unwanted hours, the least favorite flights, be the low pilot on the totem pole for the next how many years?

Her gaze locked on what looked to be a private jet flying low overhead, and more than anything she wanted to be up there. Whether she flew a helicopter or small airplane, it didn't matter. She needed the freedom to breathe that flying brought, and no matter the problems or hurt she'd feel when she left North Star—and Jonas and Carly— she couldn't get that freedom here. And she couldn't let herself forget it.

"Did I help?"

Rissa nodded, sad. "Finding balance in my life will be next to impossible."

"No, Rissa—"

"Yes. Maura, it will be. I can't plop down anywhere and fly. Which means I need to be willing to settle. And I have to remember what it's like when I *can't* fly so that I'm thankful to have a job when I find one. No matter where it is."

SKYLAR WALKED OUT of the girls' locker room and stopped for a drink at the fountain. Her mom had to work at the diner this evening so Skylar had asked her if she could get a ride to the library. It meant her mom had to drive in early to pick her up since she didn't have detention, but her mom hadn't seemed to mind since it meant a few extra tips.

She knew her mom assumed she would be meeting up with Carly, but ever since Monday when Carly had chosen to eat lunch with the in-crowd, they hadn't spoken to each other. She didn't care though. Carly was the one who'd regret it because she would have to stand up for herself from now on after choosing them over her.

Sitting in the library alone beat sitting at the cabin all night, and this way she could make sure Jonas wasn't sniffing around her mom. She wasn't staying in Loserville any longer than she had to—especially now that Carly had gone to the dark side.

"So it's a bet? The first guy to bag five cherry freshmen gets coach's tickets to the playoffs?"

Skylar froze, unable to walk away from the conversation taking place inside the boys' locker room.

"I'm going to have those tickets in no time. Give up, losers, you're toast."

She rolled her eyes. Travis. Of course.

"You've got a girlfriend, dude. You're out."

A rough laugh followed. "That's fixable. And I'm *in*." A loud slap echoed off the cement walls. "In more ways than one."

Snickers filled the air at his crude comment. The *jerks*.

"Okay, so here's the deal. All the virgin girls' names are in here. Everybody in picks five and those are the girls you go after. Nobody else's."

"That takes all the fun out of it."

"Those are the rules. Otherwise everybody'd go after the decent ones and leave the dogs alone. You want to win, you gotta get your girls."

"Guess we know Mandy isn't in there."

"Got that right."

"Or freak-girl."

Skylar rolled her eyes, disgusted by their talk, but unable to walk away because she knew this game had something to do with how nice the boys were being to Carly and a few of the other not-so-popular girls lately. Lunch had been…strange. More scenes like the one in the hallway Monday between Randy and Carly, the popular girls glaring at the jocks and exchanging angry whispers.

In that instant, she realized their bet was already in the planning stages, and they were trying to get the girls to like them, not knowing who they'd get when the names were drawn.

Low murmurs and shuffles bounced off the walls along with groans and more than one *"Yes!"*

"Hey, Trav, who'd you get?"

Skylar waited, holding her breath. *No, no, no.*

"Good ones, man. Makayla, Payton, Cheyenne, Dara and…*Car-leee.*"

"Ah, man, that girl changed overnight. Sweet!"

"Yeah, but she's so desperate she'd do anybody—even Trav."

More snickers and name-calling.

Skylar got a better grip on her book bag and took a step forward, intending to go in swinging. Someone grabbed her arm and yanked her back. "The coach is right behind me," Marcus told her. "Unless you want detention again for causing trouble and being in the boys' room, you'd best get out of here."

She glared up into Marcus's knowing eyes and blinked back tears of fury, feeling like an idiot but unable to stop. "You know what they're doing."

His mouth flattened into a line. "They're smart girls, they'll figure it out."

Maybe. *But not until it was too late.* Guys didn't understand. It wasn't the same for them. Not at all. "You're in on it, too."

"No, I'm not," he argued. "I don't treat girls like that. It's a couple of the senior losers trying to go out with a bang because they know next year they'll be nothing in college."

"And the rest?"

Marcus glanced behind him and Skylar looked as well, saw the coach talking to the principal, but walking backward toward them.

"Detention is worth bashing their heads in. I'm going to stop them."

"They're bigger than you, and nobody will believe you when it's your word against all of theirs." Marcus leaned lower, his blue eyes intense. "Think about it. You're hanging out here after all the girls are gone—"

"I'm waiting for my mom."

"You've been in trouble already, and PC or not, your looks and attitude give a certain impression. You go in there and I won't be able to protect you, not from all of them. And *they'll* say you wanted something from them—not the other way around—and are making up the story because you got caught trying to have a good time. If you want to do something, warn the girls."

She hated that he made sense. "Maybe nobody

will believe me, but if you went to the principal and said—" Skylar broke off, shaking her head when stupid tears got the best of her. She swallowed, having a hard time breathing because her chest felt so tight. "Forget it. God, guys are all the same. Every single one of you are horn-dog jerks who don't give a damn about anything but your dicks."

Skylar yanked her arm away from him and headed toward the gymnasium door.

"Not all of us."

She kept going, hating herself even more for wishing it were true.

THE NEXT DAY Carly had called Skylar's house and not gotten an answer so she'd told her dad she needed to go to the library for one of the extra-credit projects. He'd okayed it and come to pick her up, but she knew it was because he wanted an excuse to go across the street and see Rissa. Her dad liked Rissa even if he wouldn't admit it.

Now she dropped into the library chair opposite Skylar, and hoped Skylar would talk to her instead of issuing her orders like she had yesterday when she'd told her the horrible lie about Travis. "Hi."

"What do you want?"

She glanced around to make sure no one was nearby to overhear. "Um…I'm sorry about lunch the past couple days, okay? But if you knew how long I've waited to fit in, you'd understand how badly I want—"

"To screw your real friend over?"

Her stomach knotted at the look on Skylar's face, but she pressed on anyway. She had to. Nothing was going to blow her chance with Travis.

Not even Skylar.

She got up and reseated herself on the block table, closer to where Skylar sat. "Please try to understand. It's just… What you said about Travis and the others *isn't* true. It's *not*. I asked him about it and he said he broke up with Mandy because he *likes* me. You must've misunderstood or something. Travis said he's liked me for a while, but Mandy kept making such a big deal out of it that he had to say mean things to me to make her happy. After my makeover, he said she was really jealous. No wonder she's been so mean to me. She's horrible."

"She's not the only one." Skylar shoved her iPod aside and glared. "I can't believe you're taking his word over mine. He's a lying prick."

"Don't call him that, he's *not!*" She looked down, wishing she knew the right thing to say to convince her. "Travis says you're just—"

"What? What did jerk-wad say?"

Carly straightened her shirt. "He says you're jealous because I'm pretty and—and getting attention now and because everybody's talking about me and not you."

Skylar muttered a really foul word.

"He says you feel bad because you're being left out. But, Skylar, listen, we don't want you to feel bad and we—we came up with a way you can be involved, too."

"I can't wait to hear this."

Carly cleared her throat, and glanced around again. "Travis asked me to go to the dance, but my dad won't let me date. I—I need help getting out of the house to meet Travis there, and we thought maybe you'd help us so you could be involved in things, you know?"

Skylar smirked. "So I'm your friend—and *Travis*'s—if I get you out of the house without your dad finding out?"

"You're my friend either way, but I want to go. What's wrong with that?"

"What's wrong? You're supposed to be smart, that's what's wrong." She shook her head. "It doesn't work both ways, Carly. You have to choose. Me or them. Either way, I won't help you."

"*Skylar.*"

"Choose."

Carly grabbed her books and stood. How could Skylar fail her now when she needed her most? Friends? She'd never been her friend. Not really.

"If you *were* my friend then you'd help me," she told her, her throat hurting because of the lump of tears burning inside it. "I choose *them,* how's that? You're leaving town soon anyway, right?" The words came out in a gasp. "When you're gone, *I'll* still be here. That means I have to have other friends besides you. Even my dad says so."

Skylar didn't move, didn't blink. "Sounds like you've already got it figured out, and you don't need me."

"You're right. Who needs a friend like you?" She turned to walk away. "I certainly don't."

CHAPTER TWELVE

SOMETHING WAS UP. Rissa returned the phone back to its base and frowned. She'd been leaving the cabin for her shift at the diner when Skylar had called from a pay phone at school and asked if she could spend the night at Carly's house.

It was the first time her daughter had asked to stay with Carly, and the request came after a week of watching Skylar mope around the house. Rissa had immediately said yes to the request—so long as Skylar checked in and Jonas didn't mind. Skylar had called again a few hours later, but then no more. And now no one answered at his house.

Dread spread fast and Rissa told herself it was nothing. Jonas must have taken the girls to the movies again. That was all. But wouldn't he have driven to the diner to see her after dropping the girls off? He hadn't been around much this week, but he'd claimed it was due to being a man short at work. Now she wasn't so sure. Other than brief sightings of him at dinnertime when she couldn't stop to chat, he'd kept his distance, and she had to believe it was due to her reality check comment and her relief that they'd been interrupted by his watch alarm.

One of Jonas's deputies sat in the far corner of the diner. Hesitating only briefly, Rissa grabbed the coffeepot and headed his way.

"Hey, Rissa, busy tonight?"

"Not too bad. You, um, wouldn't happen to know where Jo—the sheriff is tonight, would you?"

The gleam in the man's eyes said he'd caught her slip. "He was head deep in paperwork when I left the station a few minutes ago."

"Oh. He's not off doing something with Carly tonight?"

"Not that I know of. Kevin's on vacation so we're both covering the hours."

She braved a smile and topped off his cup, her hand shaking. O-kay, now she had her answer. But was she wrong to be so suspicious? A bad mother to think the worst?

Two seconds later Rissa shoved her guilty thoughts aside and asked Charlotte to cover for her while she made a few phone calls. By the time she was ready to make the last one, she really felt ill.

"It's Rissa," she said the moment Jonas picked up.

"Hey, I was sitting here thinking about you. Listen, my deputy is supposed to be back to work tomorrow and I wondered if the girls might want to go to the movies again tomorrow night?" His voice lowered to a seductive pitch. "I'd like to talk about last weekend and…maybe we could have more time alone?"

Memories flooded her, but she shoved them aside. Once he heard the news, he wouldn't want her or Skylar around. "Jonas, did the girls ask you if Skylar could spend the night?"

He hesitated, and a squeak sounded as if he'd sat forward in his chair. "No, Carly said she was spending the night with Skylar and you were picking her up at the house after school. Why? They change their mind? It's fine with me, but I won't be off for a while. Where are the girls now?"

"I—I don't know."

"What?"

She quickly filled him in.

"Stay put. I'll be right there."

Five minutes later Rissa hopped inside Jonas's cruiser and they headed west, turning down School-house Road once they reached the outskirts of town.

"The middle school entrance is on that side of the building," she said, pointing. The structure was huge, the high school on one side, the middle school on the other, and shared a gymnasium and cafeteria between.

"There's a dance tonight. Some end-of-year

thing the eighth graders get invited to. Carly asked about it a while back, but I told her she couldn't go." He slid her a glance. "What about Skylar?"

"She didn't say anything about it."

Tension filled the car. "Then Skylar must've—"

She groaned, shaking her head. "Jonas, you can't always assume Skylar's responsible! What if she's not?"

"My daughter has snuck out once in her life and that was to see yours," he muttered darkly. "What are the odds she snuck out tonight because Skylar talked her into ignoring me and going to this thing?"

"Skylar never mentioned a dance. What if Carly talked *her* into going?"

They glared at each other before Jonas turned his attention back to the road, more accusations unspoken between them. He thought the worst of Skylar, assumed the worst, and probably always would.

Had she really thought it would be any different?

Inside the auditorium, speakers blared out a pounding rhythm that matched the sledgehammer now beating against the inside of her skull. She and Jonas wove their way through the multitude of teenagers, but saw no sign of either girl. Finally she spotted a too-young teacher sporting an employee badge and headed his way, Jonas behind her.

"Excuse me," she shouted over the din, "have you seen Carly Taggert or Skylar Mathews? We need to speak with them."

The teacher shook his head. "Haven't seen those two at all. Are you sure they're here? There's a party somewhere tonight. Heard some girls talking about it earlier."

"Where?"

The teacher shrugged.

Knowing they'd get no more help from him, they moved quickly through the dancing teens again to no avail.

"Mr. Taggert! Hi."

Rissa turned at the sound of an overly chipper voice to find Jonas already facing Mandy Blake. A group of girls surrounded her, the majority of whom Rissa assessed with a glance. Trouble with a capital T.

"Have you seen Caroline?" Jonas asked. "Or Skylar?"

Mandy shook her head, sliding Rissa a haughty glance. "Not here. They're probably at the party on the other side of town."

"What party? Where?"

"One of the football players is having it. He lives somewhere near the Wash'n Go." Mandy gave him a coy look. "I'm surprised she didn't tell you about it."

Jonas's gaze narrowed. "Why didn't you go?"

A couple of the girls snickered. Mandy lifted her chin, and after shooting her friends a killing glare, she focused on Jonas again. "Because I don't have an L on my forehead," she stated with a tight, saccharine-sweet smile. "That's why."

The girl obviously thought Jonas wouldn't understand what the phrase meant. Rissa laid a hand on Jonas's arm. She had to tug twice to get him moving, and glanced over her shoulder to see Mandy and her friends laughing. The girls were ecstatic that Carly and Skylar had obviously been caught in a lie, which didn't bode well for what they'd find when she and Jonas got to this party.

"She knows better than to sneak out. She knows better than to drink. When I get my hands on her—"

"Carly *might* have had the poor judgment to go to this party, but it doesn't mean she's done anything wrong otherwise."

Jonas shoved the door open, hurrying Rissa outside.

She glanced at Jonas as they climbed back into the cruiser, and noted his worry and upset. He looked angry and she knew it was because he thought Skylar held such an influence over Carly.

"Jonas, Carly is her own person, she makes her own deci—"

"Who's the one always breaking the rules and getting in trouble? Do you really think Skylar isn't to blame?"

Mouth set, she slumped in the seat beside him. Maybe the truth couldn't be denied and her daughter was a bomb ready to explode. What was she thinking? Pushing for Skylar to be friends with Carly? Beginning a relationship with Jonas? She should've known better, *did* know better.

She was kidding herself believing that somehow, by some miracle, things with Jonas would work out. Her daughter would always be a source of contention, always be the one behind that midnight phone call bringing disaster and, with it, blame.

"I never meant for this to happen, you know," Rissa whispered. "I thought the girls could help each other. Carly was coming out of her shell and gaining confidence, and Skylar was calming down. You have to admit the changes were good. For a while."

Jonas drove back down Schoolhouse Road, banging his palm on the steering wheel. "I saw the difference, Rissa. But it must've been too much, too soon. Skylar's still adjusting to being the new kid, trying to be cool. She probably thought since she's stayed out of trouble for a couple weeks and been on her best behavior, she could get them both out of the house and back home without either one of us finding out."

"Maybe you're right." A weak laugh left her. "What am I saying? Of course, you're right. Jonas...I'm sorry."

He glanced at her, reached across the seat and took her hand to squeeze. "Me, too, Rissa. I'm sorry, too."

They exchanged a long glance, and in that moment Rissa realized this was the end of them as well. She swallowed tightly, hoping he didn't notice the way her hand trembled. "It's been... good, Jonas. You've been a wonderful friend when I—I needed one."

Jonas didn't comment. He turned down a road, then another, and made his way back onto Main Street where he sped toward the other side of the small town. Minutes later, near the Wash'n Go, he slowed and they both leaned forward on the bench seat, searching for any signs of a party.

"At least you were a step ahead of me," he murmured finally. "You checked up on the girls when it didn't occur to me that Carly would lie and—"

"Listen— Do you hear that?"

He pulled to a stop, letting the car idle while they took in their surroundings. The motel was on their right up ahead, its grounds dimly lit, but somewhere nearby something pulsed.

"Music. We're close."

Jonas nodded and slowly drove down a darkened side street beside the motel.

"Is that— There in the parking lot behind the motel! It's them!"

He stopped in the shadows not far from where the girls stood, oblivious to the arrival of their parents because they screamed at each other with such intensity. A lanky teenaged boy leaned against a truck behind Skylar.

"Stay here and let me check this out."

"Yeah, right." Rissa opened her door and got out, hurrying toward the trio.

Jonas shook his head and sprinted around the front of the car after her, the girls' raised voices easily carrying. Jonas caught Rissa's arm and slowed her down.

Although furious at the girls and at himself and Rissa, he still had his head. And he wanted to know what had happened. Once they confronted the girls, both would shut down like they had that day at the library, and he was determined to get to the bottom of this one way or another.

"Hold it. Let's see if we can get a feel for what's going on before they clam up."

Rissa's response was cut short by Skylar. "Oh,

grow up, I told you about the stupid bet, but you wouldn't believe me! Now you're crying?"

"Travis said it wasn't true!"

"But it was, wasn't it? What'd he do? And why'd you leave the dance? I didn't think I'd find you in time!"

"This is all your fault! You *ruined* everything! My one chance and you ruined it!"

"I was trying to help you! God, why would you want your first time to be with a loser like him? Get real!"

Jonas sucked in a sharp breath, but the sound was drowned out by Rissa's gasp. He locked his legs when they threatened to cave and wondered where he'd gone wrong, anger and pain sliding through him so fast his head spun.

The teen behind Skylar shifted, suddenly aware of their presence. Their eyes met and Jonas recognized Ben Whitefeather's grandson. Marcus stiffened when he identified them, his eyes widening in alarm. He stepped forward, but Jonas waved the kid into silence, his glare daring the boy to speak. He wanted to hear it all, no matter how bad it was.

"Maybe it was true, but Travis was right about you, too! You're jealous of my new look and me eating lunch with them. You're mad because after my makeover I was popular and not sitting at the *loser* table with you!"

His daughter's shoulders shook with sobs and Jonas hardened his heart at the sight. Crying wasn't going to excuse what she'd done by sneaking out and lying and—

He couldn't think about the rest. Not now. If he did, he'd lose what little control he held over his anger.

"Are you *happy?* You got what you wanted," Carly sobbed. "Travis called me names and—and hooked up with Makayla instead. I hate you! Do you hear me, I *hate* you! This is all your fault!"

Skylar remained dry-eyed, but Jonas saw her flinch from the bite of his daughter's words. Skylar's hands were fisted, her black lips drawn tight while Carly railed at her.

In that moment, Jonas realized what she'd done, realized Skylar wasn't to blame. Realized he owed Rissa and her daughter apologies that would not come easily nor would it make anything better at this point. Especially his and Rissa's relationship, such as it was. He'd screwed that up by doing exactly what Rissa feared, jumping to conclusions and making accusations against her daughter.

Jonas closed the distance between them, Rissa at his side. "That's enough." Both girls whipped around to face them, both paled in shock.

"D-Dad?"

"What are you doing here?" Skylar asked cautiously.

"I think that's a question you two need to answer." Jonas focused on Caroline. She stood before him in one of her new outfits, but instead of the short-sleeved button-down shirt looking modest as it had when she'd modeled it for him, she'd left the material open over a tight-fitting tank that revealed the top of a lacy bra. He'd seen the same look on the covers of magazines and now cursed that it was considered stylish.

It took a long moment for the shock of seeing him to wear off, but when it did, his daughter began crying harder. His gaze shifted to Skylar, but in an instant her expression closed off and became an unreadable mask. She wouldn't look at him or her mom, but she did glance at Marcus before swearing like a pro and stuffing her hands into the pockets of her black trench coat.

"Skylar, don't," Marcus warned.

"I agree," Rissa added, "watch your mouth, Sky. The list of offenses is long enough already."

Jonas inhaled a steadying breath and found his voice. "Marcus, what are you doing here?"

The boy glanced at Skylar.

"Dad, p-please, I want to go home."

"Oh, we will," he said softly, "but first you'll

tell me why you're in a motel parking lot screaming at Skylar. What's going on?"

Rissa laid a hand on his arm. "Not like this.
She's been humiliated enough tonight from the
sound of it."

His first response was to say that she deserved
it for behaving as she had, but Rissa was right. He
couldn't talk to Caroline until he regained some
sanity. "Get in the car, Caroline. Not a word," he
warned when she opened her mouth. "Just do it."

His daughter swung around and ran away, but
not fast enough. Jonas blinked, unable to believe
his eyes when her loose shirt lifted in the breeze
and he saw the sparkling, sequined straps of a
thong visible above her low-riding jeans. Rissa's
comment that night at the library came back to
haunt him, that of not knowing his daughter as
well as he thought—or of being able to control her
or what she bought 24/7.

How the mighty had fallen.

"Come on, Sky. We'll walk back to the diner."

Skylar hesitated. "Marcus didn't do anything
wrong."

"Let Jonas decide that, please."

"Skylar, they're not going to stop until they figure
it all out. Now's the time. Just tell the truth already."

A sarcastic snort was Skylar's response.

"The truth about what?" Rissa demanded.

Jonas held up his hand. Some things had to come first. "Have you been drinking tonight?" he asked Marcus.

"No, sir."

"We heard the girls arguing," Jonas informed him. "Give us your version of what happened. Now."

Marcus shuffled his feet. "Skylar, uh, came looking for Carly at the dance."

"She wasn't there?"

The teen shook his head. "She'd already left to come to a party near here." He glanced at Skylar again and then stared hard at Jonas. "You should also know Carly's the reason Skylar's been getting into trouble at school."

"Marcus!"

"What?" Rissa gasped.

"Shut *up!*"

"Why, Marcus?" His voice shook. How much worse was it going to get?

"She's been defending Carly and…getting in fights because of it. That's why she's been in detention so much."

"Defending her from who?" Jonas pressed, his gaze darting between the two teenagers.

Skylar's whole body was strung tight. "I can't believe you—"

"The truth, Sky. Please. Marcus is right, now's the time."

"Mandy and her cheerleader friends," she muttered finally, her heavily darkened lashes hiding her eyes. "They called her names and stuff. It was no big deal."

"It was more than that," Marcus said, earning another huff from Skylar. "Because Mandy got Travis going and a few of the other jocks. Pretty soon most of the kids stayed away from her because they didn't want to be associated and risk getting slammed, too."

Jonas struggled to take it all in. Why hadn't she told him? "I see…. Exactly how long has this been going on?"

Marcus toed a rock with his boot. "Not long after Carly and some of the others started crossing over to the high school side for math and science classes."

"All *year?*" His mind might be struggling to comprehend, but his memories were beginning to confirm Marcus's words. It wasn't long after Carly had begun the advanced program that she'd become quieter, moodier, not talking on the phone, not talking period. But when she'd mentioned quitting the program, he'd urged her on, told her to stick with it. Guilt hounded him. If he hadn't stopped her from quitting, maybe—

"Until Skylar came along," Marcus clarified. "She got most of them to stop. All except Mandy."

Jonas's guilt grew by the second, whereas his upset with Caroline slowly numbed him.

"Anyway, Carly got invited to this party and even though Skylar, uh, heard some things and told her not to go, she went. We found her walking home."

"Why? What happened?" Rissa's voice sounded strained.

Marcus glanced at Skylar, a you-tell-them look on his face.

Skylar rolled her eyes. "She'd wised up and knew I hadn't lied about what I'd said about Travis."

"Which was?"

She glanced toward the car where Carly sat and Jonas quickly blocked her view. "All of it, Skylar. Marcus is right, this is your chance to come clean." The girl stared him down, but Jonas didn't blink. "I owe you an apology. I've had it wrong from the beginning, I realize that now. You've been a good friend to her and received nothing but trouble in return. I'm sorry I've misjudged you."

Skylar looked away, but not before Jonas saw the sparkle of tears in her eyes.

Marcus cleared his throat. "The guys have a bet going."

Feeling like a drowning man, Jonas forced himself to stay focused. "And you warned her about this bet, Skylar? Said she was invited because of it?"

Marcus answered for her, nodding. "Yeah.

Whoever bags the most cherr—Ah, the most virgin girls wins the coach's tickets to a playoff game."

Rage boiled. "Were you in on it?"

Skylar quickly stepped up to the boy's defense. "No, he—"

"No, sir, but I knew about it. Skylar asked me to go to the principal and say something, but I didn't. I told her to warn Carly and the girls if she wanted instead."

"Marcus would've gotten jumped if he had so don't come down on him. He helped me find Carly."

"Sky." Rissa's tone warned her to calm down.

"I'm not blaming him, Skylar. You two used the sense God gave you to look after your own safety. I only wish that were true of my daughter." Jonas stepped closer to Skylar, the cool-headed cop in him struggling with the angry dad wanting to find the party and bash heads. "Don't lie to me, Skylar, not at this point, all right? Set aside whatever mistrust and feelings you have for me and tell me the truth. Did Carly go to the party planning on having sex?"

"You need to ask her that, not me."

"I agree," Rissa insisted firmly from behind him. "Do not put Skylar in the position of telling you something that personal, Jonas. It's not right."

He wiped a hand over his face and dropped the subject for another. "Where's this party?"

After Marcus gave him the street, Jonas called for backup, giving his men very specific instructions. It was time the boys at that party realized what being a man meant. "Are there any guys there who *aren't* in on the bet?"

Marcus shook his head. "The team's divided over it. Only the guys involved and a couple girls off each of their lists were invited. There's another party next Friday with more of the girls, and after graduation next Sunday, there's a big blow-out at Trav's where the winner will be announced."

The winner. Only teenaged boys would consider what they were doing a win-or-lose situation. The night weighed on him, and there were hours left to go.

"What happens now?" Skylar lifted her chin, her expression set. "You gotta remember Carly left on her own. She changed her mind, and that counts for something. Right?"

Jonas stared into Skylar's glittering black eyes, amazed how mere moments could change entire perspectives. "She's very lucky to have you defending her, you know that? You should be proud of yourself, Skylar. She…she should be thankful she has a friend like you." Shifting his attention to Marcus, Jonas added, "Get out of here before my men show up. Go back to the dance and don't say a word about this to anyone."

Rissa walked over to Skylar and wrapped her arms around her daughter. "Let me hug you, just for a minute please," he heard her murmur thickly. "I'm proud of you, Sky. I'm *angry*, but proud. And I apologize, too. When I think of what all I've said to you…"

Skylar didn't say anything, and Jonas wondered what it would take to get the girl to open up. Whatever it was, he hoped it happened soon, for Rissa's sake.

"Poor Carly," Rissa murmured, releasing her daughter. "To have such a huge crush on a boy like that and— Jonas, are you okay?"

He tried to smile, to nod, glad to see the two of them on better terms, upset with himself and all the mistakes he'd made concerning Caroline. Mistakes he'd made with Rissa. Had he blown his chances with her entirely by jumping to conclusions? Why hadn't Caroline told him the truth?

He couldn't think of that now. Not now. He wasn't okay. And he didn't know if anything would ever be okay again.

IT HAD TAKEN Jonas three hours to wade through the mess created by busting up the party. Angry parents, hysterical girls—nearly all of whom weren't where they were supposed to be. And yet for such idiots, the boys involved in the bet had played it smart, probably due to the originator of the plan being the son of an attorney.

No alcohol or drugs were found on the premises, which meant no major charges could be filed. And everybody knew in this day and age statutory rape cases were nearly impossible to prove in court.

Jonas wasn't happy with the results of the night, not at all, and could only imagine how the other parents felt at getting that phone call to come pick up their daughters. Considering Carly had come so close to disaster herself, he felt ready to implode.

Drawing away from his thoughts, Jonas focused on the here and now, not surprised to find the clock read 1:00 a.m. He'd ordered one of his deputies to take Rissa and the girls back to the diner. Once there, Rissa had driven the girls to his house and stayed, telling him before she'd walked out the door that Caroline had ensconced herself in her bedroom and refused to talk to her.

"Why?" he demanded abruptly. His daughter's gray eyes blinked up at him, almost owlish, her body a quivering mass. "I never expected something like this from you."

"Why? Because you think I'm a kid? That I'm not pretty like mom? I'm *tired* of being treated like that! I'm the only girl in school who can't date, who can't have a boyfriend—can't do *anything!*"

"The *only* one? I think you know after tonight that isn't true." Jonas paced across the floor.

"It was just a party!"

"You lied to me. You snuck out—*again!* You not only went to a dance you were not allowed to attend, you got into a car with a boy I don't know and went to a party! One that had very serious consequences!"

Her head lowered, but the set of her jaw said she wasn't nearly ready to back down. Not yet.

"What about STDs? Pregnancy? What *did* you do with Travis before you left?"

"Nothing!" Her face flushed hotly. "Just stuff!"

"What stuff? Groping? Oral sex?"

"Dad!"

"Answer me!"

"We k-kissed and stuff."

"If you did more, I need to know, Caroline. You need to be checked out by a doctor. What if he's carrying something? You're a smart girl, you know how STDs are transmitted."

"We just kissed and—and touched a little. Then some of the other girls showed up and—and that's when I knew—" her voice caught "—Skylar was right. I s-saw the guys giving each other high fives, and heard them say s-something about tickets and—"

"And?"

"Joking about who would score first," she whispered, her head low. "One of them laughed and said Travis because I'd—I'd give it up first." She wiped her nose with her hand. "The other girls were girls like me. Nobodies and geeks. I felt sick so I went outside, and when I went back in to get my jacket *because I was leaving,* I saw—I saw Travis kissing another girl the way he'd kissed me. I yelled at him and he called me names, and…he laughed at me. Because I said I thought he liked me."

Jonas fought the pity he felt for her. Now wasn't the time for that. "Why leave then? Wasn't sex what you wanted? Because Skylar warned you and you went anyway?"

"I changed my mind," she wailed. "I was coming *home!* And I—I thought it was no big deal because Mandy and all the girls have already done it, but I couldn't so I…I left!"

Jonas glared at her, shaking at how close she'd come to disaster. "I don't get it," he murmured, his voice hoarse from the strain of holding his emotions in check. Mandy was younger than Caroline by a few months. Still thirteen and sexually active? "If that's true, *why* were you upset because Skylar and Marcus found you? Why were you yelling at *her* for looking out for you and trying to help?"

He paced across the floor and back again. Too confined, too angry. Sick to his gut and furious because this was his fault. He was a failure as a parent. Marilyn had been trying to tell him for a while, but he'd ignored her, pretended she was wrong. Now he knew how right she'd been— because she'd already seen it once in Lea.

"I was mad."

"Mad? Because she warned you about something that brought you to your senses before Travis took you in a back bedroom to win a bet? *Why* would you want some punk pawing you? Beyond being too young, do you want your first time to be with a jerk who couldn't appreciate you if he tried? He kissed the next available girl and didn't even care you were gone!"

"I *know!*" Tears streamed down her face. "I get it, okay? Nobody wants me! He didn't want me, and neither does Mom and half the time, neither do you!"

CHAPTER THIRTEEN

JONAS SWUNG AROUND in shock, unable to believe she'd say such a thing. "I don't *want* you? Caroline, do you have a clue how hard your grandmother pushed for me to sign over my rights to you when your mother left? Do you ever *think* about the fact that you're here because *I love you?*"

Her face lost its color and she gulped back a choked sob. "You told me to make friends!"

"Friends, *nothing else,*" he stated emphatically. "No boy worth dating would treat you the way you let yourself be treated tonight. Where's your self-respect? Your dignity?"

She ducked her head again. The silence between them grew. Jonas battled the tension in his body, the way his muscles spasmed and pulled until they hurt. He wanted to shout the house down, but knew it would solve nothing. He had to get through to her but how?

"Why would you even think about having sex with a boy you don't really know?" he asked, amazing himself when the question came out in a reasonably controlled tone. "Why belittle yourself that way?"

Her lips trembled. "Because it's so…*hard,*" she whispered thickly. "Dad, you don't remember what school is like! I'm not popular, not athletic, not musical, not *any*thing." Her laugh was full of tears. "I'm just a geek who doesn't fit in anywhere."

"You're not a geek."

"I *am* a geek! But then Travis and his friends acted nice after I had the makeover. They all said how pretty I was and—and then Travis invited me to the party. All I wanted was one night, *one night,* where I mattered."

"You matter to me."

"Where I was popular and…and fit in." She lowered her head even more. "I was invited to a party by the best-looking guy in school, Dad. I just wanted to go and have fun because *he* asked me. *Me!* Because he said he *liked* me." A fat teardrop fell onto her hands where they lay clasped in her lap. "And it was a lie—like always."

Jonas sighed, the bashful high school kid in him who remembered those same feelings and what he'd done to counter them warring with the father he needed to be. "Caroline, there are decent guys out there. Guys who'll see how pretty you are, and *appreciate* the fact you haven't slept with Travis or anyone else."

"Yeah, right."

"It's true. Being easy to bed might make you popular, but is that all you want to be known for? To be remembered that way when someone says your name in twenty years?"

"I guess I just thought it was better than being forgettable," she whispered, "like I am now."

"Sweetheart—"

"How old were you?" she asked abruptly, raising her gaze to meet his. "How do you know when it's right? What if I never get married? If I go to college, and have a career—*when* will I meet somebody? When will there be time?"

"It'll happen when the time is right," he told her, a mental image of Rissa suddenly filling his head.

His daughter raised an eyebrow and Jonas knew if he was going to have any credibility or say in matters such as this in the future, he had to be brutally honest right now. No more little girl sugarcoating—or depending on Marilyn to handle talks pertaining to body changes or sex. These had to come from her parent—him.

He rubbed his pounding forehead and sat next to her on the couch. "I was seventeen," he informed her with a mutter, "and really stupid, similar to Travis."

She smiled weakly at his comment, then frowned, glancing at him quickly from beneath her lashes. "You and mom weren't married when you were seventeen."

Feeling the hole getting deeper, he sighed. "No, we weren't. My first time wasn't with your mother. And like I said, it wasn't a wise move on my part, and I regretted it later when the girl turned out not to be the kind of person I thought she was. Until then I didn't realize I'd gotten things out of order, or understand that we didn't know each other well enough to kiss, much less..." He struggled for the words.

"Make love?"

He grimaced. "No, honey. What we did wasn't making love. It was sex, pure and simple, and that's the difference in sharing the experience with the right guy versus the wrong one. Travis would've used you for sex and it wouldn't have been memorable or special."

"I want it to be," she murmured, her voice low, her cheeks blood-red.

"Good. But that means being strong and mature and waiting until you're older—preferably *married*," he added in his strictest Dad tone. "Or at least until you find the right person, someone who'll treat you the way you deserve to be treated. Respect and caring lead to love and that takes time, Caro. Getting to know one another is hard enough without tossing sex in and confusing the issues. When you do that, you can't tell whether what you feel is love or lust, and inevitably someone gets hurt."

Carly shifted sideways on the couch and buried her face in his chest, her arms holding him in a tight grip. "Daddy, I'm sorry. I really, really am."

"Good."

A raw laugh warmed his chest. "I *knew* you'd say that." She sniffled. "Do you think Grandma will find out?"

He rubbed his hand over her back, her question bringing up more of his own. "I won't tell her, but the way gossip works, she could still hear it. There are an awful lot of angry people in town and you need to be prepared if she does. But right now you've got more worries to deal with—like how I'm not the only one you need to apologize to. Skylar was a good friend to you and you said some nasty things to her tonight. She was *beaten up* because she watched out for you and in return, you treated her badly. All because of the poor decisions you made."

Beneath his hand her shoulders seemed to deflate even more. "I didn't like her being right about Travis or the—the bet. She's *always* right when it comes to stuff like that and she seemed…happy about it."

"For what it's worth, that wasn't the impression I got. Skylar defended you even after everything you said to her."

She raised her head. "Really?"

He nodded. "She told me your leaving the party on your own had to count for something."

"She should hate me."

"Good friends forgive each other when they do stupid things," he told her. "Give her time and I'm sure she'll forgive you, too. But now it's late and you both need to calm down and think about things. Go to bed."

His daughter hugged him again before releasing him and moving toward the door. There she paused. "They're all going to blame me for getting them into trouble."

"Why? Mandy told us about the party. We also had an official complaint about the noise from one of the neighbors. My men went in to check things out using that as their reason for being there. I imagine some of them will try to blame you, but if you stick to the story, it'll blow over eventually."

"Are you going to send me to live with Grandma now? Because I—I messed up again?"

Jonas hesitated a long moment, his thoughts, his emotions, torn. "I probably should. After tonight, I realize your grandma was right about a lot of things I've been ignoring. I've let you get by with too much and not watched you as closely as I should have because I trusted you. Tonight you broke that trust."

"Dad, please—"

"Hear me out, Caro. I said your grandma was right about some things, but not all. For a while tonight I really considered sending you to live with her. But then I realized I can't let you go until I absolutely have to. You are my daughter, my responsibility, and I love you. No amount of anger is going to change that—although I wouldn't try me on something like this again if I were you. It's going to take a long time for me to trust you again."

Her lower lip trembled and she blinked, waiting for his final answer.

"You're not going anywhere, Caro. But for the next two months of your summer vacation, you've got my portion of chores to do on top of yours."

THE NEXT DAY Rissa stared at Skylar in surprise. *"Really?"*

"Yeah," Skylar said with a casual shrug. "Why not? It was cool. And Grace is cool, too. She showed me how to give a massage and we talked about college and training and stuff."

Rissa couldn't believe one afternoon spent with Grace giving the California executive's son physical therapy suddenly had Skylar interested in college again.

After the disaster last night, Skylar had relaxed a bit. Her daughter was a long way from normal, but it gave her hope. Small steps, the shrinks had said.

"Brandon came in, too. You know, to check on things. He said him and Zack are really close."

"Who?"

Skylar rolled her eyes. "Weren't you listening? Mr. Paxton's sons. Zack's the youngest, the one I helped Grace with, and Brandon's the oldest. He thinks he's so hot because he's got money and he's going to inherit his dad's business one day."

"Ah," she murmured, knowing exactly which teenaged boy Skylar referred to. The nineteen-year-old had his own cabin and she'd spent twenty minutes this morning busying herself by straightening one of the supply carts to avoid listening to his specifications on how he wanted his cabin cleaned. She had to find a regular flying job—*soon*.

Rissa jumped back to dodge a carefree kid running between the bunkhouse and the cabins, and smiled when he didn't even notice.

Mr. Paxton and his family had arrived that morning with their company employees and their families, and the ranch now overflowed with people. Kids of all ages played on the cabin porches, were being led around on horseback by

Seth's ranch hands and, in the case of the youngest Paxton, in physical therapy with Grace after the flight and drive to the ranch.

And through it all Jonas had been in the back of her mind. How was he holding up after last night? What had happened when he confronted Carly? "Sky…have you talked to Carly today?"

"No."

Skylar tried to act like it didn't matter, but she knew it did. "She'll come around soon. I know she will. You tried to warn her and did the right thing— except for the part about not telling an adult."

"*Mom.*"

"All I'm saying is don't doubt that, okay?" She tilted her head to the side, her thoughts flying, wondering the best approach to voice what she wanted to say.

"I'm gonna go—"

"Sky, wait." When Skylar hesitated, she continued hurriedly, knowing her daughter would probably only give her so much time before she took off, upset over something. "I was thinking this morning about…well, how you took care of Carly. Last night, at the diner and at school, and how you defended Marcus."

"So?"

Rissa wet her lips. "So…it made me wonder if you think you have to protect *me*." She searched

Skylar's face, realizing she might actually be on to something because her daughter adopted a careful expression, one she'd seen for a year now. "You're too smart for your own good, you know that? I mean, you saw and heard too many fights between your dad and me and—"

"Mom, I need to—"

"You told me about your dad's affair and things got rougher as a result, but, honestly, honey, they were bad before you ever said a word. You know that, and the sad truth is that your dad and I are at fault here for not protecting *you* from our problems."

"It's okay."

"No, it's not," Rissa countered firmly. "Last night I saw the same look on your face when you realized Carly had been caught. The look you wore when you realized the enormity of your dad's affair on our life. But it wasn't your fault. Not last night, and certainly not the past. If there's something you need to tell me, something else you've kept locked inside because you—you feel like I can't handle it, Sky, *please*, you can talk to me about it. You don't need to protect me, or—or hide behind the makeup and clothes. Trust me. I won't let you down again, not if I can help it."

Skylar's expression remained guarded, hesitant. Vulnerable? Rissa wondered at Skylar's thoughts, and then gasped in pleased surprise when her daughter charged forward and flung her arms around her in a quick hug. One that ended much too soon.

Rissa staggered a bit, both from the impact and the surprise she felt before Skylar released her and took off at a jog. She stood there in complete shock, aching because she'd been right. Now she wanted to go after Skylar, but knew she couldn't press too soon or she'd undo the progress they'd just made. Baby steps.

She had to count herself lucky. That hug was the first voluntary physical contact Skylar had initiated with her since Larry's death and it meant something. It meant a lot.

"Daydreaming?"

Rissa started and realized while Skylar had jogged over to stand by the paddock, she'd remained in the middle of the driveway. She turned to face Jonas, happy and sad in immeasurable ways. "I— It's been a strange day."

"One of several," he readily agreed. "You got a minute?"

She nodded, suddenly nervous. Wanting to share her good news about Skylar, but wondering if Jonas needed to hear it under the circumstances. What had his night been like? And after everything that happened, where did they stand? She wouldn't condone his coming down on Skylar the way he had yesterday, wouldn't allow him to blame her again. But would he apologize? Say nothing?

By mutual consent they slowly walked around the dining hall and its newly planted landscaping.

"I'm sorry. Rissa, I know it's not enough to say the words, but— You were right, I jumped to conclusions based on Skylar's looks and it was wrong and unfair. I hope you'll forgive me and trust that— I'll do my best to not let it ever happen again. Last night opened my eyes to my daughter and yours, not to mention my own long list of faults. I judged Skylar when I shouldn't have, judged you when I shouldn't have, and I hope you'll forgive me."

Last night had awakened them both to the truth. Whatever the future held, it would be better. She and Skylar were both healing, Jonas and Carly would, too. And Jonas's apology was so heartfelt and revealing, she couldn't deny him.

Jonas hesitated, but when she smiled, he lowered his mouth to hers. His tongue sought entrance and pressed deep, and for the longest time, they shared everything. Breath, warmth. The beat of their hearts, and their many problems. Friends and…more. But what?

"I needed that," he murmured against her lips. "The whole town's gone crazy over that damn party, my daughter won't raise her chin off her chest, and all day all I could think about was kissing you."

She lifted her hands to his face, the rough stubble on his cheeks. "Tough night?"

"Hell."

"Is she okay?"

"She's embarrassed and says she'll never live it down, but yeah, I think so. She's worried about school Monday."

"Skylar, too, but of course she hasn't said anything. This *is* the last week. Maybe we should let them skip it?"

"That would only make it worse," he argued, kissing her hand and nibbling. "Their absence will make them look guilty," he murmured, explaining about the noise complaint. "It'll get blamed on Carly and Skylar if they don't make an appearance. Besides, it's only three days and then it'll be summer vacation."

Three days… A lot could happen in that amount of time. Look what had happened in the last three.

CARLY CARRIED her lunch tray and hesitated before sitting down at the loser table. Where else could she sit? Nobody had talked to her all morning. Just like before.

She looked up and saw that even though she'd sat at the end away from the others, all of them had gotten up and moved, not wanting to be seen sitting with her. Everybody blamed her for her dad breaking up the party and calling everyone's parents even though she'd told them the story about the noise complaint. Why was it her fault the boys had been jerks to do that in the first place?

A tray dropped onto the table across from her. Her heart in her throat, Carly prayed she wasn't about to get the crap beaten out of her. Then she saw the rings.

Skylar's black lips were pulled down in a frown, and she glared at her a minute before she lifted her boot over the bench and sat down. Carly knew she should say something, apologize, but she couldn't make the words come. They sat there in silence, neither of them hungry enough to even look at their trays.

Then the bell rang.

Skylar surged to her feet. "Don't give them the satisfaction of making you cry. Word's getting around about the music thing. Keep your power and it'll be over soon."

"Skylar—"

She ignored her and kept going.

THE DAYS PASSED in a blur of work for Rissa. Cleaning all the occupied cabins and performing maid service took every ounce of her energy and by the time she drove to town on Tuesday to work her shift at the diner, she didn't know if she could keep her eyes open.

Grace's warning about burning the candle at both ends came to her, and she knew what she had to do, hard though it was. Rissa turned in her notice to Porter and thanked the older man for giving her a job when she needed it, but her guilt lifted when Porter told her he had a granddaughter needing a summer job and she could start immediately. A phone call later, Rissa worked her last night while training her replacement, then went home, saddened by Jonas's absence from the diner.

She told herself he was probably where he needed to be—at home with Carly—but it didn't help. She missed him, and in her mind loomed the fact their time together was limited. Already it was the end of May, the end of school. And she hoped to relocate by the end of July so Skylar could start school in August and not transfer midyear. Their time in North Star was running out.

And she was more confused than ever.

THE LAST DAY of school and early dismissal. *Finally.* Carly clutched her backpack to her chest and walked down the hall to where Skylar stood stuffing her junk into her book bag, her stomach hurting. Every day she'd sat by herself at a table until Skylar sat down with her. But other than the warning to stay strong, they hadn't talked. And even though a few of the girls invited to the party had come around and smiled at her, the entire experience made her appreciate Skylar's friendship even more.

"I'm sorry," she blurted out before Skylar could walk away again. "I know I should've listened to you, and that you—you only tried to help. And—and I'm sorry for calling you names and for waiting so long to apologize." Skylar stared at her as if she'd grown two heads and Carly shifted uncomfortably. Wasn't she going to say anything?

"Yeah, well…don't let it happen again. Choose a nice guy next time instead of a jerk, or you might not get a second chance."

She wet her lips. "Okay…so, are we friends again?"

"Maybe." Skylar slammed the door shut.

"Would you, um, like to go to the ballet with me? My grandma said I can bring a friend and—you said you liked going in New York."

"Is that why you apologized? 'Cause you don't want to get stuck alone with your grandma?"

"*No!*"

"Are you sure?"

"Positive. Do you want to go or not?"

"I guess." Skylar smirked. "But only because I can't wait to see your granny's face when she gets a look at who you invited. She's going to have a coronary."

Carly giggled and together, they headed down the hall.

RISSA KNEW EXACTLY who was the most excited about the girls going to the ballet—she and Jonas. After a long week of fetching and carrying and cleaning, and the ongoing angry calls from parents worried more parties like the one last week would be taking place, the news that Carly had invited Skylar to the ballet was…extraordinary. Even more so since Skylar had actually accepted knowing it was a black-tie event.

Jonas booked two connecting hotel rooms in Helena and presently both girls occupied the bathrooms, getting ready for their big night out. But it was nothing compared to the tension and awareness spiking between her and Jonas at the thought of an evening alone together. In a hotel room, no less.

They'd nearly made love, and she'd like to share that intimacy with him. But what then? Larry's infidelity had destroyed their troubled marriage, but Jonas had the potential to break her heart if she let him.

"Looks like heavy thoughts for what could be a wonderful evening," Jonas murmured in her ear, slipping up behind her where she stood staring blankly out the window. "Rissa, there's no pressure. Yes, I want to make love to you," he whispered huskily, "but I understand if you don't want things to get even more complicated."

What could she say? Jonas had agreed to view their relationship as short-term at *her* request. She couldn't change the rules now and beg him to want her to stay. She had too much pride for that, and she knew all too well that love had to go both ways.

Meaning she loved him?

A knock saved her from answering her panicked musings, and Jonas quickly moved through the connecting doorway to his and Carly's hotel room. She heard him greet Marilyn, and noted Jonas's voice lacked a certain warmth when he spoke to her.

But that was yet another problem. Should she and Jonas get together, Marilyn would never accept her or Skylar. What then? Ongoing verbal battles? That wouldn't be good for anyone.

Carly joined Jonas and Marilyn, her soft voice greeting her grandmother, and Rissa bit back a laugh when she heard Marilyn's sharp intake of breath all the way to where she stood. Having received Marilyn's choice of the cotton-candy pink dress replete with numerous and rather large bows from a department store in Helena, Jonas had stopped at the store and endured three females shopping to exchange the dress for one Carly liked—a trendy dark electric blue with a modest halter top and flaring knee-length skirt.

"Caroline, you—you look beautiful, dear, but what happened to the dress I sent you?"

"I exchanged it. I *love* this color, Grandma. Isn't it awesome? The saleslady said it matched my skin tone and hair much better. Thank you for getting the other one. If you hadn't, I wouldn't have gone and found this one."

"Oh…well, I—I suppose it does look nice on you. Are you ready?"

Rissa moved to stand in the doorway, and the moment Marilyn noticed her presence, Rissa's stomach dropped. The woman looked shocked. Carly obviously hadn't told her grandmother who would be accompanying them tonight.

Just when she thought about begging off for Skylar's sake, Jonas waved her forward and placed his hand on her waist in a possessive gesture. "Marilyn, you remember Rissa?" he said, his gaze daring the other woman to behave like she had at the house.

"Yes, of—of course. Hello. Caroline, dear, we really must be off."

Carly shot Rissa a worried glance. "Grandma, I brought a friend like you said I could. She'll be ready in a second."

Marilyn's expression revealed her upset. "I know what I said, Caroline, but I did not imagine you would invite—"

"Skylar used to live in New York, and she knows a lot about theater and ballet. If you talk to her, you'll see. You might even like her. And she's my friend," the girl continued determinedly, "so if you want me to go, she goes, too. It's my birthday gift, right?"

Marilyn glared at Rissa, her hands knotted in front of her thick waist. "Caroline," she murmured, her voice shaking a bit, "I understand Skylar is your friend, but…I'm also sure Skylar and her mother understand that Skylar's appearance—"

"What about it?" Skylar asked from the open doorway between the rooms.

Rissa turned, her breath catching in her throat.

CHAPTER FOURTEEN

JONAS'S HAND flattened against Rissa's waist and squeezed. His touch offered her support and strength, shared in her pleasure that Skylar had taken yet another step forward.

Still Gothlike in a long black skirt and sleeveless top, her daughter's makeup wasn't as dramatic or heavily painted. Her eyes were lined and she still wore her dark contacts, but she'd exchanged her black lipstick and blush for dark rose. The look was different, infinitely better and another example of the progress Skylar had made since moving to Montana.

Rissa blinked back tears and stepped forward to hug her, glad that this time the embrace lasted longer than the previous one. "You look *beautiful*. Doesn't she look beautiful?" She turned, her arm around Skylar's shoulders.

"Absolutely," Jonas murmured, his gaze gentle and proud. Skylar said nothing in response, but she didn't glare at him, either. "You look fantastic,

Skylar. Both you girls do. Here, stand together and let me get a picture."

Marilyn remained quiet and disapproving while Jonas teased the girls into smiling naturally. Rissa's attention was torn between the girls and the woman, wary of sending Skylar out with Marilyn under the circumstances. Especially after Skylar had made such a concession on Carly's behalf. The daughter she'd raised was trying to make the night go more smoothly for her friend. But what about her?

"Is it time to leave, Grandma?"

Carly's question pulled Marilyn out of her dazed state and she nodded. "Oh. Yes, dear. Yes, it is. We'd—we'd better go or we'll be late."

"Have fun but be careful," Jonas warned. "And stay with Marilyn at all times."

Carly made a face. "Daaad, we know."

Rissa hurried forward and pulled a fifty from her pocket, slipping it into Skylar's palm.

"Mom, you don't—"

"Take it just in case. And have fun." She hesitated, then pretended to quickly hug Skylar again. "Do *not* let that woman treat you badly. Stand up for yourself and if she leaves you behind, fine. Call me and I'll come get you."

When she reluctantly let go and stepped away, Skylar frowned, her head down. "Thanks... Mom?"

"What?"

"Don't do anything that'll make you sad later… when we leave."

Rissa barely suppressed a gasp of unease. Skylar had considered the fact she and Jonas would be there in the rooms alone. A glance at Carly made her groan. They *both* had. But while Carly obviously didn't mind the thought of her and Jonas getting together, Skylar hated it. And it was obvious.

"Skylar, come on!"

The girls walked out the door carrying their shoulder wraps and sparkling bags. Skylar slid her one last look before Marilyn blocked her view. Marilyn remained quiet, frowning, but she'd managed to keep her thoughts to herself after Carly's passionate declaration of friendship.

Jonas shut the door behind them and waited a long moment before he slipped the lock into place. "Wow."

She raised her hands to her face and fought back tears. "Do you think she'll be all right? Marilyn was not pleased to see who Carly had decided to bring. And after all Skylar had done to try and fit in better. Maybe we should—"

"They'll be fine." He closed the distance between them. "And I know the perfect way to distract you."

She shook her head, her thoughts on her daughter. "I'm really worried about them. I mean, what if—"

A rough chuckle sounded before Jonas swung her up in his arms. "Hush," he ordered. "They'll be fine. You, on the other hand, are at my mercy," he threatened, his mouth hovering above hers.

With that one look from Jonas, Rissa's protests died on her lips. She stared up at him, watched while scorching need flared to red hot desire in his eyes. The reflection of hers?

"Well?"

She palmed his face and brought his mouth low. Jonas brushed his lips against hers, his tongue seeking entrance. She curled her arms around his neck and deepened the kiss while he lowered her to her feet long enough to dip her backward and yank the coverlet off the bed. Vertical again, Jonas raised his head, smiled into her eyes and then gently pushed her backward. She fell with a surprised gasp that turned into a laugh when he pulled his shirt over his head and followed her down, snagging one of her jean-clad knees with his hand to settle himself comfortably between her legs.

The hard length of him pressed against her and she shifted her hips slightly to better feel him, a low moan rising in her throat. He kissed her again, breaking contact to skim her throat and tease her.

Rissa curled into him even more, wanting, craving, the culmination of what had built between them these last few months.

Jonas propped himself on an arm and set to work unbuttoning her blouse. With every button he released, he pressed a kiss to the skin exposed, the slow bend-and-kiss moving his lower body in breath-stealing nudges that ground him against her, a poor simulation of what they both wanted.

But no matter how much she enjoyed Jonas's touch, no matter how much she wanted their clothes removed and him to make love to her, her daughter's words kept intruding. She'd be sad later. If she slept with Jonas and left, she'd be sad. No question about it.

"Rissa?"

She gripped Jonas tighter, slid her hands from his shoulders to his face and gently drew him away from his pursuit and back to her mouth. She was an adult who knew what she wanted, needed. A full-grown woman who deserved the tender loving of a good man after the painful marriage she'd endured for too many years.

She fastened her mouth to his and a rough chuckle rumbled out of his chest. After quickly freeing the last button, Jonas followed her urging, slanting his mouth purposely over hers. His hand slid up her exposed stomach to cup her breast and

Rissa gasped at the sensation, raised her knees and tried to get closer. It wasn't enough.

Jonas pulled the cups of her bra aside and covered her with his hand, touching her delicately at first. She arched her back off the bed and relished his strength surrounding her, anchoring her, supporting her, and yet—

Jonas ended the kiss to view what he'd uncovered, smiling when her body instantly reacted. His eyes were slumberous, his lashes low, and he'd never looked sexier or more handsome than he did in that moment. She wanted him, wanted more. But when she closed her eyes she saw her daughter's face. Knew Jonas would never be able to handle Skylar's many moods.

Jonas played with her, his thumb wreaking havoc with her ability to breathe because it brushed back and forth across the tip of her breast.

"What's wrong, sweetheart?"

His voice caused a shiver to run through her. Husky and deep, the low timbre rasped over her senses the way his thumb stroked over her skin. She tried to push the worries away, to respond to his touch, but couldn't.

"Nothing." The word was weak and layered with frustrated tears. A lie and a poor one at that.

His expression tightened. "Are you thinking of your husband?"

"No. Jonas, *no*, it's—it's not that. Not him. Please don't ever…don't ever think that. We weren't…good together," she whispered. "Not like this, not like…us."

He held her gaze for a long moment before breaking eye contact and staring longingly at her breasts. With one last, lingering kiss to the pointed tip, he smoothed her bra back into place.

"Jonas—"

"Shhh. Come here."

He pulled her close, and she clung to him, the moment gone.

JONAS ROLLED OVER and took Rissa with him, cradling her against his chest. He ran his fingers down her back and smiled ruefully when she squirmed. Thank God. For a minute he'd been afraid he was the only one ultrasensitive after what they'd just shared, or nearly shared. What had started off as hot and heavy passion had cooled with Rissa's obvious indecision. Now he had to get himself under control so that his arousal didn't cause him quite so much discomfort and then find out what happened.

Minutes passed and slowly his body cooled. They lay there snuggled close, the night ahead of them, and a lot unsaid.

"What were you thinking about?"

She shifted against him and rested her hands on his chest, raising up to prop her chin on top. She slid him a sheepish, questioning look that was vulnerable and sad. "I'm thinking of how grateful I am that you're a good man. I—I'm sorry, Jonas. Not that I changed my mind, but that…things got a bit out of control before I did. You've stopped, not once but twice now, and you haven't once treated me like a tease."

"You're not a tease, Rissa, I know that. We both have things we need to figure out."

Her lashes lowered over her eyes and once again Jonas saw the sparkle of tears. He rubbed her back, soothing the tense muscles, and waited for her to continue. Whatever it was, she needed to talk about it. He'd like to think her indecision was based on her need of him, in wanting more, maybe some confusion as to whether or not she wanted to leave Montana and him behind. Was that too much to hope for? God knew he felt more for Rissa than he'd ever felt for Caroline's mother. They'd been too…opposite, Lea too into herself to be much of a wife or mother.

"You don't realize it, but you gave me something special just now."

He raised an eyebrow, knowing his teasing expression would indicate his thoughts.

She lifted her head long enough to whack him

gently with her hand. "Okay, so maybe not *that*," she said, resuming her position with a soft laugh and a quick kiss to his bare chest. "I meant something else."

Jonas shifted in the bed, rolling so that she landed on her back, her unbuttoned blouse falling open to the mattress beneath them. He propped his head up on his fist and leaned over her, careful to maintain skin-to-skin contact. "What?"

He liked how her shoulders were dotted with freckles. They spread down her arms, across her chest. He fingered the edge of her bra, and noted with satisfaction that her breathing immediately quickened. Maybe one last kiss? Something to hold onto and dream of when she—

Rissa pasted a weak smile on her lips and swallowed with a little shake of her head, apparently still trying to gather her thoughts. The sight ended his debate, and the movement of her throat drew his touch. From there he ran his fingertips back down her neck, over her collarbone, across her chest to her breast, squeezing gently. Touching her was torture considering it wasn't going to go any further tonight, but he couldn't help himself. And if he were honest, he liked the closeness, being with her. Sex or no sex.

This was the kind of connection he'd told Caroline she needed to find before making love. He saw it, felt it, he even thought Rissa felt it. But for whatever reason she was suppressing her feelings for him, shutting down. Was she afraid? He was.

Her eyes revealed her doubts, the words that needed to be said but neither could say, and he bent and dropped a kiss on her mouth. "It's okay."

"It's not," she said thickly, shaking her head. "I *want* you, but Skylar…"

Just as he feared. But what could be done about it? Rissa wasn't going to put her own happiness over her daughter's, not after what Skylar had been through. And he couldn't expect her to. He'd be a hypocrite if he did.

"I understand. We'd be good together, Rissa, but until you figure out what you want in here," he said, gently smoothing his fingertip over her heart, "and come to terms with Skylar's dislike of me in relation to what you want for yourself when you think of us and our future, you can't take the next step."

But he'd been ready to do just that. Make love to her because he—

Her eyes widened, and Jonas realized he'd said way more than he'd meant to. Declarations from him were the last thing she needed to hear, not when she was trying to sort through her feelings. And then there were the girls. Carly loved Rissa already and she and Skylar had made up after their fight. But Skylar…who knew what the girl would do if faced with staying in North Star? He certainly hadn't gained any ground where she was concerned.

Rissa looped her hands around his neck and pulled him close for a kiss. Jonas entered the sweet interior of her mouth, slow and easy, wanting to show her how special he thought she was and how much he cared, praying she'd decide to stay and then—

What? Sneak around so Skylar wouldn't get upset?

"Thank you," she murmured against his mouth before breaking contact and snuggling her face into the hollow of his neck. Her breath hit his skin.

"For what?"

"For being you. Jonas, no matter what happens, please know I—I'll always…cherish the time we've spent together. Cherish this."

That sounded too much like goodbye. Needing some distance, Jonas gave her one last kiss. Only time would give her the answers she needed, allow her to realize what they could have together if she wanted it. But time was running out and he knew it. He loved her, but would she realize she loved him before it was too late?

Skylar's "transition" was occurring little by little, and tonight was another step forward.

Summer would be gone in a flash…and Rissa would be gone with it.

"WELL?" Rissa asked, opening the door with a strained smile. "How was it?"

Carly glanced at her grandmother before saying, "It was okay."

"It was *great*," Skylar informed her, crossing over the threshold first. "The music, the costumes. It was awesome!"

Her back to her grandmother, Carly wrinkled her nose, and Rissa had a hard time smothering a laugh. "And you said thank you to Mrs. Wells?"

"She did," Marilyn confirmed from where she stood outside the hotel room door. "Your daughter was…a surprise," she admitted, appearing reluctant. "If not for her unfortunate choice in appearance and, at times, speech, she seems to be quite nice."

Rissa glanced over her shoulder and saw the girls disappear into the opposite room, bantering the merits of the ballet and ignoring them entirely because they'd remembered a favorite show on television they simply couldn't miss.

Biting her tongue, Rissa forced another smile. "Thank you."

Marilyn peered into the room. "I'd like to speak with Jonas. Is he here?"

The smile was hard to keep pinned to her face,

but she managed, leaning her shoulder against the door when she remembered how quiet Jonas had been when he'd left. She'd thought things would be simpler in Montana, but they'd proven to be more complicated than ever.

"No, actually, he isn't. He couldn't get a cell signal from here so he went for a walk to call work and check in."

"I see." Marilyn's frown deepened, her expression cynical. "Or perhaps you were pressuring him in some way?"

Nothing like unsheathing the claws when no one was around to hear her. She deliberately widened her smile. "I'm a no-pressure kind of gal, Marilyn. Would you like to come in and wait for him? He should return any minute and you can ask him yourself."

The woman's chin lifted. "I should. I should wait and tell him exactly what I think of what he's doing."

"And it would be your business in what way?"

"My daughter—"

"Isn't here—as I believe Jonas, Carly *and your daughter* can attest to. Mrs. Wells, I'm not the enemy here," she said, shaking her head slowly back and forth, her gaze direct. "Nor will I allow you to make me the scapegoat for your arguments. You will *always* be Carly's grandmother. No one can take that from you, and if you'd really look, you'd see Jonas isn't trying to, either. He's a good man who's trying to be the parent your daughter couldn't be. Why can't you give him credit for it, back off and let *him* do what he needs to do as a man and Carly's father before—"

Rissa snapped her mouth shut, appalled that she'd gone off on such a rampage. But after the tenderness of the night in Jonas's arms, Marilyn's interference and judgmental attitude rubbed her the wrong way. Jonas didn't deserve to be treated that way. By Marilyn Wells…or herself.

"I…apologize," she said stiffly. "It's not my place—"

"No. No, you're—" Marilyn's eyes filled with tears, and she opened her purse and began searching inside. "You're right."

Hesitant, Rissa found herself in an awkward position, pained that she'd caused another person to hurt whether it was due or not. She ran to the desk and grabbed a handful of tissues from the dispenser there, gently closing the connecting door between the rooms along the way. Gulping in steadying breaths, she pressed tissues into the woman's trembling hand and led Marilyn to one of the chairs.

"I'm sorry." Marilyn dabbed her face, but the tears kept coming. "I didn't—you're right. Oh, you're right," she sobbed. "Lea isn't coming back. She's said it often in her letters. My own child won't give me a return address or a—a phone number! She sends letters like she sends to Caroline, but only when she wants…. When she feels she must tell me how good her life is. But she always assures me that she's moved on and won't ever be back. She not only abandoned them, she abandoned *me*. I always knew Jonas would meet someone eventually but—I'm so *scared!*"

"Scared of what?" Rissa seated herself on the corner of the bed.

Marilyn shook her head back and forth, her shaking fingers fiddling with the damp tissues. "Everyone talks about mother-in-laws, makes jokes. It's one thing if Jonas would've left and Lea had custody of Caroline, but Jonas—he's not my son. If he marries and he and his new wife shut me out of Caroline's life, I'll—" She looked up at Rissa, her expression that of one mother to another. "I'll have *nothing* left. Nothing at all. I *know* I've made mistakes, *horrible* mistakes! And I've taken my fear and frustration with Lea out on Jonas because he's—he's *here*. But Caroline's all I have left of my daughter and I *can't* lose her, too, so I…I push, say too much to a man who's been what you said. Good and kind and the p-parent Lea couldn't be. Dave tells me, warns me, to stop.

He always sides with Jonas and then we fight. He says I put too much pressure on Jonas and that I'm driving them…"

Rissa glanced at the door connecting the rooms, glad the TV blared on the other side. "You're driving them away," she finished for her. "By behaving this way, you're pushing them further away instead of helping them stay close. You do understand that, don't you?"

Marilyn nodded, sobbed. "Yes. Yes, but I don't mean to! I look at her and I see Lea. Her expressions, her temper, and then— Poor Jonas. He is a good man, I know that. But the words come and— I've given him such a hard time because I'm *so scared* of losing Caroline, too, and I simply can't bear it happening again."

Rissa patted Marilyn's hand, easily able to understand her motives. Another person hadn't taken Skylar away, but whatever had happened before the accident *had*. She identified with Marilyn's fear.

"I'm sorry, R-Rissa. I don't mean to—to act this way. I need to go. I don't want Jonas to see me like this or—"

"Too late," Jonas murmured from the doorway. He stepped into the room and shut the door before moving to the bed. Rissa scooted over to give him room.

"And Rissa's right. You'll always be Carly's grandmother, and I'll do my best to make sure you're involved in her life, but I won't let you run her life—or mine. We need to get that clear right now, once and for all."

"Yes, yes, I know," Marilyn said, sniffling. "I'm sorry. Dave's told me to back off many times. Says that a man doesn't like orders and demands handed down like I do to you."

A wry smile curled his lips. "He's right, and now that you've admitted that, I'm going to ask that you listen to him for your own sake so that we don't have to talk about this again. You need to be prepared, Marilyn. I've held my tongue for far too long and made Carly do the same to not hurt your feelings, but we're done now. Hear me? As of right now, we're through with that. Carly is my daughter and I'll raise her as I see fit."

Marilyn nodded, wiping more tears and seemingly accepting of his declaration of change. Of a new future.

"But, in return I won't ever forget you're the only grandmother Caro has, you have my word on that."

Marilyn broke down and sobbed quietly, went through two more tissues and issued a dozen more apologies, then finally pulled herself together enough to get out of the chair to hug Jonas. She surprised them both by urging Rissa to join in.

"Thank you." She released Jonas only to turn and hug Rissa alone. "Thank you. Thank you so much. My Lea… I wish she could have been stronger, Rissa…like you."

JONAS DROPPED the three of them off at the ranch at nine o'clock the next morning. By nine-thirty, she was back to work cleaning cabin number one, and Skylar and Carly were putting in their first day as full-time babysitters for Mr. Paxton and his many company employees.

"Good news!"

Rissa shielded her gaze from the sun to look at her cousin. "Shouldn't you be fixing lunch?" she asked, gripping her cleaning bucket of supplies. She stepped off the porch of cabin number nine and noted the time. "Wait—I *missed* lunch?"

"Worked right through it," Maura confirmed. "Someone must have something on her mind."

Rissa made a face, but didn't respond. "What's the good news?"

"Seth is taking Mr. Paxton and his entire gang on a slow ride into the mountains to camp."

She stared at her, her mind unable to fathom the logistics of such a thing. "And the good news is?"

"The girls are going along to help with the kids, and *you* will have the weekend free once the cabins are taken care of. Which from the looks of things, won't take you long."

"Skylar agreed to go *camping?*"

Maura fell into step beside her along the path to cabin ten. "She's packing now. Carly contacted Jonas and gained permission, and this afternoon everyone will be on their way."

"What about you and the kids? Jake?"

"Jake's taking Lexi, but I'm keeping the boys here. Mr. Paxton wants a big dinner when they all get back on Monday night so I lucked out and don't have to go." She grinned. "The boys love playing in the dining room when no one's around. Cooking will be easy. But that leaves you and Jonas. How'd last night go?"

Rissa paused there on the path and looked at Maura, her expression unguarded.

"You're in *love* with him," Maura said, her excitement quickly dulling. "But you're not happy about it. Oh, Rissa, honey, what's wrong?"

"What's wrong?" She laughed uneasily. "Everything! We *agreed* to be friends, to take things slow, and even though I wanted to make love with Jonas while we were at the hotel, I couldn't because—" She ran a hand over her hair, smoothing the tendrils that had escaped her ponytail only to have it fall back into her face again. "Maura, this is temporary, remember?

Some women out there wouldn't have hesitated, but no matter how much I care for Jonas, I knew it would only hurt worse when we leave. And we *will* leave because Skylar—" She broke off, unable to go on. "How could everything get so complicated? We came here to simplify things, not make them worse!"

"Okay, Skylar aside, why do I get the impression you're more upset that you're not sure you *want* things to be temporary?"

"Because I'm not sure."

"That's great!"

"It sucks," she countered, borrowing one of her daughter's favorite phrases. "Maura, it doesn't mean *he* wants more. Jonas has never said a word about the future, and if I do, I'm changing the rules. Larry hated that kind of thing, said women constantly inferred things that weren't there. He was no doubt talking about sex and his affairs, but—"

"It sounds like you and Jonas need to sit down and talk about you-the-couple rather than always discussing the girls. Maybe somehow along the way you can let Jonas know you're teetering on the edge of wanting to stay in North Star and he'll say something?"

Maybe. She shook her head, hating that the insecure part of her was leaving such a monumental decision up to what Jonas said. It was her life, her decision. *Her* future on the line. Hers and Skylar's. If she could get a job, find a house. There were too many things to consider.

But Maura was right. She needed to talk to Jonas, be open and honest about her feelings for him. His response would be the deciding factor in whether or not she'd start World War Three with Skylar.

She'd told Skylar she could trust her again. How hard would it be to get her to understand that if Jonas felt the same way about her, then he and Carly would be a good thing, not a bad one?

HER BUTT WAS KILLING HER. Skylar shifted in the saddle and grimaced, glad she'd at least ridden a horse before. Now if only she could figure out how she'd wound up on a freakin' camp-out. No one had said anything about that when she'd said she'd babysit all summer.

But she'd felt really guilty when her mom had pressed the fifty-dollar bill into her hand last night. She wasn't blind. Her mom looked tired from working all the hours she worked, and even though she'd quit the diner, she still had to lug that stupid cleaning bucket around all over the ranch. Her mom was a pilot and Skylar had caught her staring up at the sky so many times it was obvious she missed it. Maybe she could help her search online for jobs? Her mom had had less and less time lately to search through all the listings. Yeah, she'd do that. After all, she definitely owed her.

She'd given the fifty back, but...not the thousand dollars she'd spent when she'd taken her credit card. Helping her mom find a job was the least she could do. But then what? She kind of liked North Star now. Not school, but Carly was cool again, and Marcus, well...she really liked him. Leaving meant leaving them.

"Skylar, keep the kids hemmed in," Jake ordered from behind her.

Jerked from her thoughts, she picked up the pace and kept Mr. Paxton's secretary's kid from pretending he was a jockey. All in all there were about twelve kids to watch, but that included several older kids around ten or so that were supposed to help look after their brothers and sisters.

Jockey-boy strayed again and she pushed her horse faster, nudging the pony back in with the others on the wide path. She glanced over her shoulder to see how Carly was doing and Brandon flashed her his bleached-white smile. He was hot, sure, but for some reason he didn't compare to Marcus.

The slow-moving group topped the hill and Skylar sighed in relief when she spotted the campsite. *Finally.* If she had to answer one more stupid *knock-knock* joke she'd scream. Half of them didn't even make sense.

"I need a break," she said when the kids bounced on ahead and Carly rode slowly up beside her. "Wanna take a walk?"

Carly stared at her in horror. "Are you kidding? If I manage to get off this thing without falling on my face in front of everyone, I'm not moving again until tomorrow."

Skylar shrugged. "Whatever. I'm going."

RISSA SET MAURA'S appetizer on the table and then stood back to look at her handiwork. In an effort to help Rissa have a romantic evening, Maura had cooked a delectable dinner while she took a bath and hurriedly cleaned up the cabin.

The good news was that the bath had calmed her and freed her thoughts. She forced herself to imagine leaving North Star, leaving Jonas and Carly behind. Multiple scenarios played out in her head, but in each and every one of them, the end was the same. She wanted more because she wanted what Maura had—balance. Balance and a life with Jonas.

A car drove up and pulled to a stop outside. More nervous than ever, Rissa smoothed her sweaty hands over the simple black sheath dress she wore. Sleeveless, it came to her ankles and had a slit up to her thigh. *For easy access.*

Rissa blushed at the errant thought. Yeah, well, there was that, too. If things went well, if Jonas liked what she had to say… She couldn't go there yet. Not when her willingness to stay in North Star could very well send Jonas running for the hills. Who knew what his reaction would be?

It took everything Rissa had in her not to rush to the door and lock it tight. What if he only wanted temporary? What if he was *counting* on it being temporary? Her nerves faded a bit when she swung the door wide and his eyes revealed his appreciation of her appearance. A slow grin spread across Jonas's features. One she could get used to.

"You like?"

He whistled. "I like. What's the occasion?"

She stepped aside so he could come in. "Maura made us dinner and I—I thought we could eat and…talk." She wished she didn't sound so anxious.

"I see. And the candles?"

"Do they bother you? I can blow them out." She shut the door and moved to do that when Jonas caught her arm and pulled her gently toward him, his intent clear. Tilting her head, she parted her lips and wasn't disappointed when his mouth covered hers in a light, but heady kiss.

A combination of heat and dizziness swept through her. "Come on." Her voice sounded throaty and not at all like her own. The last thing she wanted to do was push him away, but there were things that had to be said first. Important things.

"Where are we going?"

"First let's eat and then…we need to talk."

CHAPTER FIFTEEN

THINGS HADN'T EXACTLY gone as planned. Half an hour later the remnants of Maura's feast remained on the table and Rissa was in his arms. They swayed back and forth with the music and it was one of those moments when she wanted time to stand still. The feel of Jonas holding her, the strength and breadth of his shoulders and chest.

"Time for that talk yet?"

Unable to avoid it any longer, she reluctantly lifted her head from his shoulder.

"You've been nervous all night." A muscle worked in his jaw, spasming because he had it clenched so tight. "Did you find a job somewhere? Did you do all this to tell me you're leaving?"

They stopped dancing. Rissa smoothed her hand up to his face and rubbed the lightly stubbled skin with her thumb. "No." Was he relieved?

"Then what is it? Something has you tied up in knots."

Apt description, she thought, swallowing again.

"Actually, I—I've decided that maybe North Star isn't the end of the earth like I first believed." She figured it was better to get it out before she chickened out. "Skylar has come a long way and is doing well and—and I have family here. I thought—I'm thinking," she corrected, gasping for air when it seemed to be in short supply, "of s-staying. But," she said, holding up her hands when he opened his mouth to respond, "my doing so is no pressure on you at all."

She turned away from him. "Really, Jonas, all I'm saying is it's a—a possibility and I'd like to know what you think. Get an opinion. B-but I want to make it clear I don't expect anything from you since we agreed to be friends."

He swung her back around so fast it made her head spin. "What if I do?"

Her mind went blank. For a pilot who had to make snap decisions, she didn't seem to be all that capable at the moment. Not where he was concerned. "Huh?"

"What if I expect more from you? Want more?"

She blinked up at him, only then remembering she hadn't put on her sandals, which would have given her a bit more height and enabled her to look into his eyes without putting a crick in her neck. "Like what? If we're talking going public with a relationship, you'd—you'd have to get used to people commenting on Skylar's appearance. The psychologists said to let her come out of it on her own."

"I've come to terms with that. I'll do my best to get along, Rissa. You'll just have to trust me on that."

"You have? Oh." Rissa bit her lips, afraid to hope. She pulled away and started pacing. "Okay, well, there's also Marilyn—"

"I think after last night we've both got a handle on her. You'd have no worries there, and I'd support you completely."

"We'd also have to think about Carly. She's wonderful, but she might not like—"

"My daughter loves you and Skylar both," he said firmly, moving into her path so that she had to stop or run into him.

"Then there's Skylar." She shook her head, unable to fathom her daughter's anger and dislike of Jonas. "I told her we wouldn't stay in North Star long, and it won't be easy trying to talk her into it."

"Maybe if we came up with a good approach? A compromise? I don't know what—something."

Rissa laughed softly at his inability to come up with anything that might appeal to Skylar. She hadn't had any luck, either. Relegating that to another time, Rissa resisted the urge to blurt out what she really wanted to say. "Well, then I guess that's…that's it."

"Not by a long shot."

His tone of voice forced her to lift her head and meet his gaze. Dread spiraled through her. "It's not?"

He shook his head. "What about flying? A job? Can you find one in Helena?"

"Maybe eventually, but not right now. I checked before moving out here, and they have my resume on file, but…there aren't openings or anything."

"So until something changes, you're willingly grounding yourself?"

Did he look relieved again?

"I'm not giving it up completely, Jonas. Ever. I can't. Flying is in me, it's in my blood. Could you stop being a cop?"

He shook his head. "I'll just always worry—"

"That I might have an accident on the job?" she asked pointedly. "That worry goes both ways and is justifiable, but it doesn't change who we are at heart. While I've been here I've played the role of traditional woman with the jobs I've worked to make ends meet, but that's not really me. You need to know that. If I can get back in the air, I will. The question is whether you can handle that on top of Skylar and everything else."

"Everything else?"

She wet her lips. "If we stay… What I'm trying

so hard to say right now is that…Jonas, if I stay, you have to know I'm staying because I love—"

"You."

Rissa froze, afraid her mind played tricks on her. *Please, God, don't let it have been my imagination.* "What?"

Jonas closed the distance between them and pulled her into his arms. "I said, I love you." He smiled down at her. "And I knew you weren't a traditional woman the moment I saw you crawl out from under your car."

She didn't know what to do. Laugh, cry, scream? This was what she needed from him. These words, the look in his eyes. The one that told her she hadn't imagined anything.

Rissa surged up onto her tiptoes and kissed him, a no-holds-barred, you-can't-take-it-back kiss that left her breathless. Last night had been nice, but this, oh, this was what she'd dreamed of, what she'd needed to know before taking that final step. Skylar—she'd break the news to her somehow. Make her understand that things would be changing, but they were good changes.

The kiss went on. Their lips meshed, tongues entwined. Happiness and joy gave way to a hunger only Jonas could appease. "Mmmm, oh, no," she mumbled against his lips.

"What?"

"The—the bed," she said dazedly, knowing exactly how the night was going to end.

"What about it?" Jonas reluctantly pulled away to look around the impossibly small cabin. "Where *is* it?"

"I sleep on the couch—it folds out." She smiled ruefully, breathless. "We needed to talk and—I didn't know if things would work out, or if you'd make a run for it when you heard we might stay and… I couldn't have you thinking I only wanted you for your body."

His arms tightened around her, one hand drifting over her hip to grip the material of her long dress and pull it upward. Jonas held her gaze the entire time, watched her reaction with an all-male expression.

"Do you?"

When he had the material bunched at her waist, he pulled the dress over her head and dropped it to the floor.

"Yes." She tugged him to her again, her lips nibbling at his. "I want your body. Your heart… your love. I want to be with you."

He made quick work of her bra and panties, and stood there staring at her with such heat and love she knew no matter what the future brought with their daughters—with Skylar— they'd work it out.

"I'm, ah, feeling a little underdressed here."

Smiling, he raised his hands in supplication, and Rissa set to work on his clothes, stripping him with fumbles and ten thumbs, and kisses she felt compelled to give. When his clothes were gone, Jonas lowered her down onto the couch, but before she could pull him closer, he stopped her with a murmur.

"You're sure, Rissa?" He raised a hand to her face, his thumb sliding gently over her lips. "Honey, I love you, but you have to be sure."

He wasn't questioning their lovemaking, or her love for him. No, he questioned the sacrifices she and Skylar would both have to make if they stayed here in the little Montana town.

Removing his hand from her face, she laced their fingers and nodded, raising their hands above her head to stretch full-length beneath him. "Until I can fly again…you'll just have to take me flying another way."

Smiling, Jonas caught her mouth with his, his tongue sweeping inside. Careful to keep his full weight off her and ignoring her husky murmurs to join them, he stroked her. Her breasts and waist, the inner flesh of her thighs. He touched her, brought her need to a feverish level before he entered her in a long, smooth stroke.

"That's it. Sweetheart—"

Forehead to forehead, his body moving steadily in hers, the tension built, taking her higher and higher until—

"*Jonas.*"

"I love you, Rissa. That's it, honey—fly with me."

SKYLAR DIDN'T KNOW he was there until he was almost right behind her. She jumped and turned, almost falling into the wide stream. "Are you following me?"

Brandon Paxton grinned. "I needed to stretch my legs. Besides, we haven't had any time alone at the ranch."

"For what?" she asked bluntly.

Brandon stepped closer, his green eyes roaming over her jeans and black T-shirt. It was too hot to wear her concealing trench and she'd taken it off, but now she wished she had its bulk when his eyes fastened on her boobs and stayed.

"I like the tough-girl image."

She rolled her eyes. "Get real. I'm not interested."

"Sure about that?"

Before she knew what was happening, Brandon swooped down and planted a big one right on her mouth. Skylar couldn't believe his balls and shoved him away, as hard as she could.

Time stood still for a moment. Brandon swung his arms like a windmill, slow motion, before he landed on his butt in the stream. Water soaked him up to his waist and gave him a good, cold shower, his expression priceless.

She laughed loud and hard, the sound echoing across the water. Seconds ticked by, and Brandon continued to look up at her, anger giving way to surprised disbelief and then...what kind of look was that?

"All you had to do was say no."

That was all the warning she got before he slapped his hands against the water and sent it spraying all over her. Her clothes, her face, her hair.

Then he was the one laughing. "What's the matter? You one of those girls who can dish it out, but can't take it?"

Her mouth dropped at the challenge. "I wouldn't talk considering *you're* the one on his butt. Maybe you shouldn't consider yourself God's gift to females and give us lowly humans a chance to actually get the word out!"

They stared at each other and a split second later both hurled water toward the other like human water cannons.

"Skylar? Hey! *Hey!* What's going on?"

Skylar paused when Brandon did, both of them breathing heavily from a combination of laughter and exertion. Brandon raised an eyebrow in question, a grin creasing the dimple at the side of his mouth. Exchanging a smile, they turned at the same time and doused Carly.

The battle raged on a long time, and it wasn't until later that the three of them collapsed on the bank, soaking wet and tired.

Skylar groaned. "I can't believe you've never had a water fight before."

"I can't believe you two ganged up on me." Brandon rolled onto his side and propped his head on his hand, a blade of grass between his lips. "So what *do* you do here?"

"Nothing," Skylar and Carly said together.

"Jinx."

Skylar smiled, but didn't comment. After staying up late last night, watching the kids all morning, riding almost three hours and then the water fight, she was beat. She closed her eyes, glad they weren't stinging anymore. She'd lost her contacts in the stream, but it was time for her weekly change so it wasn't a big loss.

She settled herself more comfortably in the fading sunlight and sighed, aware of Brandon's presence since he'd come on so strong, but confident she'd gotten her point across. What an ass.

Seconds later she felt someone staring at her and blinked her eyes open, squinting a bit. "What?" she asked, meeting Carly's gaze as she pushed herself into a sitting position. Brandon sat up as well, and

Skylar quickly glanced behind her to make sure they weren't about to get eaten by a bear or something. "What is it?" Everything was blurry.

"Skylar?"

"What?"

"Why do you wear the goop?" Brandon demanded suddenly. "When you're prettier without it?"

He gazed at her face, searching. Up close she could sort of see.

"And *blond?*" he continued, looking at her eyebrows. "Why do you dye your hair?"

Skylar quickly raised her hand to her face to shield it and shoved herself to her feet with the other. Carly caught her arm before she could stand, and off balance, she fell on her butt. "Hey!"

Carly scooted closer, still holding on to her, and stared at her like she'd never seen her before.

"A friend of mine in L.A. did the Goth thing. She was really cute, too."

"Why do you say it like that?" Carly asked suspiciously.

"Everybody thought she did it to be cool because it was in, but then she had a nervous breakdown and told people her stepdad and his brother had been raping her. She'd done it to get them not to like her."

Skylar pulled her arm away from Carly and

glared before turning her attention to Brandon. "Get real. You think I'd go down without a fight if somebody tried that? I took care of you, didn't I?"

Carly gasped. "You mean you tried to—"

"No way! I kissed her, that's all. And believe me, I won't try it again. Not unless she wants me to."

Skylar snorted. "Do me a favor and hold your breath while you wait on that to happen, okay?"

"Why do you wear it?" Carly asked, insistent. "*Did* someone try something with you?"

"No! What's with all the questions? You wear makeup now and the whole reason why you wanted it was so you could—" She broke off just in time.

Carly's mouth dropped open in horror of what she'd almost said, but snapped shut after a leery glance at Brandon.

They sat there in silence a long while.

Skylar pulled her knees to her chest and crossed her arms on top. She stared out at the little sparkles the sun made on the water, the conversation reminding her of what her mom had said about trusting her to handle things now. Was it true?

"Anybody else cold?" Carly asked.

"I'm hungry."

"All you do is eat. I've never seen anyone ride a horse and eat a sub sandwich at the same time." Maybe if she told her mom the truth, all of it... Would she believe her?

"I'm a growing boy." Brandon stood, holding out both his hands to pull them up at the same time. "Come on, let's go back to camp."

"I CAN'T SEE WHERE I'm going," Carly whined. She didn't want to sound like a baby but—

"You can see better than I can. My contacts are in that stream. Everything's blurry."

"Blurry? You're leading us," Brandon groused.

"Because *you* led us away from camp!"

"Guys, don't fight! Please." She swatted a tree limb out of the way only to hear Brandon curse behind her. "Sorry!"

"We've walked for miles and now we're nowhere near the stream!"

Skylar stopped so fast Carly ran into her. She mumbled an apology and stepped back.

"You want to lead again?" Skylar challenged Brandon. "Fine! But at least follow the path. The stream should be up ahead."

"Says who?"

"There's a path?"

"Haven't you two paid attention at all?"

Carly struggled to hold back tears while they continued to argue. She didn't want to cry in front of them, but camping sucked. She was sore from riding, being eaten alive by the bugs. Wet and cold and hungry and—

"I'm leading now." Brandon pushed past them. "Move out of the way. I never should've let you lead. I'm older, the *guy*. I shouldn't have let you go this long when—*ahhh!*"

Carly had her back to him, but spun around at Brandon's cry, horrified when she didn't see his white T-shirt gleaming beneath the half moon overhead.

Skylar dropped to her knees and scrambled forward. "Brandon!"

Carly caught Skylar's belt and yanked her back. "Don't! You'll fall, too!"

"Brandon! Are you all right? Can you hear me?"

No response, not even the normal sounds of the night. Everything was quiet except their rough breathing, like they were the only people on earth. So weird. So scary.

"We have to get down there!"

"No!" Carly held tight when Skylar tried to edge closer to the bank or ledge or wherever they were. "We can't see him! You don't know how far he fell— Skylar, we've got to get help!"

"We can't wait that long! We're lost in the freakin' forest!"

"I know, but we can't do this on our own!" Carly could barely make out the glitter of Skylar's eyes, but she heard the way her voice shook. If Skylar was scared enough to cry, she'd lose it for sure.

Why had she come on this stupid trip? All she wanted to do was go home.

"Fine—I'll stay here with Brandon. You keep walking. See if you can find Seth or—or Jake and—"

Carly gulped, the thought of walking on alone making her sick to her stomach. "Wouldn't they want us to stay together?"

"Brandon's *hurt!*"

"I know, but—Skylar, *I* didn't know there was a path, either! Even without your contacts you could see it when we couldn't!"

Skylar sat back on her heels beside her. "*Brandon!* If this is a joke, it's not funny! *Say something!*"

They both held their breath and listened. Nothing. Carly started crying.

"I'm going."

"By yourself?" she choked out.

"What else can we do? Someone has to stay here with him. What if he wakes up? He'll think we left him. And if he doesn't, we won't know where to look for him unless you're here."

She swallowed repeatedly, but couldn't stop the noisy sob from bursting out of her chest. She flung her arms around Skylar and hugged. "Please come back."

Skylar snorted, but she hugged her back and

released her. Two seconds later, her black T-shirt and jeans were swallowed up by the woods.

LOUD POUNDING brought both Rissa and Jonas awake instantly.

"Rissa? Jonas! The girls are missing!"

In an instant they both scrambled off the sofa bed. Jonas grabbed his pants and pulled them on while Rissa found her dress and yanked it over her head. Seeing she was decent, Jonas flung the door wide.

Maura stood on the porch, shaking and pale, one of Seth's older ranch hands behind her. "The girls are gone—along with Mr. Paxton's older son, Brandon. They went for a walk and—and never came back to camp."

Jonas swore. "I'll get my men on it. Maura, call all your neighbors and get their ranch hands out on the search."

"Wait for me. I'm coming with you."

"You're staying here," Jonas ordered. "Help Maura contact everyone."

She'd already begun pulling clothes from a drawer, but now she swung to face him. "I'm going with you to help find them."

"What's a New Yorker going to do in the mountains? You'll get lost, and then we'll have to search for you!"

"I do need help," Maura interjected softly.

"Whenever this happens we call the churches and ranches and—"

She ignored Maura's comment. "I'm not helpless! Jonas, I've logged a lot of hours doing search and—"

Before she could finish, Jonas gave her a brief, rough kiss and took off out the door where Seth's ranch hand waited.

Rissa watched them go, fear and anger and upset boiling inside her until she shrieked. "I needed two minutes to get dressed, that's all! Two lousy minutes!" She whirled around and returned to the open drawers, grabbing the first items that came to hand and mumbling to herself and cursing stubborn, egotistical men who thought women should stay home and keep the fires burning.

"I'll go start those calls," Maura told her.

Still muttering, Rissa pulled a sweatshirt over her head and followed Maura, lifting a Yankees ball cap from the hook by the door. If Jonas thought she was a sit-back-and-wait kind of gal, he had another thing coming.

She had a phone call to make herself. One way or another, no matter the cost or the damage to her already overloaded credit cards, she was getting into the air.

SKYLAR PRESSED her hand against the rough bark of a tree and did a couple deep squats. The muscles in her legs were bunching and sore from walking at an angle.

The wild cry of something big filled the air, everywhere at once. She scanned the darkness, but didn't see anything. Walking again, slowly, her head pounded from the effort it took to focus on the path. It didn't take an idiot to figure out the trail wasn't made by humans. It twisted and turned, back and forth, and sometimes even made circles around sets of trees. It would be her luck to be following a mountain lion or something.

Don't think of that, think of Brandon.

She stumbled over a root and caught herself by grabbing a tree. The rough bark jabbed into her palm and cut. Her toes throbbed, but she kept going. She had to. She'd been walking forever, and with every step she'd been thinking. She had things to say to her mom. She needed to talk to her about what had happened and how important it was that her mom know she loved her, that she was sorry for being such a brat.

Skylar ducked beneath a branch and stumbled on another root, her already blistered feet and throbbing toes taking a beating in her wet boots. She ripped the air with curses, too tired and scared to care if the noise brought the wrong kind of attention from whatever animals were out there.

Her mom used to tell her about flying, how

disorienting it could be up in the air which was why she had all those machines. What she'd give for one of those GPS things now. She knew enough to know the ranch was south of the camp, and they'd gone east to the stream. But in the water fight they'd apparently come out on the other side, which meant they'd walked for hours going the wrong way even though Brandon had been sure it was the right one. She hadn't noticed until it was too late.

Sharp pain streaked up her calf, reminding her of ballet class and toe shoes. Her foot cramped, hard enough she actually sat down where she was and rocked on her butt, frantic to get her boot off to rub the pain away. Another gasp left her when her sock pulled off skin.

What was she thinking? She couldn't do this. She'd never find her way out and even if she did, she'd never be able to lead the others back to Carly and Brandon. Breaking the stupid limbs every few feet wouldn't be enough. She'd never get to tell her mom she was sorry for all the things she'd said to her, never get to—to tell her the truth. And she wanted to. She really wanted to. Maybe her mom would understand. She was different now than she was a year ago. They both were.

A moan sounded and it took her a minute to figure out it came from her. Before she knew it, she bawled like a baby. She hadn't even cried at her dad's funeral. She'd been numb with pain medicines and shock, yet here she sat in the middle of nowhere, blubbering away. Just freakin' perfect.

Images filled her head. Her and Nic dancing on stage, her mom always there with an armful of flowers and a video camera. Her dad being lowered into the ground. Nic's dad teasing her, laughing—

What had she done? "I'm sorry," she whispered, choking. "Oh, God, I'm *sorry.*" She sobbed, rocking back and forth, the pain too strong, too deep, too much. It just kept coming up out of her, like someone ripping her to shreds, stabbing her again and again. Her nails dug into her skin, the muscle, and she drew blood, but that pain didn't come close to matching what she felt inside. She raised her face to the sky overhead, unable to see it because of the tears. "I didn't mean for it to happen. Please, God, I didn't mean it! I'm *sorry! I'm sorry!*"

CHAPTER SIXTEEN

RISSA DIDN'T BOTHER waking Ben. She wasn't going to take no for an answer, and if it meant stealing the helicopter and Jonas tossing her in jail, so be it. She'd at least find the kids first.

It had taken her ten minutes to get Maura to tell her where Ben and Marcus lived, and the half hour drive seemed more like an hour. Now she stared at the latch holding the huge double doors closed and tried to think positively even though it was nothing but rust. Not a good sign. If Ben couldn't take care of a simple latch, what were the odds the heli would fly? Ben said himself it was rusting on its rails.

Let it fly, let it fly, let it fly. Her heart pounded in her throat, but she refused to give up. The metal bar moved with a lot of pushing and grunting and squeaking, and Rissa grabbed the door to pull it wide.

"Damn drug smugglers— I'll shoot!" The sound of a rifle cocking from the house backed up the angry man's words. "You ain't stealin' my bird! No's no!"

"Wait!" Rissa swung around to face him. "Ben, it's me! It's Rissa! From the diner!"

"Are you crazy? What are you doin'?"

"There are three kids lost in the mountains—my *daughter!*" She indicated the building. "You said you should've sold it, that it's rusty, but does it fly?"

"'Course it flies!" he returned, sounding insulted. "My legs might be shot, but my hands are still good!"

A shadow appeared behind Ben and took the gun from him, exchanging it for his canes. A porch light was flipped on, and Rissa watched Ben painstakingly make his way out onto the porch. Marcus followed and once Ben was on solid ground, Marcus broke into a run toward her. Rissa blamed her imagination, thinking the teen looked unusually pale.

Silent, they pulled the doors wide.

IT DIDN'T TAKE Jonas long to get to the campsite. He and the ranch hand had just arrived when word came in that Jake had found Skylar, and that the kids weren't together. Waiting for Jake and Skylar to get back to the base camp was torture. Where was Caroline? Why hadn't they stayed together?

Finally the group returned, but other than a shocking glimpse at Skylar's drawn features, he had to wait like the rest of them to speak to her until after Grace helped Skylar change into warm, dry clothes and checked her out.

Now Jonas locked his jaw and stared at Rissa's daughter, more than a little astonished. Minus her makeup, Skylar looked like a different person. And the difference was so incredible, it made him all the more curious to what made an otherwise beautiful girl behave as she did.

"How badly was Brandon hurt?" Mr. Paxton demanded.

"She's already said twice she doesn't know." Jake glared at the man, unable to sit still, and Jonas felt his frustration.

"He followed *her* to the stream! She said so!"

"And then Brandon apparently led them out the wrong way. It's not Skylar's fault, and we're wasting time. My daughter is out there, too." Jonas was aware of Skylar's wide-eyed surprise that he'd taken up for her, but there was no time for that now. Carly had to be found. She was out there surrounded by millions of acres of forest with a teenaged jerk who might or might not be hurt or even dead. How would she handle that?

Look what had happened to Skylar after the accident.

"Let's get the details and get there without giving her a hard time or pointing fingers. The important thing is finding them both," Grace interjected, her tone calm. "Skylar, honey, do you have any idea how far you walked to get back to the stream?"

She shook her head. "Seemed like forever, but I had to go slow because I couldn't see and kept tripping. Definitely a few hours. Maybe three?" She rubbed her nose with the blanket draped around her shoulders.

"Where? What direction? Can you take us?"

"She needs a hospital." Grace looked up from where she sat next to Skylar, her gaze sharp. "She might look okay, but she's still hypothermic and her hands and feet—"

"I'm okay," Skylar said firmly. "I won't leave."

Jonas walked over beside her, noticing for the first time that Grace had bandaged both Skylar's hands, and over the bandages on her feet, Skylar wore several pairs of socks, no shoes. He squatted down in front of her and stared her straight in the eyes. She stared right back, but this time he didn't see any attitude or anger, just worry for her friends.

"Carly's okay," she whispered, her eyes glazing with tears. "And I promised her I'd come back so if you go, I go. I—I followed a path and broke little branches all along the way, big ones when I had to go a different direction. But you won't find them without me."

A wry smile caught him by surprise. She was

so much like her mother. Determined, headstrong. Protective. Skylar hadn't let his daughter down before, and she was determined not to do it now.

"Then you can come with me, and we'll go find them together."

IT HAD TAKEN Rissa some time to check things over for herself. No pilot worth her weight climbed in and took off trusting that everything was as it should be, and she ran through the check-list she'd memorized years ago. Now the steady *wump-wump-wump* of the helicopter's blades filled her ears and gave her a measure of calm while she flew Ben and Marcus toward the ranch.

Jonas might have been right about her lacking knowledge of the woods, but she knew the air. This was her territory. And it was the only thing keeping her panic at bay because it required her full concentration.

"Got it! Jonas always uses this channel." Ben grinned at her raised eyebrow. "An old man gets bored," he said in defense.

Over the headphones she heard static inter-mixed with voices she didn't recognize, relays between the base camp and searchers out looking for the teens east of the stream. Chatter filled the air, something about a cliff and one of them falling, possibilities of where they might be.

"Who?" she demanded. "Who's safe and who fell?"

"We're almost there," Ben said gruffly. "The ranch is over that next ridge."

Jonas's voice filled her headset then, ordering someone to double-check that she'd been contacted at the ranch house and knew Skylar had been found safe, that she was with him on an ATV.

"Oh, thank God." She flew over the ranch and kept going, found the nearly abandoned base camp lit with several fires. From there she headed east. A minute later, she flew over the widest part of the stream, the woods beyond. Trees blocked most of her view, but in the early morning light there was no mistaking the spots of color worn by the search crews.

She nodded to Ben to open the radio frequency. "Jonas, it's Rissa. Where's Skylar? Can I talk to her?" She had to hear her baby's voice.

"Mom? I'm okay. I…I love you."

Her heart clenched at the words and she fought back the instant sting of tears. Blinking rapidly, she said, "I love you, too, Sky."

"I'm sorry—"

"Shh, hush, it's nobody's fault. Everyone knows no one plans to get lost. Okay?"

She heard a choked "okay" in response. Sniffling, Rissa cleared her throat determinedly. "Tell me what's going on down there. Where are Brandon and Carly?"

"Brandon fell on the path and went over a—a cliff or something, and Carly stayed with him so we'd know where— So he wouldn't be scared when he woke up."

Leave it to Skylar to think of that. "And you walked out alone to find help? Oh, honey, you did good. Can you describe it? Were there a lot of trees? Maybe not so many?"

"I could see the sky and there was a breeze. We were on a hill and it was really rocky."

"Perfect," Rissa murmured even though the description could've been the side of any mountain. "Where's Jonas?"

A click sounded. "I told you to stay at the house. What are you doing? It isn't safe for you to be flying under the circumstances, you're too involved."

"And I'm going to stay that way. Any idea where the cliff is or how far they walked?"

Obviously reluctant, Jonas gave her what information he could about outcroppings and drop-offs nearby. "Be careful, Rissa."

"Always." Signing off, Rissa slowly zigzagged above the trees looking for breaks in the foliage along the mountainsides. She didn't see anything at first and prayed for patience, guiding the heli back and forth. She monitored the gauges, her feet pushing the pedals to move the aircraft left and right, the automatic movements as familiar to her as breathing. Her sweaty hands gripped the cyclic and collective controls, adjusting their altitude and direction while they buzzed over the terrain.

Ben and Marcus peered out their windows, silent, the chatter on their headsets from the search teams making up for the lack of noise in the cockpit. Suddenly a crackle sounded.

"We found them!" Skylar shouted over the air. "Brandon's awake. His leg is broken, but Jonas dropped a radio down and Brandon caught it. Jonas is going to try to lower himself down and see if he can reach him."

"What?" Rissa shook her head in protest, heading west again since the searchers couldn't have covered much ground after she'd last seen them.

"There!" Ben pointed farther down a ridge where Skylar had spotted her and now waved her blanket, her trench coat flapping in the wind. Carly stood beside her, another blanket around her shoulders. Both looked okay, and Rissa breathed easier for the first time since getting the news.

One look at the scene told her what she needed to know. Brandon had fallen over the edge of an outcropping and was now balanced on a narrow ledge beneath. Below that, the mountain sloped steeply into a ravine.

"Jonas, wait," Rissa ordered, hovering overhead. "Is Brandon in good shape?"

"He was knocked unconscious by the fall."

"I didn't hit my head," Brandon said, joining the conversation. "I, um, passed out when my leg broke."

Paxton's son sounded strong, clear-headed. "Brandon, if we toss out a lifting harness, think you can get yourself strapped in so we can pull you up?" Thank goodness Ben had had the foresight to insist they attach it to the heli and bring it along.

"No, Rissa. You'll be too close to the mountain."

"Yeah, I think so," Brandon said. "My leg is completely numb, and I haven't passed out or anything since I woke up."

"Rissa."

She smiled, tolerant of Jonas's worry because she knew it would take time for him to trust her skills. "Jonas, I'm good. Now help me get into position so that Brandon can catch the harness. When he's on, I'll pull back and lift him over the ravine up to you."

Glancing over her shoulder, Rissa made sure Marcus was strapped in tight before allowing him to open the sliding side door and push out the rope and harness attached to the cargo hook. From her vantage point, she saw the harness drop and get carried toward the mountain by the draft off the helicopter's blades. Now the trick was edging in close enough that Brandon could catch it.

Minutes ticked by, and more than once Ben muttered to himself when Brandon missed the harness and it swung away from him. Sweat beaded her forehead and ran down her temple, but Rissa didn't let it break her concentration. On the fifth try, Brandon snagged the harness, and they all breathed a sigh of relief.

"I'm in," Brandon said, his voice high-pitched with excitement from the ordeal.

"Fasten it tight and hold on," she ordered. "Jonas, you ready?" Once she got the okay from Brandon, and the rescue team above the ledge, Rissa lifted the chopper back and up until the rope was nearly taut. She held her breath and prayed when Brandon's feet left the ledge. Carefully, she raised him above the jagged rock formation and inward to where Jonas and the rest of the team waited.

"Got him," Jonas said, pride and relief in his voice. "He can't feel a thing, but his leg is in bad shape. What's your fuel level? Can you fly him to the hospital?"

Rissa ordered Marcus to pull the rope back into the aircraft so it wouldn't swing into her tail rotor before she radioed the Helena airport tower and the hospital, quickly getting the information and coordinates she needed to answer Jonas's questions. "No problem. I'll pick him up at the clearing by the stream."

"THERE YOU GO, Skylar. And do not get those bandages wet, okay? The medicine will ease the sting and help those cuts heal faster." Grace tucked the end of the bandage inside one of the folds around her hand and then taped it down like she had the other one. "Jonas and Jake said you must've broken a thousand or more limbs along that path. Your poor hands."

Done, Grace grabbed the bowl of dirty water and poured it down a nearby sink, her eyebrows raising when she turned around. Skylar looked over her shoulder and saw Marcus standing in the doorway of the physical therapy room.

"Hey."

"Hey," she whispered. What was he doing there?

"Um…I'm going to go see if I can give Maura a hand with the food. You'll be okay?"

She nodded at Grace. "Thanks for…this. I didn't want to go to the hospital."

"No problem. It's not every day I patch up a heroine," Grace said with a wink. "Marcus, will you keep an eye on her?"

"Yeah, sure."

Skylar sat there and stared down at her hands.

At least Grace hadn't bandaged up her blistered feet as much.

"You okay?"

She nodded, embarrassed. She wore no makeup, looked huge due to wearing a couple layers of clothes because she'd been so cold, her feet wrapped up like a mummy's. Okay? She was a mess, and Marcus looked cute as ever.

He walked over to where she sat on one of the tables, hesitated, then sat beside her. "Mr. Paxton said Brandon followed you to the stream, and that's how you got lost."

"He led us out of the clearing the wrong way, and I was so tired I actually followed him." She rolled her eyes. "Figures, huh?"

"Why'd he follow you? He try something?"

The tone in his voice had her jerking her head up to stare at him. "Why do you care?"

Marcus leaned a hand on the table beside her hip and stared at her. "Because even with your hair the wrong color and scratches all over your face, I think most guys would want to kiss you."

Meaning him? *Whoo-yeah!*

"Then again, when they get hit with all that attitude—"

She elbowed him to shut him up, rolling her eyes again.

Marcus laughed softly and captured her arm,

held on and tugged her closer. Skylar stared up at him, wishing more than ever she could change things. Wishing she hadn't done something so royally stupid because she couldn't take it back. Couldn't fix it.

"What's wrong? You okay?"

Suddenly fighting tears, she shook her head and closed her eyes.

"Hey, tell me." He lifted his other hand and wiped a tear from her cheek. "It's okay now, you're here remember?"

"It's not that."

"Then what? Something's bothering you."

She sniffled. How could she explain? "It's just...I can't stop thinking about something... Something I need to tell my mom but...when she finds out she's going to lose it. I screwed up so bad."

"With Brandon?"

She glared at him. "*Forget* Brandon. No, it's— Did you ever do something really stupid—really wrong—and then wish you could take it back, but you can't because it's too late?"

"Yeah. Did he kiss you?"

"Yeah, he did. Can we move on?"

"Did you like it?"

"No. What did you do?"

He nodded once, as if her not liking Brandon's kiss was a good thing. "A long time ago, I was mad at my parents for going on a trip without me. I was just a kid and it was their anniversary, but I didn't care. When they dropped me off at Granddad's, I wouldn't say goodbye or hug them or anything. It made my mom cry because it was the first time they'd left me anywhere."

"But you said you were just a kid. Did she stay mad for long?"

Marcus reached over and fingered one of her bandaged hands. "No, she hugged me anyway and said she loved me, but I wouldn't say it back. Then on the way my dad stopped for gas and my mom went in to pay. Some guy decided to hold the place up. When my dad heard the screaming and the shots, he ran in after my mom. They died together…. And I didn't tell them goodbye when I had the chance."

She couldn't breathe. He'd lost *both* his parents? At once? She and her mom fought a lot but she—she didn't know what she'd have done without her this past year. "I'm sorry."

He nodded, his expression sad. "What about you? What can't you tell your mom? It can't be that bad."

She opened her mouth but quickly shut it. Marcus would never look at her the same if she told him. Her hesitation registered because Marcus stiffened.

"Fine, be that—"

"Wait." Marcus started to stand and she stopped him, her hands on his thigh. "I want to tell you but... Please don't be mad. I just *can't*." She closed her eyes and hated the stupid tears because she couldn't seem to stop crying now that she'd started in the woods. "Please, Marcus, try to understand. It's...my mom won't understand and neither will you. Nobody will." She lowered her head. "I don't want either of you to...to hate me."

"You make it sound bad."

It took everything in her to raise her head and look him in the eyes. "It is."

Marcus stared at her a long time, his gaze searching hers until she couldn't stand to look at him anymore because she was afraid he'd be able to tell, to see, the truth.

"Then will you please tell your mom? Or Grace? You've got to tell someone and let them help you."

He didn't know what he was asking. In the woods she'd decided to tell her mom the truth, but now...

"I think you should. Your mom is cool. She looked down the barrel of my grandfather's rifle and didn't even flinch. That woman can handle anything you throw at her."

"Seriously?"

He nodded, smiling a little. "She was desperate to find you and nothing was going to stop her. Because she loves you. Skylar, she can handle it."

"What if you—I mean, what if she…hates me?"

"We couldn't."

A wave of tears hit her again. Did he mean it?

He leaned closer, his smile fading. "Close your eyes."

Feeling silly, she did—and felt his lips brush her cheek.

Against her skin, he said, "Lexi says that teardrop you painted right here is symbolic—and so is this."

She blinked up at him. "Meaning?"

He shrugged. "Maybe if you quit giving your mom a hard time and decide to hang around until you're older…you'll find out."

IT WAS ALMOST five o'clock that evening before Rissa flew Mr. Paxton back to the ranch to rest while Brandon slept off his pain meds. Broken in two places, he'd spent an hour and a half in surgery and now sported a thigh-high cast. Both girls had refused treatment so Rissa had yet to do more than give Skylar a hug at the clearing.

Jonas had also stayed behind, his hands full since the press had picked up the story and surrounded the Second Chance looking for a headline. She set down not far from the cabins and watched his cruiser speed up the drive, but while she wanted to wait on him, she got carried along on the wave of well-wishers and employees into the dining room, a glass was pressed into her hand.

"To our heroine!" Mr. Paxton called, garnering even more cheers from those around her.

"And to everyone who pitched in to find them before I got there," she added, not wanting the remaining ground searchers mingling with Paxton's people to feel slighted.

The door opened and Rissa saw Jonas enter the dining room. He shook hands with several people before their gazes locked and held. Rissa smiled, hoping he could read her thoughts, feel her love.

"Thanks to you all!" Mr. Paxton raised his glass in a salute. "But most especially to Rissa for her skills today. The doctors said irreparable damage could've occurred if Brandon hadn't made it to the hospital so quickly. And as a much deserved reward, I've made Rissa a very generous offer to be my company's pilot and asked her to come join us in California. I hope you'll all help me convince her to take the job. You can't hide someone's true talent, and she proved that today, did she not?"

Cheers abounded, but Rissa ignored them. She'd wanted to tell Jonas about the offer herself, before he heard it like this. Jonas's expression darkened, and without a word to anyone, he turned around and headed toward the door, tugging Carly behind him.

Rissa set her drink aside and hurried after him, but the crush of people made it difficult. "Jonas?" She got outside just as Jonas opened the cruiser's door. "Jonas, wait!"

"Dad, why are we leaving?"

"Get in the car."

"Jonas!" She ran to catch up with him. "Where are you going? We need to talk."

"Take the job."

Rissa tripped to a stop. *"What?"*

Jonas swung around and cupped her face with his hands, his gaze dark, turbulent. Bleak. "Take the job," he repeated firmly, staring at her like he'd never seen her before. "I can't compete, Rissa. You're glowing, and not because of us. Because you were *flying* again." He dropped his hands and turned away with a curse. "Take the job. I can't give you what Mr. California in there can, and I'll never be able to."

"Have I asked you to?" she demanded, breathless with pain.

"You'll be miserable if you stay here knowing you could be back up in the air!"

"I'll find a job here."

"When? What if it takes a year? *Five* years? I won't be blamed for causing another woman to grow so embittered and resentful of being here with me that she takes off anyway. I'm giving you your freedom, Rissa. *Take it.*"

"Jonas, I'd never—"

"You wouldn't be able to help it, but I won't be left behind again. Rissa…take the job." Jonas slid behind the wheel, ignoring the fact she stood there dazed, shocked at how things had changed within a matter of minutes. She couldn't move, couldn't speak. Her heart slammed against her chest, breaking with every beat.

Rissa watched Jonas drive away, Carly's pale face staring at her from the passenger seat. She watched him pick up speed until the only thing left of their presence was the dust coating the air.

"Where's Jonas going?" Maura asked when she walked up behind her. "Isn't he staying for the cele— Rissa, what happened?"

"Mom?"

A strained laugh betrayed the thread of hysteria she barely kept in check. First the kids, the day, now this?

"Skylar, go get your mom something to drink, okay? Something sugary."

"He told me to take the job."

Maura wrapped her arm around Rissa's shoulders and led her away from the dining hall, prodding her clumsy steps on until they reached Seth and Grace's back porch. "Sit down and tell me what happened."

"I don't know! He—he said he wouldn't be left

behind again, but he could give me freedom and—What kind of crap is that?" Tears battled with anger. Fear. He loved her, she knew he did, but—

"Ex-wife crap," Maura murmured suddenly. "Jake and Jonas are fairly good friends because they attended high school together, and Carly's mom was from here, too. Jake said she blamed Jonas for forcing her to come back here, and that she never stopped talking about leaving and going somewhere bigger and better, even after Carly was born and Jonas became a deputy. Then one day she up and did."

Oh, poor Jonas. Poor *Carly*. No wonder neither of them liked to talk about her. She'd gotten more information from Marilyn the night of the ballet than she had from either Jonas or Carly. "And now he thinks I'm her?"

"Rissa, you're hurting right now, but open your eyes. He's *afraid*," Maura said soothingly. "The thing about not getting left behind should tell you that. He left you before you could leave him. Give Jonas some time to calm down and come to his senses. He'll come back."

"What if he doesn't?" A choked laugh escaped her. "All I wanted was a job that put me back in the air. But then I figured out it wouldn't be the same if it meant leaving Jonas so I go and tell the man I love him—and he *leaves?*"

Maura lowered herself to sit on a step, but stopped when something crinkled. Her worried expression brightened as she reached into the pocket of her denim jumper, retrieving an envelope from the folds. "Then how about you go after what *you* want and let him know without a doubt that it's him? I have a feeling this might help." Maura handed her the envelope with a smile. "It came by special courier yesterday evening, but with everything that's happened…"

Rissa stared at the address in the corner. Talk about timing. She slid a shaking finger beneath the sealed edge. Inside was a letter of notification. The life insurance money, all two million dollars worth, had been electronically deposited into her account. "I don't believe it."

"Is that what I think it is?"

"Yeah." Only now the joy wasn't there. Every ounce of it had been sucked away.

"Makes that decision about leaving a little easier, doesn't it?"

"I'm *not* leaving!" Skylar declared from a few feet away, her bandaged hands awkwardly holding a soda can and a plastic cup. "Mom?"

Rissa couldn't get her brain to work. All she could do was look at Skylar's beautiful blue eyes, stare at her beautiful face. Her *clean* face. This was it. This was what she'd waited for, prayed for.

Now she could afford to get Skylar back into counseling. Pay off her debts. *Live anywhere they wanted to live.*

"Why do you want to leave? I thought we were staying the summer? What about you and Jonas? What about Carly?"

What about them? She wanted to track Jonas down and rail at him for making her fall in love with him. Instead she sat there, numb, overwhelmed, wanting more than anything to go somewhere quiet to curl up and lick her wounds. How dare he order her away?

"You like it here?" Maura asked, giving Rissa a worried glance when she remained silent. "Enough to want to live here permanently?"

"Maybe." Skylar searched her face. "Mom, if this is about Jonas and me… He's okay. When we were up in the mountains he didn't blame me for what happened or anything, not like the other times. I thought you, I don't know, I thought you liked him?"

"I'll leave you two to talk," Maura said quietly. "Rissa, come find me if you need me."

Skylar walked over and sat down, laying the cup and soda beside her on the step. "Are you okay?"

Rissa squared her shoulders. "Yes, I am," she said with more conviction than she felt. "How are your hands? Grace told me you'd cut them."

"The stuff she put on them made them stop stinging. Are you sure you're okay? You look... sick."

She felt it, too. "Sky, I meant what I said. You aren't responsible for taking care of me."

"Yeah, but...tell me what happened."

Fresh tears stung her eyes at Skylar's concern and she determinedly blinked them away. "I...do like Jonas, but he told me to take the job."

"Oh."

"But, whether or not I do," she said, trying to sound okay with it, "is up to us. I don't want you worrying about this. Especially not after the day you've had."

"But you more than like him...don't you?" Skylar pressed, refusing to drop the subject. "Maybe even...love him?"

She stared at Skylar in surprise. "We've grown close over the last few months," she admitted carefully, "but sometimes love has a lot of complications."

Skylar digested those words with a frown. "Are you sure...are you sure he didn't say that because of me?"

"Oh, honey, no. Jonas and I... We both carry some heavy baggage emotionally. That's the problem, not you." She reached out to her, tentatively laying her hand on Skylar's shoulder, rubbing gently. "I was so worried about you. Thank God you and Carly and Brandon are all right. Is there…do you want to talk about it?" Rissa waited, wanting to press but knowing from experience not to. "I like your new look."

In typical Skylar fashion, she rolled her eyes with a snort. "Whatever. It seemed kinda stupid to put it back on when everybody saw me out there anyway and—" she held up her hands "—Grace wrapped them up so much I wondered if she did it on purpose."

Rissa laughed at the wry twist of Skylar's bare lips. Whether Grace had done it on purpose or not, she was thankful.

They sat there a long moment, silent, both of them lost in their thoughts, her hand on Skylar's tense shoulder and back.

"Mom…you were right about something."

"I was?"

Skylar wouldn't look at her. "I—I didn't tell you some things because I…felt like I couldn't. After Dad died and—and the problem with the insurance and bills, I felt like you couldn't— I don't know, *deal*, you know? I know I could've told you, but you didn't need another problem."

Clearing her throat, sensing the moment had finally come, Rissa tried to slow her rapidly beating heart. "I was a mess afterward," she agreed. "You're right. I should've been stronger for you. I'm sorry I wasn't, Sky."

"It's not your fault."

"Yes, it is. You've always acted so grown-up sometimes I'd forget you were a child—my *daughter* instead of my friend. I won't forget again. I hope you won't *let* me, and that you'll call me on it if I do. You can tell me anything, baby. I'm back on my feet now, I'll do my best to help if I can."

Skylar stared at her hands, the tips of her fingers visible, her black nail polish chipped and worn away. "When Dad died...he died because of me. If I'd kept my mouth shut and not said anything to you about Dad and Nic's mom—"

"I'm *glad* you told me, I needed to know. I'm just sorry you found out at all and wound up caught in the middle."

"Rick was mad that Dad had slept with Cindy."

He wasn't the only one. "That's understandable, no one wants to find out their spouse cheated."

"But...that's not all that happened."

After wishing her heart would slow its racing, it did in an instant. Seemed to stop entirely in preparation of the news Skylar was about to impart. Sitting there on the step with the bright sunshine and beautiful day around them, Rissa knew true fear. A chill ran down her spine, laced with unadulterated terror at the look on Skylar's face. She'd never forget it in a million lifetimes.

"What, Sky? Tell me."

Jaw tight, Skylar fiddled with the bandaging. "Before the—the accident…before I saw Dad and Cindy… I stayed there a lot, remember?"

"You and Nicole were very close."

She nodded, shrugged. "I liked it there because…Nic's dad—he always teased us and goofed off. Played games and, you know, hung out with us, took us places. He was…cool." Skylar glanced at her quickly then looked away. "Nic and I still talked some after things blew up. And sometimes when I went over Rick was there…." She wet her lips. "D-do you remember how he would always joke around and tease me?"

Rissa's mind whirled with the potential scenarios, things she didn't want to consider, but did due to Skylar's tone. Spots danced in front of her eyes, and Rissa knew she was close to fainting for the first time in her life. If Rick had—

"I—I kind of had a crush on him, a really big one. Sort of like Carly was with Travis. You didn't know that, did you?" Skylar didn't look to see if she responded. Her gaze remained unfocused, her breath, her words, coming faster. "Anyway, after Dad and Cindy, Rick k-kissed me."

"Sky—"

"And then one weekend when N-Nic was away we...something happened."

An invisible fist punched her in the stomach, the impact of Skylar's words more powerful than any physical blow she could've imagined.

"I didn't mean for it to go so far. We were goofing around, wrestling over the stupid remote and then— I swear I didn't mean to, but—" Skylar began to cry, couldn't sit still. She rocked on the step, back and forth. "We k-kissed some more and— He said things l-like how much he liked me and cared for me and l-loved me. That he was l-lonely because—because of what Dad had done. I felt sorry for him and Nic called and said she and her mom were staying with her grandma and not coming home. Rick was upset because Nic was supposed to spend the weekend with him, the three of us were going to the zoo and stuff, and I knew I should leave but—" Skylar broke off with a vicious curse. "I didn't." She closed her eyes and grimaced. "God, what an idiot. Mom, I didn't come *home*."

Rissa was too stunned to comment. Too horrified. Too numb, and not nearly numb enough.

"I...I spent the night there. Just me and—and Rick."

Anger overtook the numbness, and Rissa grabbed Skylar by her shoulders, turning her so fast Skylar winced. "He took advantage of you! Skylar, oh, dear Lord, there are *laws*—"

"*I wanted to!*"

Rissa's horror returned. The air left her lungs in a rush and she stared at Skylar, realized the words weren't said in defense of Rick, or what happened. Tears flowed freely down Skylar's face, but her expression gave truth to her words.

"I *wanted* to." Skylar met her gaze numerous times before she quickly looked away again, her face pale. "Mom, he— Rick didn't *make* me do anything. I wanted to. I didn't mean for it to happen, but he *didn't* rape me. You need to—to know it wasn't like that."

"Sky—"

"There's more."

God give me strength.

Skylar pulled away and distanced herself again, averting her face so that all Rissa could see was her profile. That and the way she curled in on herself, her shoulders hunched.

The rocking motion started again. "I c-came home and everything was fine. You—you and dad didn't think anything about it because I—I always stayed over at Nic's and you were all pretending everything was okay even though me and Nic had heard all the fights and knew…But then Nic called. Dad picked it up and sh-she talked to him, asking permission for me to c-come over because she'd been gone. D-Dad started questioning me, w-wondering where I'd been and what I'd done and then…I slipped. I s-said Rick's name and—"

"He knew," Rissa finished dully. "That's why Larry called my cell so many times." Dizziness washed over her. "That's why the tower didn't patch a call through. He wanted me to land first before he told me—" Her gaze narrowed. "You and your dad were on your way to Rick's," she said suddenly, piecing the events together. "That's where you were going when you—"

"See?" Skylar demanded, her whole body trembling. "It *is* my f-fault. If I'd kept my mouth shut you and Dad wouldn't't've—and Rick and I— None of it would've happened. *None of it.*"

Rissa put her arms around Skylar, her concern for her daughter's broken state overriding everything else.

Skylar reacted blindly. She lowered her head to Rissa's lap and clung to her like she had when she was a little girl.

She was *still* a little girl. But whatever had happened in the woods had released the hold, giving her courage and strength to face the future—and the past.

"I felt like such a—a whore. Every boy at school already hit on me and said nasty things because of my boobs, and they thought—they thought just because I cheered I was easy, but then Rick... I really *liked* him. He m-made me feel good about... Said I was pretty and not sleazy. Then after the accident...he came to the f-funeral." She cursed again, the words coming out accompanied by strangled sobs. "He offered to *c-comfort* me to m-make me feel better." A caustic laugh followed, bitter and full of tears. "Nice, huh? I—I couldn't believe he'd *say* something like that. Not when he *knew* what happened. When he *knew* it was our fault Dad died."

"Baby, don't—"

"He—he really liked my hair. He got mad when I cut and—and dyed it. He actually *ordered* me to change back, but I t-told him if he didn't leave me alone I'd say he raped me. He didn't, Mom, really, but that—that shut him up. Stupid ass. If Nic and her mom knew what an SOB he really is..."

Rissa wrapped her arms tighter around her daughter's quivering body and lowered her head onto Skylar's back, giving into the tears she'd somehow managed to hold in check. She rocked them both back and forth. Slow and easy, back and forth. The motion soothing, automatic. Controlled because she couldn't control anything else.

How could she not have known? Not have realized?

The rational part of her knew she'd been reeling from the affair and knew a divorce was inevitable, but that didn't excuse—

She shoved the guilty thoughts aside to deal with later and concentrated on the here and now. "We're going to get through this, Sky. We are. I'm so glad you told me. That you—you trust me enough to be honest. I'm sorry, too. I'm sorry I wasn't there for you when you needed me most, but we're going to get through this," she crooned, pressing a kiss to Skylar's dark head. She petted her, held her, tried to make up for a year's worth of lost time and a lifetime of pain. "I'm sorry he hurt you, I'm sorry I didn't know…I'm sorry I wasn't the mother you needed me to be, but regardless of what you've told me, it's *not your fault.*"

She made Skylar sit up and wiped her tears away. Staring into eyes so like her own, she tried to convey her love. "Skylar, listen to me. Every girl has a crush on a friend's dad at some point, but Rick should've been man enough not to take his anger out on you for something your dad and Cindy did. He lied, Sky. Honey, if Rick cared for you at all, he would've left you *alone.*"

Fresh tears rolled down Skylar's cheeks. "I know. I know that now, but Dad—"

"An accident," Rissa insisted, ignoring her own tears because she refused to remove her hands from Skylar's face, refused to let her look away. "Skylar, we are not in control on this earth. We're not invincible, we're not infallible. We're human and we screw up. We make poor decisions, but they keep us humble and make us try harder, to be wiser. And sometimes...things just happen, bad things and good, and it's all out of our hands and in God's. All we can do is face our mistakes, grow from them, and move on."

Skylar blinked rapidly, her expression seemingly torn between hope and disbelief. The girl Skylar had been was easy prey for a grown man bent on revenge. A man who knew the right things to say to get her to do the unthinkable.

"You mean...like Jonas dumping us? Are you taking the job?"

Rissa stared into Skylar's blue eyes, the exact color of the deep blue sky overhead. Montana sky that couldn't be replaced with city streets and smog or even a pilot's job. Eyes that begged her to be the mom she should've been before. To make a firm decision and settle their future. "Like Jonas dumping us."

Skylar wiped her nose on the back of her hand. "Do we have to move because of him? I—I will if it would be too much for you to, you know, stay and see him." She sniffled. "I didn't want to move here, but, I was glad I wouldn't ever see Rick again."

Rissa forced a smile, wondering what, if anything, she could do about Rick's behavior now, especially when she refused to put Skylar through more than she'd already endured. "We'll see." She glanced up at the heavens, knowing in her heart Rick would indeed face a punishment more harsh than any she could inflict on Skylar's behalf.

She looped her arms around her daughter's shoulders, wanting to touch her as much as possible now that she was allowed to. "How about we go to our cabin and—"

"Eat some chocolate?"

Her daughter knew her well. Rissa laughed and squeezed Skylar tight. "Works for me," she said, kissing her cheek. "Let's go get some brain food and…talk. Okay?"

Fresh tears filled Skylar's eyes. "You don't… you don't hate me?"

Rissa wiped them away. "I could never hate you. You're my baby girl, Sky, and I'll always love you."

"Mom?"

"Yeah?"

"I want you to be happy."

"I want *us* to be happy."

"Then can we stay?"

CHAPTER SEVENTEEN

A WEEK LATER Jonas glared out at the stretch of highway outside town that was so inviting to speedsters, and tried to tell himself it had nothing to do with the first time he'd met Rissa.

The town was buzzing with all sorts of gossip. Skylar's transformation, the fact that Mr. Paxton's vacation was over and Brandon was out of the hospital. How they'd all packed up and gone home, leaving behind a generous donation for Seth's ranch after Brandon owned up to his involvement in getting them lost.

Rumor also had it that the Paxtons had flown out of North Star via helicopter.

Which meant Rissa had accepted the job.

Carly moped around the house, refusing to talk to him about the goings-on at the ranch because he'd "ruined everything" by telling Rissa to leave. All she'd say was that Rissa and Skylar were both upset with him and for good reason. Yeah, well, that much he knew.

A loud, shrill beep sounded right before the radar gun flashed wildly. Jonas sat up, blinking in horror when Whitefeather's helicopter headed right toward him and skimmed the roof of the cruiser. Jonas ducked down in the seat, amazed it hadn't taken the lights off the top. The old fool was liquored up again, no doubt trying to get himself back in the air now that Rissa wasn't there to do it for him.

He scrambled out of the car, unsure of what to do. The helicopter did a quick turn midair and headed back down, right toward—

Jonas hit the dirt when it flew over again, low enough that he squeezed his eyes shut and told himself it was from the grit flying through the air instead of the instant flash of regret he felt for not swallowing his pride and begging Rissa to stay. He opened them in time to see the chopper turn yet again before setting down in the field next to the road with barely a bounce.

He stared in disbelief, scrambled to his feet and took off running for all he was worth. He had to get to the helicopter before Ben took off again. Jonas was almost there when the blades powered down and slowed, the door opened, and the pilot got out removing his—*her*—headset and ball cap.

Rissa?

Her expression carefully guarded, Rissa pulled something from her pocket and flung it through the air toward him. "You're going to give me a ticket this time, right?"

He caught the small plastic card instinctively, but a quick glance down had him doing a double-take. The shiny, newly issued license listed her home address as North Star, Montana. White-feather's place? "You bought him out?"

She nodded. "I thought I'd stop by and tell you that Skylar and I decided we're staying," she informed him, her gaze narrowed. "But you need to realize something, Jonas. *We* chose to stay on our own. You didn't make us, and we're not the least bit embittered about it."

He closed the distance between them, uncaring about the details so long as it was true. He pulled her into his arms, wanting to kiss her, to make love to her. "No one will ever believe you managed to get that crazy old man to sell."

Her expression softened. "They just hadn't made him an offer he couldn't refuse. All I had to do was promise to take him up every now and again."

Ingenious. Jonas stared at her, tension filling him. Hope. More love than he'd ever dreamed possible. "Will you make me one of those offers? One I can't refuse?"

She swallowed. "Perhaps… After you apologize for being so dense you told me to leave."

A smile pulled at his lips. "I'm sorry, sweetheart. I didn't mean a word of it, but my pride wouldn't let me beg you to stay." He waited, impatient for her to speak. "My offer?"

Raising an eyebrow, she wet her lips, and Jonas had a hard time concentrating.

"I'm a pilot, and I'm going to start up a charter business. I'm a horrible cook and not a great housekeeper, and if you've got some preconceived notion that I'll give up flying to become June Cleaver—"

"I understand." He winked at her. "Trust me, when I think of you, I see way more than June Cleaver."

Her chin lifted. "Good."

"What else? I want more than you simply living in the same town, Rissa. I've always wanted more from you, that was the problem from the beginning."

She inhaled shakily. "Well, maybe we could work something out where…Carly could have a best friend and sister rolled into one. Maybe, under the right motivation, more?"

"More," he repeated, liking the idea despite the two teenagers giving them both fits. "That would require you making an honest man of me," he mused aloud. "And I'm afraid I still don't understand. You're going to have to spell things out for me and be more specific. Just so we're clear."

Her gaze narrowed a bit more, but her smile was unmistakable. "It means I love you and I want you to marry me," she said, finally giving voice to the words he was about to say himself since she couldn't seem to get them out.

Rissa's gaze held his, soft, warm. Full of love. "I can't promise it'll be easy, but I do promise I'll see it through, Jonas. To the very end. You and Carly won't ever be left behind again, not if I have any say in—"

Jonas lowered his head and kissed her. His tongue swept inside her mouth and the taste of her filled him, eased the tension and pain he'd carried ever since that day at the ranch. He'd missed her so much. Loved her even more.

Her arms rose to curl around his neck, but he pulled them down, capturing her hands behind her back long enough to quietly slip the cuffs from his belt.

"I accept your proposal," he murmured against her lips. "And we're getting married soon. I don't want to wait."

"What— Jonas, what are you doing?"

He snapped the cuffs into place around her wrists and smiled down at her. "You were speeding, Mrs. Taggert. Second time I've caught you, too."

Her surprised expression turned to one of sensual promise. "And my punishment?"

He kissed her again, deeply, leaving both of them breathless and panting. "Fifty years to life."

* * * * *

Happily ever after is just the beginning...

Turn the page for a sneak preview of
DANCING ON SUNDAY AFTERNOONS
by
Linda Cardillo

Harlequin Everlasting—Every great love
has a story to tell.™
A brand-new line from Harlequin Books
launching this February!

PROLOGUE

Giulia D'Orazio
1983

I had two husbands—Paolo and Salvatore.

Salvatore and I were married for thirty-two years. I still live in the house he bought for us; I still sleep in our bed. All around me are the signs of our life together. My bedroom window looks out over the garden he planted. In the middle of the city, he coaxed tomatoes, peppers, zucchini—even grapes for his wine—out of the ground. On weekends, he used to drive up to his cousin's farm in Waterbury and bring back manure. In the winter, he wrapped the peach tree and the fig tree with rags and black rubber hoses against the cold, his massive, coarse hands gentling those trees as if they were his fragile-skinned babies. My neighbor, Dominic Grazza, does that for me now. My boys have no time for the garden.

In the front of the house, Salvatore planted roses. The roses I take care of myself. They are giant, cream-colored, fragrant. In the afternoons, I like to sit out on the porch with my coffee, protected from the eyes of the neighborhood by that curtain of flowers.

Salvatore died in this house thirty-five years ago. In the last months, he lay on the sofa in the parlor so he could be in the middle of everything. Except for the two oldest boys, all the children were still at home and we ate together every evening. Salvatore could see the dining room table from the sofa, and he could hear everything that was said. "I'm not dead, yet," he told me. "I want to know what's going on."

When my first grandchild, Cara, was born, we brought her to him, and he held her on his chest, stroking her tiny head. Sometimes they fell asleep together.

Over on the radiator cover in the corner of the parlor is the portrait Salvatore and I had taken on our twenty-fifth anniversary. This brooch I'm wearing today, with the diamonds—I'm wearing it in the photograph also—Salvatore gave it to me that day. Upstairs on my dresser is a jewelry box filled with necklaces and bracelets and earrings. All from Salvatore.

I am surrounded by the things Salvatore gave me, or did for me. But, God forgive me, as I lie alone now in my bed, it is Paolo I remember.

Paolo left me nothing. Nothing, that is, that my family, especially my sisters, thought had any value. No house. No diamonds. Not even a photograph.

But after he was gone, and I could catch my breath from the pain, I knew that I still had something. In the middle of the night, I sat alone and held them in my hands, reading the words over and over until I heard his voice in my head. I had Paolo's letters.

* * * * *

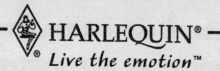

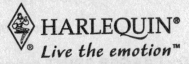

HARLEQUIN®
INTRIGUE®

BREATHTAKING ROMANTIC SUSPENSE

Shared dangers and passions lead to electrifying
romance and heart-stopping suspense!

Every month, you'll meet six new heroes
who are guaranteed to make your spine tingle
and your pulse pound. With them you'll enter
into the exciting world of Harlequin Intrigue—
where your life is on the line
and so is your heart!

THAT'S INTRIGUE—
ROMANTIC SUSPENSE
AT ITS BEST!

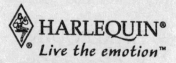

HARLEQUIN®
Live the emotion™

HARLEQUIN®
Presents

The world's bestselling romance series...
The series that brings you your favorite authors,
month after month:

Helen Bianchin...Emma Darcy
Lynne Graham...Penny Jordan
Miranda Lee...Sandra Marton
Anne Mather...Carole Mortimer
Susan Napier...Michelle Reid

and many more uniquely talented authors!

Wealthy, powerful, gorgeous men...
Women who have feelings just like your own...
The stories you love, set in exotic, glamorous locations...

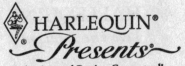

HARLEQUIN®
Presents

Seduction and Passion Guaranteed!

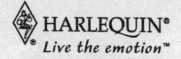